LENDON

THE ART OF WAR

-

'The art of war teaches us to rely not on the likelihood of the enemy's not coming, but on our own readiness to receive him; not on the chance of his not attacking, but rather on the fact that we have made our position unassailable.'

Sun Tzu

(544 BC – 496 BC)

Anthony Turner

IN MEMORY OF

Paul Steer

5 November 1946 – 12 April 1990

'One in a million for all the right reasons.'

-

Derek William Vingoe

26 April 1937 – 20 September 2018

'A kind and generous man to one and all.'

-

Patrick English Nunn

18 May 1926 – 15 February 1992

'Without whom I would never have passed Maths O level.'

ABOUT THE AUTHOR

Anthony Turner is a retired police officer who joined the Metropolitan Police Service in 1981 before transferring to Hampshire Constabulary in 1986. From there he finally hung up his truncheon (those were the days!) along with his Asp, CS Gas, Quick Cuffs, Body Armour (dustbin lids back in the day!) and a variety of other toys. Anthony and his wife, Lee, live in Southsea on the south coast of England with their menagerie of Dobermanns and Parrots all of whom seem to enjoy it when Dad settles down to put pen to paper or fingers to the keyboard. In this, his second novel featuring Superintendent Alex Lendon, he again draws on his personal and professional experiences to piece together a contemporary thriller which explores the potential for renewable energy and to answer the question of just how far a superpower might go in order to protect its assets

PROLOGUE

The Sheik listened to the BBC World News anchor…

'In the advent of Brexit, Prime Minister Taylor, President Thorne and Prime Minister Dubois have announced plans for a tri nation alliance between the UK, US and Canada which could bring an end to the Middle East and Russia's global domination of the oil and gas industry…

Setting aside Armani in favour of a check Keffiyeh and pure white Dishdasha, the Sheik's handsome features gazed out across the panoramic landscape which, only a few decades ago had been a desert, but was now a glittering landscape of opulence and, he admitted to himself, no small amount of gluttony.

The revolution in renewable energy, Prime Minister Taylor told the press conference, will ensure existing oil and gas reserves are, to all intent and purposes, sufficient to serve our respective needs for many years to come…

He was not a fool and only too aware the avarice of his own countrymen had contributed to this potential economic downturn for the OPEC countries. Indeed, to make matters worse, dwindling reserves across the Arabic world meant that unless spending was curbed dramatically then bankruptcy within the next ten to fifteen years was a real threat.

So, with a Treaty between the three countries due to be signed after the forthcoming World Energy Summit in London, is the world order about to change?'

A buzzer interrupted his thoughts. Checking his Rolex, he muted the television and walked across the marble floored lobby towards a pair of cherrywood double doors. Pausing briefly alongside a Baby Grand, he delicately ran his fingers across the glossy black surface and released a small control panel beneath the keyboard. A moment later, the muted sounds of the CNN reporter were replaced by Rachmaninoff's Piano Concerto No3.

PART 1

'La vengeance est un met que l'on doit manger froid'

(Revenge is a dish best served cold)

Charles Maurice de Talleyrand-Perigord

(1754-1838)

CHAPTER 1

Behavioural indicators associated with suicide bombers remain as entrenched in the minds of police officers today as they were in 2005 when, on the 7th July, Jean de Menezes was mistaken for Hussain Osman and shot six times in the head by plain clothes specialist firearms officers.

That the shooting took place on the London Underground was not lost on Gary Bushell as he stepped onto the Northern Line's southbound tube from Tottenham Court Road. Placing the Hamleys carrier bag on the bench seat next to him, a present for his six year old daughter's birthday, he glanced up and looked round at the other passengers, not that there were many in the carriage at this time of day. One of the benefits of working a late shift he thought as his eyes settled on the slight figure of a clean shaven young Asian lad sat diagonally opposite, maybe half a dozen or so places away.

Zipped up to his chin and face partially covered by the fur lined hood of an oversized parka style jacket, he was chewing frantically while staring straight ahead at the empty seat opposite. Not indicative in itself by any means and aware of being labelled a racist should he call it in, Bushell couldn't help but feel an increasing sense of unease as he watched the lad out of the corner of his eye.

Introduced in the aftermath of 9/11, 'Operation Kratos' came from a delegation of Metropolitan police officers visiting Israel, Sri Lanka and Russia to learn more of their experiences when dealing with suicide bombers. Of the twelve possible behavioural indicators identified from these trips, Bushell had just ticked three off his mental checklist.

Although the operation name had since been removed, this didn't detract from the remaining nine indicators, eight for a woman, the disparity relating to the shaving of a beard to blend into a crowd. That there was no crowd in the largely empty carriage inferred this was not the intended target should his suspicions prove to be accurate.

Of those remaining indicators Bushell knew that most were subjectively linked to signs of stress and anxiety in the build up to an event. After all, it's all well and good being the big I am among your peers, boasting of a willingness to sacrifice your life in exchange for a place in paradise and however many virgins, but when push comes to shove and reality hits home, it's hardly surprising that sweating, panting and fidgeting all become par for the course. While these were signs he was unable to determine from his current location, that was about to change as the train pulled into Leicester Square and the lad stood up. Right hand holding onto the handrail and the left dipping into his coat pocket as if to assure himself something was there, he walked passed Bushell towards the exit.

Waiting for him to leave the carriage, Bushell grabbed the Hamleys bag and slipped through the doors just as they were closing. Following on from a safe distance, further indicators began to fall into place. The strange floral smell of herbal essences mixed with sweat as he passed him in the carriage. Apparently it was important to smell nice when entering paradise. The mutterings that began as soon as he stood up and now, as he approached the escalator, the hunched almost robotic walk of a man on a mission, weighed down by whatever lay beneath his coat. Not a full house, but enough for Bushell to reach into his pocket for his mobile phone while at the same time looking round for any BTP officers of which, typically like a bus just when you needed one, there were none.

Reaching the upper level and following the exit signs, Bushell was grateful for the relatively low number of commuters as he quietly relayed his concerns to the Silver Commander in charge of MP, the Metropolitan Police Service Control room.

Staying on the line he could hear the Inspector deploying Armed Response Vehicles along with a relatively recent addition to the fight against terrorism, CTSFOs, Counter Terrorism Specialist Firearms Officers.

Permanently on patrol across the capital, this gave Bushell cause for cautious optimism as they emerged into the open air and turned left into Cranborne Street. Closing the gap, Bushell maintained a running commentary using his hand to muffle his words as the suspect – he was now definitely a suspect – crossed Charing Cross Road heading west towards Leicester Square.

Come rain or shine London's West End teams with life pretty much 24/7 and today was no exception as the suspect weaved his way in, out and around the crowds of tourists enjoying a bright winter's afternoon.

At the north west corner of a park at the centre of the square, Bushell could see crowds gathering in front of a platform erected to the left of the entrance where a press conference was being held for an up and coming boxing match. Beyond that, the not unusual sounds of police sirens could be heard in the background as the suspect picked up speed, both arms now swinging freely as he pushed his way passed the crowds of onlookers and entered the park where, beyond a statue of William Shakespeare, Bushell could see what he now realised must be the suspect's final destination.

Perhaps one of the busiest places in London at this time of day, the 'Leicester Square Box Office' attracts hundreds of people looking for tickets and last minute bargains to West End shows playing later that evening. Joining the queue and only two places behind, Bushell kept a careful eye on the suspect's left hand as he looked round for the tell-tale signs of plain clothed firearms officers converging on the box office from the periphery of the Square.

Guessing, not the best thing to do in this type of situation, but nonetheless having no real option, Bushell figured the suspect was looking to get in amongst the mass of bodies rather than on the fringe of the queue so the contents of what lay beneath the parka, like as not nails, ball bearings and any manner of deadly material would have a maximum effect on detonation.

While it was good this bought some time, Bushell also knew that for the firearms officers to reach the suspect without causing a disturbance was going to be difficult particularly given the great British public's aversion to people pushing in. This was a prophesy which came true seconds later as a voice called out, 'Oi! What do you fink you're dooin!'

All eyes turned to the source of the exclamation as a man and woman could be seen trying to ease their way through the crowd. Had they averted their gaze then perhaps they might have got away with being a couple behaving badly, but instead human instinct had kicked in, their focus on the one individual being only too recognisable as he responded to their approach.

Reaching for his pocket, the suspect screamed, 'Allahu Akbar!' as Bushell, dropped the Hamleys bag, shoved the two bodies in front of him to one side and launched himself at the suicide bomber.

Hitting him full in the back, Bushell wrapped his arms tightly around the bomber as both men were propelled forward into a tangle of bodies, arms and legs. Pinning his arms to his sides as they hit the floor, Bushell could hear the plain clothed police officers yelling for the public to get back as they tried desperately to reach the deadly struggle taking place only a few metres away.

Wriggling and squirming beneath him, Bushell, now very much aware of what lay beneath the parka, was grateful for his additional bulk as he rolled onto his back and literally held on for grim death as he locked his arms and legs around the bomber's slight frame.

The officers shouts were drowned out by screams of the public as they star burst away from the two men and although it felt like a lifetime to Bushell it was only a few seconds later that both officers knelt down beside them.

'Hold on,' said the female officer as she grabbed hold of the bombers hair, pulled his head away from Bushell's, rammed the muzzle of a Glock 17, 9mm pistol into the base of the skull and without hesitation fired two hollow point rounds up and through the medulla oblongata at the top of the spine. Not that the bomber's finger was on the trigger, but had it been then this would have prevented any form of reflex action accidentally detonating the device. Likewise, the use of hollow point rounds negated a 'through and through,' leaving both rounds firmly embedded in his skull.

Uncoupling himself from the deadweight, Bushell took a deep breath and carefully eased the body to one side. Laying there for a moment he looked up at the sky and whispered a silent prayer as the shadow of the male officer blotted out the sun.

'Good job,' he began to say, but then, noting the inevitable shakes kicking in. 'You'll be alright in a minute, matey,' as he reached down to help his colleague to his feet.

Let's hope so were Bushell's last thoughts as the sound of a ringtone rang out from the body alongside him.

CHAPTER 2

TERROR in the CAPITAL

MISSED chances to foil BOMBER

By **Ron Luce** *and* **Roy Folland**

As London comes to terms with the latest terrorist atrocity, counter terrorism agencies face awkward questions after it emerged authorities were aware of suicide bomber, Behdad Khadem's links to British based jihadists.

In the aftermath of the explosion which killed 40 innocent people waiting to buy theatre tickets from the concession stand in Leicester Square, sources suggest that authorities were informed of the danger posed by Khadem on several separate occasions.

Despite these warnings, Khadem was able to travel frequently between the UK and Egypt where it is believed he used his cousin's connections to an Islamic Fundamentalist Group to cross the border into Libya where he trained in bomb making.

With Prime Minister, Geraldine Taylor, on her way back from Canada, Home Secretary, Alan Hillary, chair of yesterday's emergency COBR meeting, conceded Khadem was known to the intelligence services, but would not be drawn further given the ongoing investigation.

The Prime Minister stormed into the Cabinet room, dumped the newspaper on the boat shaped table and focused her attention on two men stood with their backs to a bank of Georgian windows that overlooked the walled garden to number 10.

'Well, I'm back now and frankly, gentlemen, enough is enough!' she exclaimed, her anger self-evident as she settled herself into a mahogany armchair. Upholstered in red leather and a nod to the seat of power, it was the only one of twenty or so otherwise identical chairs around the table with arms. 'Take a seat please.'

From above a marble fireplace, immediately behind the PM, the portrait of Sir Robert Walpole, the de facto first Prime Minister of Great Britain, appeared to glare, much like the incumbent, at the two men as they did as instructed and took their places opposite.

Both wore charcoal grey pin stripe suits, crisp white cotton shirts and colourful ties, but that was where the comparison ended.

Alan Hillary, the PM's Home Secretary and trusted ally, was of average height and build, clean shaven, with a smattering of grey hair around the ears that propped up a tanned bald pate. Alongside him, Sir Henry King, former Metropolitan Police Commissioner and strategic head of the UK intelligence services rested a huge paw on a black leather folder in front of him. Reminiscent of a giant silverback, King had the air of pending doom for those who crossed him. Yet, beneath the gargantuan exterior was a man of great intellect and calm authority, a slight twitch of his neatly trimmed grey beard, the only indicator of what was to come from this meeting.

Two hours later, King emerged from No 10 and stepped into the passenger seat of a gleaming black Jaguar XJ saloon, pretty much the only vehicle in the range able to accommodate him comfortably.

'Good meeting, Guvnor?' enquired his driver.

Testament to King's character and commitment to his men and women, Jim Well's was one of his former detectives who'd been invalided out of the job after poor intel on a crack house raid in Clapham led to an encounter with a shotgun, a prosthetic leg and the need for the car to be an automatic.

'Interesting, Jim... in fact very interesting,' replied King thoughtfully as the car eased away from the kerb and approached the black wrought iron gates that would see them out onto

Whitehall and north towards Trafalgar Square. 'Have we heard back from Lendon yet?'

CHAPTER 3

Mountains either side of a broad valley, heavy snowfall and swirling cross winds buffeted the Boeing 737-800 as we made our final approach into Innsbruck. Three attempts to land had already been aborted so, as white knuckles gripped armrests and sick bags began to fill, passengers waited anxiously for the Captain to decide whether to give it one last go or give up and head for Munich. Choosing the former and with what felt like a tongue in cheek reminder to 'fasten seatbelts and remain seated until reaching the terminal building,' the aircraft, like a drunk on his way home after a bender, slewed left to right, up and down until eventually the tyres hit terra firma, bounced a bit, then settled back down to cheers and rounds of applause as reverse thrust kicked in.

The purpose of the trip, aside from the obvious when visiting Austria in January, was to consider a job offer from, Sir Henry

King.

As a former member of SO13, the Metropolitan Police Anti-Terrorism Branch, I'd moved to Hampshire Constabulary shortly after its merger with SO12, Special Branch in 2006 to form the Counter Terrorism Command, SO15. The move coincided with my father passing away and having inherited the family home in Portsmouth, it seemed like an opportune time for a change and to leave behind the smoke of the big city, anyone whose worn a white shirt in that environment will know what I mean, in favour of a more relaxed and less polluted lifestyle.

So having arrived in the second largest provincial force in England and Wales, behind Thames Valley, it turned out there were no operational vacancies for Inspectors. So instead, I took up a temporary post as Staff Officer to Sir Henry King, Henry King then, who at the time was Assistant Chief Constable for Specialist Operations, a neat fit given my prior role in the Met. Anyway, what started out as a temporary posting lasted two years before the boss moved to the Met as a Deputy Assistant Commissioner and I went through the rank of Chief Inspector to become Superintendent in my current role, on paper at least, as Operations Commander within Specialist Operations.

I say 'on paper at least,' as off the back of three separate yet interconnected terrorist incidents last year, the first which resulted in personal tragedy for me, I'd been reunited with Sir Henry and now it was time for me, again, to consider my future. 'Trouble shooter, man without portfolio, call it what you will,' he'd said. The offer to work directly for him a second time and on a more permanent basis was worthy of serious consideration and one without any external influences. So I'd decided to book a week away in the mountains from where I hoped clarity of thought would ensue and a decision for the next chapter in my life would be made.

As the last flight of the day, it was approaching dusk by the time the taxi dropped me off outside my hotel. From its elevated position at the base of the Spieljoch mountain, the Hotel Bruno looked down on snow laden rooftops and the twinkling lights of Fugen. A picturesque village that dotted slopes either side of the Ziller valley, huge dumps of snow had descended since Christmas which made for a classic picture postcard scene. More importantly from my perspective though, the conditions bode well for perfectly groomed pistes the next day. Taking a last look and deep breath of fresh mountain air, I turned back to the entrance and lugged my suitcase, skis and boot bag up the granite steps and into the foyer.

'Ah! Welcome!' exclaimed Frau Erlebach as she surged round from behind the reception desk and enveloped me in an all-encompassing bear hug. The travel company said there'd be a warm welcome from the owner and they weren't kidding.

'*Danke Frau,*' I replied as I uncoupled myself and took in my surroundings. A small office set back behind the reception desk. An elevator, signposted down to a bootroom and wellness spa. A pair of smoked glass doors that led to a corridor off which I could spy a cosy lounge and most importantly, a roaring log fire. '*Das ist perfekt,*' (What more could you want).

'Your German ist immer noch gut,' she said with a broad smile. 'But please… call me Isobela.'

A literal twist in the helix of my DNA gave me a penchant for languages. The fancy name is hyperpolyglot, but whatever the title, it was something which had proven useful in the past, both at work and of course on holiday.

'Now,' she continued, getting down to business as I filled in a registration form and pocketed the keycard to my room. 'No skis or boots in your room. You must use the bootroom. There is an outer door that stays open until seven after which you must use your card to enter the hotel here, then use the elevator to go down and put your skis and boots away.'

'Yes. Ma'am,' I said with a smile.

'So,' she pressed the button and the elevators doors opened. 'Put these away, then return to the foyer and I will show you to your room.'

By the time I got back, I could hear Isobela on the phone in her office so I decided not to disturb her and instead went native. Extending the handle on my suitcase, I backed my way through the glass doors and wheeled my way along the terra cotta tiled corridor to a second elevator handily located next to a small bar area and a restaurant full of guests having dinner. The number 301 on my keycard gave the game away so I felt fairly safe in doing this on my own as I entered the elevator and pressed the button for the third floor.

Tucked away in the eaves, the room was a typical alpine affair which matched perfectly the A-frame exterior of the hotel. Simple pine furnishings. A television I wouldn't be watching. A bed my feet would dangle off – pretty much the same wherever I go – a small en-suite and a balcony that promised glorious views of the mountains in the morning. Just the ticket for the next few days. That said, it was a pre-dinner beer in front of that cosy log fire I was looking forward to, so I quickly unpacked and made my way back downstairs.

Further up the valley and a thousand metres above Fugen's sister resort of Hoch *High* Fugen, tiny flecks of snow drifted lazily off the WedelHutte's roof. Nestled beneath the Marchkofp summit each unique, tiny crystal glistened in the moonlight as they fused together to blanket the terrace in a sea of white that come morning would be swept clear in readiness for guests and visitors alike to eat al fresco and bask in what promised to be a glorious sunny day.

Accessible only by the *Zillertaler Shuttle*, the evenings were inevitably reserved only for guests of the WedelHutte to relax and enjoy the warming splendour and intimate atmosphere of open fires and contemporary log cabin luxury that only the wealthy could afford. Sat alone at a rotunda bar overlooking the terrace, a woman, simply dressed in figure hugging jeans and cream roll neck sweater, ordered a second mug of hot glühwein from the attentive barman who for the last two weeks had been doing his best to bed this beautiful Fraulein. Combining Bavarian efficiency with Tom Cruise like 'Cocktail' flair, he presented her with the deliciously warming liquid. Strangely appealing in his lederhosen of knee length leather trousers and matching suspenders, he *was* good looking, she thought, and on another occasion she might have been tempted, but no, not on this trip.

Over time, she'd learned to assume many roles. On this occasion though, her natural beauty with only a few minor adjustments to hair colour (red) and eyes (green) were all that was necessary for her to blend in among the beautiful people so attracted by this most luxurious of hotels.

Savouring the warm aromas of cinnamon, cloves and orange that gave glühwein its distinctive flavour, she casually checked out her fellow guests. Force of habit, she supposed as she slid off her barstool and with a smile for the barman, made her way through to the restaurant.

Having foregone the customary five course, gourmet dinner in favour of a light supper of goulash soup and salad, she returned to her room from where she changed then stepped out onto her balcony and gazed out across mountain peaks illuminated by the full moon. Come morning the vista would offer stunning, uninterrupted views towards Italy and Switzerland, but tonight the focus of her attention was a hundred metres or so up the slope to her right where the head of the *Zillertaler Shuttle* lay in darkness. Doubling as the only means for getting guests to the hotel during the winter season, the last of the arrivals were now safely ensconced in the bar and the skidoos used to ferry them down from the station were being put away in the garage beneath the hotel. The only other sign of activity came from the lights of piste bashers dotted across the mountain as they worked through the night to prepare the slopes for the following day.

From this vantage point, high above the tree line, the temperature was significantly lower than down in the valley, a balmy minus five degrees Celsius compared to the minus twenty she was now experiencing. She'd chosen her change of clothing carefully. Not simply white or black. A mix of shades to replicate the terrain. Not too many layers. Just enough to keep her warm, but not so much to restrict her movement. Satisfied there was no sign of activity immediately outside the hotel, she took the wooden fire escape down to the side of her balcony and ventured out onto the freshly groomed piste. Pausing a moment to strap on a pair of snowshoes, she adjusted her rucksack to fit snuggly into the small of her back and with a final look back to the hotel, set off across the slope.

Born and raised in Fugen, Gerhard and his brother Sebastian grew up on the ski instructor circuit before following in their father and grandfather's footsteps as third generation mountain rangers. A vital element of the job included testing for potential avalanches, specific concerns for which had been raised earlier in the day due to the presence of a warm weather front approaching from the west. This also accounted for the brothers after-hours presence on the mountain as they took advantage of the clear moonlit night to check the area in readiness for the morning when upwards of two thousand skiers and snowboarders per hour would be spewed out across the mountain.

Traversing the fracture line above the gondola station they were taking it in turns to test the snowpack for signs of weakness while the other remained at a safe distance in the event of any problems. By digging pits at intervals, Gerhard was using state of the art radar technology to identify 'planes of weakness' caused by the proximity of ice beneath the surface. The warm temperatures prior to the recent snowfall across the Alps had caused much of the upper layers of snow to melt then re-freeze, effectively creating frictionless sheets of ice on which the new snowfall had settled. Once detected, the brothers would need to set charges to trigger mini avalanches in order to clear the problem, hence doing it at a time when the mountain was free of people, or at least when it should have been.

'Scheisse!' exclaimed Sebastian quietly, as he spotted torchlight further down the mountain. Fucking idiot, he thought as he reached for the radio handset on his lapel.

Yet to set any charges, Gerhard responded to his brother's call and worked his way back up the slope.

'There,' said Sebastian, pointing down the mountain to an area just above the tree line where moving torchlight could be seen clearly working its way down the edge of the piste.

'What the fuck does he think he's doing?' said Gerhard.

'I don't know,' replied Sebastian, shaking his head in amazement. 'Pissed probably, thinking he can walk back to the village.'

She heard the motor seconds before the headlamps appeared. Heading directly towards her, she had nowhere to go, so instead, stood still and waited for the skidoo to pull up alongside her.

'*Staatsangehorigketeit?*' (Nationality?) demanded the

pillion passenger as he stepped off the back of the skidoo.

'I'm sorry?' replied the woman.

Being bilingual was part of the job for all mountain rangers and instructors and with English the second language taught in Austrian schools, Sebastian followed up with, 'What do you think you're doing?'

'I love the night air and just wanted to go for a walk. Why? Have I done something wrong?'

Clearly she was not pissed, but that didn't make her situation any the less dangerous. 'You could get yourself killed out here alone at night,' Sebastian responded, his voice tight with anger at the stupidity of this woman.

'Well I'm not alone now, am I,' she smiled.

Her coy response did nothing to abate Sebastian's anger. Although wolves were only prominent in the Haute region of the French Alps, the Marchkoph was home to several other creatures, such as wild boar, that could cause a person harm. 'What is your name?' he asked.

'Lisbeth, Lisbeth Harrington,' she replied.

'Identification?'

As the woman slung her rucksack round from her back and dropped it on the floor, Sebastian turned to his brother,

25

*'Kontaktieren Sie den Kontrollrau Gerhard und sagen Sie ihnen,
dass wir diese dumme Frau zur Befragung hereinbringen werden.'*
(Contact the control room, Gerhard and tell them we will bring this
stupid woman in for questioning).

While her German was not fluent, a classical education,
plus the tone of the man's voice told Harrington all she needed to
know as she rummaged around in her rucksack. That she was
beautiful and petite was something which had always given her an
advantage in life and this situation was no exception as she used
the rucksack for cover to attach the suppressor onto the barrel of
the Glock.

That neither man saw the woman as a threat left them
woefully unprepared as she pulled out the weapon, swung her arm
up and *pfft, pfft* fired twice, both rounds hitting Sebastian in the
chest. A look of confusion then shock appeared on his face, yet
before his body had time to register what had happened, the
woman was already on her feet and in a smooth arc repeated the
process as Gerhard, unfamiliar with the sound of a suppressed
weapon looked up from the mainset radio mounted on the front of
the skidoo.

Annoyed, not so much by the intrusion, more by the wasted
time, the woman put the weapon back in her rucksack and
considered how to dispose of the bodies. What these two were
doing on the mountain at this time of night was not something she

had prepared for and the last thing she wanted was for another patrol to find her. With that at the forefront of her mind, she dragged the body of the Ranger who had spoken to her over to the skidoo and lay him across the back seat. Repeating the process with the second body, she found a coil of rope in a cage attached to the back of the skidoo and strapped them tightly to the machine. Maybe fifty metres or so further down the mountain she could see the top of the tree line which she figured would be her best bet even though it would mean having a short hike back up the hill when done.

Straddling the skidoo with her backside propped up on Gerhard's body, she examined the controls and decided it was nothing more than she was familiar with on a motorbike. Pressing the electric start button, she put it into first gear, let out the clutch and motored gently down the edge of the slope. On reaching the tree line, she looked down off the side of the piste. Satisfied with what she saw, she left the engine in first gear and keeping her hand on the clutch, stepped off to the side of the skidoo. Once satisfied there was nothing that could get snagged, she released the clutch and watched as the engine engaged and the machine, with its two inert passengers, slid off the edge of the piste and dropped down into a copse of pine trees which, come morning she hoped would be enough to hide them from view until her task was complete.

*

I guess the beer, dinner and mountain air must have done some good as for the first time in months I'd slept through till dawn. Okay, perhaps not the beer so much, but it still felt good as, in track suit and Beanie hat, I set out for a run before breakfast. Too cold for stretching, I began slowly maintaining a gentle pace as the orange glow of a beautiful new morning sketched a jagged line across the peaks above the village.

Again breathing in the pure mountain air, perfumed by occasional wafts from nearby cowsheds, I stuck to the gritted roads and headed downhill towards the centre of the village where a mix of traditional and modern hotels and homes reinforced the picture postcard theme from the night before. Dodging the odd snow plough here and there, I spent the next half hour or so navigating my way round the village before cutting across a park that ran parallel to the valley road. Pumping legs high to clear the near waist high snow, at the far end and with the thought of breakfast beckoning, I hopped over a wooden fence and turned back uphill towards home.

After a quick shower, hot, not cold, I'd leave that for the likes of Mr Bond, I headed back downstairs for breakfast. The buffet was, as advertised, a combo of cereals, cold meats, cheeses, yogurt and fruit all of which I passed in favour of a plateful of scrambled eggs, bacon, a couple of Kaiser rolls and by the time my guide appeared, two pots of coffee.

She wasn't quite what I expected, but perhaps that's just me getting old. They do say todays forty something is yesterday's thirty something so perhaps I shouldn't be surprised. Anyway, brown hair, pigtails, hazel eyes, freckly nose and a cheeky grin beamed at me as she dropped a rucksack on the floor and plonked herself down on a chair opposite.

'Hi, I'm Olivia,' she said, reaching out across the table, 'and you must be Mr Lendon?'

'Alex, please,' I replied, returning her handshake and infectious grin.

It turned out Olivia was older than she looked. In her mid-twenties, she'd recently qualified as a BASI level 2 ski instructor and this was her first job. Obviously keen to make a good impression, she ran through some basic health and safety stuff, including that due to the recent heavy snowfall, off-piste would be off the cards today due to avalanche warnings across the region.

So, having mapped out a plan for the day, I headed for the boot room to collect my gear and arranged to meet Livie, as she preferred to be called, outside the front of the hotel.

Stepping out of the shower, Harrington toweled off and reached for a fluffy white robe hanging on the back of the bathroom door. Wiping steam from the mirror she checked her contacts. How well they hid, not just the colour of her eyes, but also the anger behind them. Brushing out her hair, she shivered briefly, not with the cold as ski resort hotels were always warm, but in silent expectation of what was to come. Taking her time to brush her teeth, she left the bathroom, poured a coffee from the pot left by room service and opened her laptop.

It was a ten minute walk to the Spieljochbahn, the gondola station that would take us up the mountain. Ski buses were already arriving in droves so we hustled up the stairs and joined the huddle negotiating the electronic turnstiles. Edging forward into a bottleneck designed to provide controlled access to the individual gondolas, or bubbles as they're more commonly known, we waited patiently amidst the excited banter and multi-coloured ski apparel that would do London fashion week proud. To be fair, it was a pretty slick operation and within a couple of minutes it was our turn to board as bubble after bubble swallowed up the steady stream of skiers and snowboarders.

After an initial surge on exiting the station, each bubble settled down to become part of a giant, slow motion rollercoaster wending its way up the mountain. Lost in my own little world as we snaked through dense snow laden forests of pine, I gazed out of the plexiglass window at tiny snowflakes, cast adrift from the needles by a gentle breeze, creating a gorgeous rainbow of colours in the dappled morning sun.

'Good eh?' said Livie.

'You bet,' I replied. 'It doesn't get much better than this.'

Okay, time for a reality check. There are days when you can barely see your gloves in front of your face, but as we gazed through the plexiglass windows that surrounded our bubble, I could literally feel the mountain working it's magic on me.

'Oh look!' said Livie, interrupting my reverie. She was leaning forward from the bench seat opposite me and pointing down towards a gulley in the snow that come springtime would be a stream. 'Matta deer tracks.'

I leant forward and was about to say it, then just looked at her, shook my head and instead said, 'Nice try cookie girl!'

'So what brings you to this part of the world?' she asked, now she'd got my full attention.

I wasn't about to tell her the real reason for my trip so instead, I settled for, 'I got a map of Austria, closed my eyes, stuck a pin in it and here I am. How about you?'

'Kind of similar, I guess,' she replied. 'My Dad paid for my instructors course, but I had a few months to spare before the season got underway, so went travelling with my girlfriend.'

'So how did you decide where to go?'

'Like I said, a bit like you. We bought a round the world ticket and so long as we kept heading east we kind of did the pin thing each time we were ready to move on.'

'Good plan,' I said, grateful for the distraction as she went on to tell me about her journeys across Europe, Asia and Australasia before returning home to prepare for this, her next adventure.

It wasn't long before we broke free of the tree line into a dazzling snow bowl, crisscrossed by a series of chairlifts and topped by clear blue skies, interrupted only by occasional wisps of cotton wool hovering over the mountain peaks. It really doesn't get much better than this.

A few minutes later we reached the head of the gondola station and trudged, there's no elegant way to walk in ski boots, out into the snow. Dropping our skis down, we stepped into our bindings and with a double click of Livie's poles, set off down an easy blue. Despite the average ski holiday being one week a year, two if you're lucky, once you've got over the initial trial, great fun as it is, of re-acquiring the basics, skiing really is like riding a bike. So it wasn't long before blue runs became red and red became black as we took the Panoramabahn gondola to the summit and from there onto what Livie told me was a brand new skytrain that linked Fugen to the neighbouring higher resort of Hochfugen.

This time we had a bubble to ourselves which meant Livie

had room to spread the piste map out on her lap. 'Apparently, before this was built,' she said, 'you had to ski down the back of the mountain to pick up a bus to get up the valley.' She leant forward and pointed out the spur road that connected the two resorts. 'Now all we need to do is hop off here and…'

I smiled as she pointed to a symbol on the map that showed where this conversation was going. She'd told me earlier about a hutte above Hochfugen that had the most amazing views and 'burgers to die for.' That a shortish red from our next stop would take us to the base of a gondola station from where the hutte could be reached was clearly part of her forward planning.

'Early lunch it is then,' I said.

'If we must,' she replied with a grin as she re-folded the piste map and tucked it inside her jacket. 'After all, it has been a long time since breakfast.'

A faint blip appeared on the laptop screen. Gradually increasing in strength, Harrington waited until the final destination was clear before reaching for her ski jacket and helmet. A few moments later she stepped out of the bootroom into the hustle and bustle of the Wedelhutte's crowded lobby.

In a past life she would have relished the chance to be part of the melee looking to find a table for lunch. The warm atmosphere amidst pine clad beams and open fires couldn't have been more perfect. As was the sun clad terrace crowded with multi-coloured revelers. But now things were different. Despite her privileged, non-ethnic background, her transition from a confused student trying to make sense of life to one of radicalisation was not an uncommon path. Under the guidance of her mentor and lover, her time at University had become one of learning. Not for the course she had signed up for, but one which would ultimately end with a failed attempt to murder thousands of innocents and the death of her lover.

It was not survivors guilt that prompted her to beg for the opportunity to exact revenge on her lover's killer. Her part of the operation had gone according to plan and she was not to blame for the failure of the mission. But, she knew that if, as a woman, she were ever to be taken seriously and not simply used as a one off mule for delivering explosives into a crowded place, she would have to prove herself if she were to continue on the path her lover had set.

So now, as she retrieved her skis from the rack outside the hutte, it was almost time and Allah, in his infinite wisdom, would determine his fate.

It was relatively quiet as we shushed to a stop outside the base of the *Zillertaler Shuttle*. Lunchtimes had a habit of doing that.

Stepping out of our bindings, we picked up our skis and pushed through the turnstiles. With no one ahead of us we waited for the next bubble to make its way slowly round the giant bull wheel then, stashing our skis in the racks on the outside of the doors, stepped inside.

'Let's hope we're not too late to get a table,' said Livie, as she stretched out on the bench seat opposite me and slid the tips of her ski poles underneath my bench.

'Don't panic,' I laughed, as I stood to flip down the transom window and let in some fresh air. 'I'm sure we'll be able to perch somewhere.'

Looking up towards the summit as we began our ascent, I had a clear view of the gondola train ahead. Although designs have moved on since Robert Winterhalder invented the first iron beamed ski lift in 1910, the basic principles of propulsion have pretty much remained the same.

Supported by a single arm, each bubble uses a spring loaded clamp at the top of the arm to grip an endless loop of steel cable that travels between a series of towers positioned at intervals between the bottom and top of the mountain. Dependent on the terrain, this can mean going down as well as up as the path follows the contours of the mountain. When each gondola reaches a tower, the clamp rises automatically as it rumbles across a series of idler wheels fixed to a teeter-totter frame before freeing itself on the far side and moving onto the next.

This almost mesmeric process invariably focuses my attention on the towers ahead, today being no exception until Livie tapped me on the knee and pointed back down below.

'Look,' she said.

'Not again,' I laughed.

'No seriously,' she said, more urgently. 'Look.'

I did as I was told and saw a group of skiers and snowboarders clustered together along the edge of the piste. Following their line of sight down and into a gulley beneath the gondola train I could see what looked like the back end of a skidoo sticking up and out of the undergrowth.

'Okay, that doesn't look good,' I said.

'No, it doesn't,' replied Livie. 'I'm sorry, Alex, but we're going to have to miss lunch.'

'Of course,' I said.

Despite being one of only a few independent ski companies operating across the region, much like a ship stopping for another in distress at sea, it was the same for all instructors when there was a problem on the mountain. As Livie reached for the radio transmitter in her rucksack, I looked up to see how far we had to go to reach the top station. Clearly outlined against the backdrop of blue sky, maybe a couple of hundred metres away, it was instead the change in outline of the approaching tower that caught my eye. What looked like a small dark object sat alongside the ascending teeter totter wheel. I suppose it could be some form of monitoring device, but the hairs on the back of my neck told me something different.

Having taken black from the red that led away from the hotel, Harrington had swept round underneath the path of the gondola train, increasing her speed by taking the fall line down the mountain until she reached her predetermined vantage point. From there, she'd stopped on the edge of the piste and pulled an iPhone from a pocket in her ski jacket.

The last thing I remembered as the explosion rocked the mountain was hitting my head on the plexiglass window and being thrown around the inside of the gondola like a lottery ball in a tombola. I don't know how long I'd been out, but it couldn't have been long, as from my new location on the floor, the bubble was still rocking wildly from side to side as it sought to regain its equilibrium.

How the cable held fast heaven only knew, but that wasn't my immediate concern as I tried to clear the ringing in my ears and check on Livie who lay unmoving, wedged half under me and half under my benchseat. I needed to make some space. But as I tried to move, a searing pain ripped through my shoulder and sweat began to pour off me. Forced back onto the floor, I turned my head away from Livie and with a silent apology, vomited. It must have been the adrenalin, nature's very own anesthetic, that prevented me from immediately recognising the extent of the injury, but one quick look told me my right shoulder was at best dislocated. Trying to put it out of my mind, I took several deep breaths, pumped my left fist and clenched my butt cheeks to try and raise my blood pressure. It wasn't going to do either of us any good if I passed out again and although it didn't help with the pain, at least the nausea passed as I used my good arm to slide under the bench from where I could reach Livie's neck and check for a pulse. Low and steady was good news, but then, as muffled screams broke through the ringing in my ears, what followed was not, as a series of cracking, pistol like sounds began to reverberate around the mountain.

Looking up and beyond what was now a spider's web of cracks in the plexiglass, I could see my hopes for the cable holding had been short lived. Individual strands of steel were pinging off, whipping back and forth furiously as the whole thing began to unravel. With the inevitable seconds away, I used my good arm to pushed Livie completely under the bench then, laying out in the footwell alongside her I just had time to jam my legs against the doors of the gondola as the final strand parted.

*

As the gondola train plummeted down through the canopy of pine trees, Harrington listened dispassionately to the screams that echoed across the mountain. Such had been her indoctrination into the world of terror, she felt no remorse for the victims. Instead, she was simply grateful for the angle of descent as the train landed on, in and around the skidoo. This quirk of fate that would hamper the investigation into the deaths of the two mountain rangers was something she would take advantage of in making her escape, but for now, as she watched the clouds of snow billowing up through the trees, she knew her ultimate goal would only be complete once she had sight of the lifeless body of her lover's killer.

Daylight filtered through a thin dusting of snow. Our bubble was on its back, plugged in the snow like a golf ball in a bunker. With Livie still unconscious as she lay alongside me, I managed to ease myself up between the two benches and rest my back against the wall opposite the double doors. Cradling my injured arm against my chest, I thanked God for small mercies. Only the week before, I'd been disappointed to hear there had been little more than thirty centimetres of compact snow on the upper slopes which would have barely covered the rocky outcrops in the gulley beneath the gondola train. Now though, and thanks to the recent heavy downfall, the depth must have been nearer ninety centimetres.

Not that this made the downward trajectory of our fall any the less painful, but at least this time, not having lost consciousness, my senses were on full alert as a weird silence which had descended on the mountain was broken only minutes later by the sounds of scrabbling outside the bubble's double doors.

Too soon for mountain rescue and with those onlookers who'd spotted the skidoo unlikely to risk the descent to our location, I instinctively reached for a ski pole and waited as one of the skis, amazingly still held in place on the outside of the doors, was plucked out of the rack and jammed in between the opening. Worked back and forth, the doors cracked open slightly after which the edge of the ski was replaced by a pair of gloved hands and ultimately, as the doors eased open, the slim figure of a woman wearing a black and white, one piece ski suite. A serious looker, perhaps in her mid-twenties, she had a shock of blond hair held in place by a black headband. In clumpy ski boots she balanced precariously on the edge of the footplate, her left hand holding onto the doorframe to steady herself while the other held a Glock 9mm semi-automatic pistol, complete with suppressor.

Although different to the images captured on CCTV, there was no doubt this was the final and its believed only surviving member of a terrorist cell involved in two terrorist attacks on UK soil last year.

The precursor and reason for those attacks took place at the launch of a luxury cruise liner in Southampton to which I and my girlfriend, Bronagh Foley, had been invited. It had been a glorious summers evening at the end of which I'd planned to propose. Instead, it went tragically wrong as a group of Islamic fundamentalists attempted to kidnap the billionaire owner of the cruise line. It transpired that the leader of the group was looking to move up the terrorist food chain under the guise of fighting for independence in Kashmir, a region of north west India plagued with problems since rendition in 1947. That they'd ultimately been unsuccessful meant nothing to me as a stray round from a discharged handgun had taken B's life. Ironically it was this incident that brought me back to the attention of Sir Henry who himself had moved on to pastures new. Seconded from my day job in Hampshire as Operations Superintendent he tasked me with investigating a sensitive piece of intelligence on the group which told of the leader's desire for revenge off the back of the failed operation and the need for him to save face among the terrorist fraternity.

That I'd been responsible for taking the life of his nephew during the failed kidnapping added some spice to the occasion and ultimately led to two subsequent incidents.

The first, a bombing in Portsmouth during which a police dog handler tragically died and for which the woman balancing on the footplate in front of me was responsible and second, well that was more ambitious and involved two IEDs (Improvised Explosive Devices) in the Blackwall Tunnel.

Spanning the Thames from the Isle of Dogs to the borough of Tower Hamlets, one was directly beneath the O2 Arena, formerly known as the Millennium Dome and the other mid tunnel. Her role in this incident had been to murder the engineers from the control room and prevent the floodgates located at either end of the tunnel from closing. Had the devices detonated, thousands attending a Princes Trust concert above would have been murdered and having breached the tunnel midway beneath the Thames, flooding to the north and south of the river would have been devastating.

As the suspected lover of one of the cell members killed during the attack, this went some way to explain this less than welcome turn of events. While 'revenge' as they say is 'a dish best served cold,' the irony of our location made this thought somewhat more poignant. That her lover's part in the operation had been one of a suicide bomber seemed to have passed her by and although I knew I was about to play with fire, the best I could hope for given our current predicament was to keep her talking and hope for a miracle.

'So this is personal,' I said, looking up at her as my hand closed on the ski pole.

'I really wouldn't bother,' she replied, gesturing towards

the pole with her gun. 'And yes, you're right. This is personal, but don't over estimate your importance Mr Lendon. You are nothing more than a loose end.'

'Charming,' I said. 'So I guess we're looking at another "Allahu Akbar" moment?'

'Very funny,' she replied. 'But yes, *God is great.*'

This wasn't *my first rodeo*, but at least in the past, I generally had a contingency plan. Hammad, my old oppo from SO13 having been on point the last time someone tried to send me on my way. But not today. Even if I were able to bridge the gap between us, gammy shoulder and all, she would still have more than enough time to pull the trigger. Three rounds in a second to be precise.

'You can't blame a man for trying now can you,' I said, easing my good arm behind my back. Perhaps if I could at least lever myself up and…

'I suppose not,' she said, as an incongruous rumble of thunder echoed across the mountain. Distracting her momentarily, her eyes left me to look up the mountain.

Grabbing the ski pole again I went to thrust it up and towards her exposed belly, but as I tried to gain some purchase, the ground beneath the bubble began to shake. Not dissimilar to the beginnings of an earthquake, it was enough to knock me back against the wall and send another crippling bolt of pain through my shoulder. Gasping for breath, I looked up, expecting to feel worse from the 9mm. Instead, both her hands were occupied, her precarious position on the footplate meaning she had to use both hands to brace herself against either side of the bubble's doorframe. So with the Glock no longer in play and me unable to move, we ended up in an almost comical stand-off as she fought to maintain her balance until… the bubble flipped up in the air and the lights went out.

PART 2

'Morituri Non Cognant'

(Those Who are About to Die, Just Don't Know)

Tom Clancy

12th April 1947 – 1st October 2013

CHAPTER 4

'Darling! Have you seen my cravat?'

'The paisley?'

'Yes, that's the one.'

'Same place as last time, you old fool. In the wardrobe, third drawer down on the left. Now hurry up, breakfast's nearly ready.'

Jim Kirby smiled as he opened the wardrobe doors. They'd been having this type of ritual for years and he loved every minute of it. Married for forty, never a day went by without him thinking he was the luckiest man alive. Yes, the house on Eaton Square, the Bentley and the villa in Nice were all splendid, but none of that meant a jot without Mary-Jane to share it with.

'So what culinary delights have you got lined up for me this morning?' he asked, as he walked into the kitchen and perched on a stool alongside the granite topped island.

'If by that, you mean something other than boiled eggs and soldiers, you'll be sorely disappointed,' responded Mary-Jane, as she spooned an egg from the saucepan into a waiting cup and lay another on the side.

'Fry up tomorrow then?' he asked hopefully.

'You'll be lucky, but if you keep being good and your cholesterol levels return to normal, then we'll see,' she replied, as she shook out a linen napkin, tucked it under his chin and gave him a peck on the cheek. 'Can't have his Lordship with egg on his face now can we.'

'No dear,' he replied demurely, as the doorbell chimed.

'Stay there and finish your breakfast,' she said. 'I'll get it.'

'Amanda not in today,' he asked doing as he was told.

'It's her day off,' she replied as she disappeared down the corridor.

Gentleman Jim Kirby, as known to his contemporaries, had been a member of the bar for the best part of four decades and Queen's Counsel for twenty five. A staunch advocate for the right to a fair trial, his attention to detail and reputation for thoroughness were beyond compare, something which had earned him enormous respect among his colleagues and others, including the former

Commissioner of the Metropolitan Police.

'Darling, it's…'

'Yes, yes, my dear, I can see,' said Kirby as he looked up at the familiar figure filling the doorway. 'Henry, dear fellow,' he continued as he dabbed his mouth with the napkin. 'Stop blocking out the light and come in.'

'I'm sorry to disturb you on a Sunday, James,' said Sir Henry King, as he reached for the mug of coffee proffered by Mary-Jane. 'But there's a question of some import I'd like to talk to you about.'

'Yes, of course, Henry,' Kirby responded and rose from his stool. 'Nothing like a spot of intrigued to wet the whistle on a weekend. Come along, bring your coffee and we'll talk in the study.'

CHAPTER 5

According to the news coverage, the avalanche had swept down the mountain from a deep fracture above the *Zillertaler Shuttle*. Picking up more and more ice and snow as it sped down the mountain, the good news for those skiers on piste was the trajectory took it down the valley beneath the gondola train from where it engulfed the bubbles in a protective layer of debris until such time as mountain rescue could get to us. Quite what happened to ours was still unclear, but it seemed the combination of the doors being open and the woman on the footplate resulted in the bubble being flipped over, a circumstance which effectively saved our lives, for had the snow entered the bubble then like as not we would have crushed and or suffocated. As to what happened to the woman? That was something I was looking forward to finding out, but it had to wait as my first stop had been an airlift to Innsbruck University Hospital.

Thankfully the shoulder was only a partial dislocation, so

having checked up on Livie who was back in the land of the living, albeit whinging loudly about being kept in for observation, I'd been given the all clear by the medics, dosed up on anti-inflammatories and had taken the first available flight home. From there I went to Flint House, the Police Rehabilitation Centre at Goring-on-Thames, where I spent the next couple of days in the hands of a sadistic team of arch manipulators going through a series of stretching and strengthening exercises. That said, by the time I left, things were a lot better and I was ready to follow up on an invite from Sir Henry to join him at his new digs in the city.

Approaching the nondescript building on the corner of Whitehall and Trafalgar Square, I was mindful of 'Universal Exports,' Ian Fleming's fictional headquarters for MI6. In reality, and far less romantically in my opinion, the top floor had been given over to the government by the Royal Bank of Scotland which occupied the rest of the building.

'Morning Moneypenny,' I said to Di Brooks, Sir Henry's personal assistant, as I sauntered into the outer office. If only I had a trilby to lob at the coat stand in the corner, the scene would have been complete. 'Am I to be hung drawn and quartered or sent to the dungeons?'

Di looked up at me over the top of her glasses. 'All of the above,' she said, swiveling her chair around to get up and give me a careful hug. A pocket rocket, fifty something, I never dared to ask, a forever tan and bleached blond spikey hair, Di had been Sir Henry's PA from way back in the day when he was Assistant Chief Constable for Specialist Operations in Hampshire. 'Go on in and I'll bring the coffee.'

'Perfect,' I said, then out of habit, knocked before opening the door to the inner sanctum.

Reminiscent of a bygone era, wood paneling into which recessed bookshelves were stacked with scholastic tomes, a crackling fireplace and the feint aroma of lingering cigars gave the place the air of a gentleman's club. In front of a bay window that looked out and across to the top of Nelson's Column, Sir Henry was sat behind an old regency style desk, banging out a two fingered assault on a keyboard. Stopping momentarily to look up over his glasses – must be catching – he pointed towards the fireplace in front of which an array of deep cushioned, brown leather armchairs were dotted around a black marble topped coffee table.

'Make yourself comfortable, Alex. Just need to get this off to the Home Sec and I'll be with you.'

I nodded as Di appeared with a tray on which sat a pot of coffee and three cups and saucers.

Sir Henry's empire had expanded little since his appointment as Head of the UK Intelligence Services. As was his want, he preferred to rely on a trusted, close knit circle of confidants on whom he could rely not to treat him like a mushroom. One such person was Charlie Irving, the protégé of GCHQ Director, Sir John Bradley. Following on behind Di, Charlie, was in his late twenties, a keen triathlete and Cambridge first with an MPhil in Advanced Computer Science. His early achievements in computer programming and code breaking quickly brought him to the attention of Sir John and by default, Sir Henry. Having helped bring down the terrorist plot in London last year, the last I'd heard was that Charlie was working in the Computer Network Operations department at GCHQ.

'Morning, Charlie,' I said, as he took my cue and slumped into another of the armchairs.

'Hi, Alex,' he replied with a casual grin.

'Help yourselves gentlemen' said Sir Henry, easing himself out from behind his desk, 'and pour me one please.'

Joining us round the fireplace, Sir Henry settled himself comfortably into another of the armchairs and reached for the cup and saucer proffered by Charlie. 'It seems your vacation turned into quite an adventure, Alex.'

'You could say that,' I replied, shifting slightly to ease some residual discomfort in my shoulder.

'How's it doing?'

'It could be worse,' I smiled. 'A lot worse.'

'Good point. What about the girl?'

'Concussion, whiplash and seriously pissed off that she's had to miss the rest of the season.'

'We need to do something about that...' he half closed his eyes. 'Leave it with me. I'll get Di on the case.'

'That would be good,' I said. 'She didn't deserve to get tangled up in this mess.'

'Quite. Now, I expect you're looking forward to some answers?'

'You could say that,' I replied.

'The good news and despite rumours to the contrary, Brexit hasn't affected our relationship with Europol which meant we were given unrestricted access to the subsequent investigation by the European Counter Terrorism Centre. Indeed, a team from SO15 were invited over to shadow the investigation.'

'Do we have more information on the casualties?' I asked. I'd read that the numbers were low which seemed incredible, but there'd been few details in the paper and of course there was one I was particularly interested in hearing more about.

'Believe it or not, very few,' he replied. 'It seems that emergency clamps on the towers above and below yours engaged as soon as the cable severed which resulted in only your section of the gondola train being affected. That, coupled with the heavy snowfall since Christmas meant the depth of snow in the gulley beneath the gondolas reduced serious casualties to a minimum. Broken bones, concussions, cuts and bruises, but thankfully no fatalities, at least not in terms of passengers.' He paused to pick up his coffee cup. 'It turns out the bulk of the avalanche followed the line of the valley beneath your gondola train.' He took a sip, clearly enjoying the build up to the climax of his story. 'And it would appear your nemesis was flung from your gondola and slammed into the one behind.'

'Dead?' I asked. 'There was no mention of a fatality in the papers.'

'Oh yes,' he replied. 'Broken neck. The Austrian authorities were keen to keep it quiet. The last thing they wanted was to admit to a terrorist incident on home soil, especially in a ski resort. Any reports of a fatality would have led to no end of awkward questions, not to mention the impact on tourism.'

'So what was their explanation?'

'Let's just say Dopplemayr aren't going to be very happy when it's declared as a technical fault.'

'Some technical fault,' I replied. 'So what happened to the body?'

'Airlifted to Innsbruck, where the post mortem confirmed the broken neck.'

'And, it's definitely her?'

'No question. Her clothing was seized, along with a hotel keycard and much like the one used to detonate the bomb in Leicester Square, a mobile phone used to trigger the explosion.'

'So who is she or should I say was she?'

'Passport in the name of a Lisbeth Harrington. Facial recognition confirms her as our missing female from both incidents in Portsmouth and London last year.'

'Did she have any connection to Bronagh's murder?'

'Timing's wrong' said Sir Henry. 'She only came on the scene after Bronagh's murder. Turns out, as we suspected, she'd been radicalised by her lecturer and lover while a student at the London School of Economics.'

Who I'd subsequently dispatched in the tunnel and so it goes on. 'I assume the keycard was for a hotel on the mountain?'

'Your lunch destination by all accounts.'

'Makes sense, but how could she know which gondola we were in?'

'I'll leave that one for Charlie to explain,' he said, replacing his coffee cup and settling back in his armchair.

'A laptop in her room was linked to her mobile,' responded Charlie, 'along with a tracking device hidden in your ski boot.'

'What?'

'Don't ask me how it got there.'

After a moment's thought I said, 'I know,' and told them about the insecure boot room at my hotel. 'But how did she know I was even in the resort in the first place?'

'It looks like Hampshire's mainframe was hacked,' he continued. 'Your calendar showed you on leave with a contact number for the travel company. We got someone to have a quiet word with your management assistant and apparently she put it in so she could get hold of you in the event of an emergency. Once they had that, they did the same to the travel company and up came your name and a booking for the hotel.'

'Okay,' I said, 'but how was Harrington able to get the timing right? I'm assuming she must have set the charge the night before otherwise it would have been discovered during an inspection?'

'Travel manifests showed Harrington as having flown into Innsbruck two weeks earlier and booked herself into the hotel. According to the owners of your travel company, they received a call a week or so before from a prospective guest keen to know the routine for a typical week of guided skiing for solo travelers. This was unusual, hence they remembered the call. Anyway, the guest, a woman was all they had, didn't follow up with a booking, but it's fair to say that was Harrington.'

'Makes sense,' I said.

'It does and also ties in with what you said about the bootroom scenario. A similar call was put through to Frau... he looked down at his notes.'

'Frau Erlebach,' I said, remembering the bear hug.

'Apparently the caller was concerned about her skis and wanted to know the security arrangements for the bootroom. Had a pair pinched once on a trip to Slovenia apparently. Armed with that information, it was a simple matter to wait for you to check in, plant the tracker in your boot and then, the following day wait for it to appear on line and well, you know the rest.'

'Now, Alex,' said Sir Henry as Charlie sat back in the armchair, his job for now done. 'Before we go on to other matters, have you had any more thoughts on my offer?'

To be honest, I'd thought of little else since my return from Austria and couldn't help but feel whatever Sir Henry had up his sleeve was something I wanted to be a part of. So the answer was quite simple.

'When do I start?'

CHAPTER 6

The Sheik had arrived in Dover after a circuitous journey across Europe. A tiresome yet necessary subterfuge given the nature of the operation, once on UK soil he'd hired a car using one of several false identities at his disposal. Nothing too fancy and certainly nothing to which he would otherwise be accustomed, he took advantage of the plethora of minor country roads, not covered by any form of traffic surveillance, to make his way north until eventually, two days later, arriving at his current location, a lay-by overlooking the Scottish Port of Grangemouth.

From his perch on the side of the hill, the Sheik nodded in satisfaction. The Russian had chosen well he thought as he watched the container being raised from the cargo hold of a battered old merchantman and loaded onto a trailer attached to the back of an lorry. Midway between Edinburgh and Glasgow, at the centre of Scotland's industrial heartland, Grangemouth, which handles in excess of one hundred and fifty thousand containers per year provided the ideal destination for the shipment. Yes, all were screened, but having taken the right precautions, the container, one of many to arrive from the Latvian Port of Riga, would soon be heading south on the M9.

With time to kill before the lorry and its precious cargo cleared customs, the Sheik reflected on the visit from Nikolay Kamenev, the once head of SVR, *Sluzhba Vneshney Razvedki*, Russia's external intelligence agency and equivalent to MI6, the UK's Secret Intelligence Service. The meeting had gone well, their mutual concerns having caused significant rumblings in the labyrinthine corridors of the Kremlin. He also knew that with Kamenev now distanced from his former seat of power, the Russian became the perfect foil for President Vasily Ulyanov to, in the words of John Dean, legal counsel for disgraced US President Richard Nixon, wear the cloak of plausible deniability should the result of their conversation in the desert ever come to light. But of course, this wasn't going to happen, after all, despite their countries past differences, *'the enemy of my enemy…'* remained as true today as it did in the 4th century BC when first penned in Sanskrit as part of India's economic and military strategy.

CHAPTER 7

The lights were still on when I got home. The white clapperboard façade of a three storey property in Bath Square backed onto Portsmouth Harbour and was a welcome sight after a long day. Sliding the key quietly into the lock I could hear soft music playing in the background as I gently pushed the door open.

The ground floor was an open plan mix of dim lighting, wood paneling, lathe and plaster walls, beams and pillars, the latter supporting the upper floors to which a spiral staircase provided access. At the far end, the kitchen extended the entire width of the building with a bank of windows that offered spectacular views across the harbour, especially during a storm. To the right and just beyond the staircase, a pair of French doors opened out onto a wide terrace. Surrounded on two sides by high walls, the third was open to the water from where a mooring, once used by HM Customs to collect duty from trading ships as they entered the harbour, was now home to *Trinidad*, my father's pride and joy. A sleek mahogany slipper launch, think of a comfortable old leather slipper and you'll get the idea in terms of its shape, was more suited to the tranquil waters of a river or lake rather than the Solent, but on good days there was nothing better than pottering round the harbour or taking short trips along the coast to Hayling Island or Chichester Harbour where it was possible to moor up and enjoy some local hospitality.

Back inside, a central walkway connected the front of the property to the rear, either side of which were recessed areas in the floor that provided an ever present reminder of the building's original purpose in the mid 1700's, that of a saltwater bathing house. To the right, three steps led down a study while to the left, the dying embers of a log fire played centerpiece to a scattering of armchairs and a large sofa on which two bodies were sprawled out fast asleep.

Not much of a guard dog perhaps, but as a former bomb dog, Scrumpy had been second to none until the bombing in Portsmouth last year killed his handler and left him stone deaf. But as they say, when *'one door closes...,'* the subsequent decision to retire him meant he was now very much a part of the Lendon household.

Not that a dog like Scrumpy needed his hearing to know I'd arrived home. The scent of his new Dad was enough to fire him up and like an ICBM, fly over the back of the sofa, scuttle across the wooden floor and crash into my legs as the second, bleary eyed head appeared over the back of the sofa.

Brushing a hand through a mop of tousled blond hair, she said, 'Hello stranger.'

Hampshire chief inspector, Jill Dennison was head of the Marine and Joint Specialist Search Unit with Thames Valley and like so many others had come too close for comfort to losing her life last year. But now, how can I put it… she was a good friend and an occasional sitter for Scrumpy.

'Sorry,' I said. 'Had to detour via the old man's office.'

'No worries. Was it worth it?' she asked, squinting at the clock on the fireplace.

'You could say that,' I said.

'Something you can share?'

'Could be.'

'There's beer in the fridge.'

'Even better,' I said and grinned as I headed for the kitchen. 'By the way, have you ever thought of becoming an escort?'

CHAPTER 8

They say a week in politics is a long time, a truism applied equally to my new role as beneath azure skies, I looked across crystal clear, cobalt blue waters towards the Kas peninsular.

A remote fishing village on the Mediterranean coast, Kas is some 700km, give or take, south west of the Turkish capital of Ankara. This popular tourist destination of narrow cobbled streets, bustling markets and bougainvillea laden whitewashed buildings would, under other circumstances, have made for a perfect holiday destination. But not today. Today was all about business, although you could be forgiven for thinking otherwise, given the looks our table was receiving from the lunchtime clientele at the rooftop bar. Despite offering stunning views across the harbour, it was the two girls at my table that were attracting the most attention, from the men for one reason and from their partners entirely another.

Sat alongside Jill and in her late twenties, Nici Matthews was a stunning strawberry blond and every inch the typical English rose. An undercover officer with the National Crime Agency, she'd been approached for this operation by Sir Henry on Jill's recommendation. Having worked together on several jobs in the past, this was a familiarity which could well prove essential over the coming few hours. To be fair Jill didn't look too shabby either, a comment which had met with a firm slap earlier in the day. But, most importantly, bikinis and near transparent sarongs, hung loosely from narrow hips, meant both girls fit perfectly the profile for our target's tastes.

As to what we were doing in Kas, well, that became apparent as soon as I'd agreed to Sir Henry's proposition.

It turned out Charlie was able to download a list numbers from the iPhone found on Harrington's body, one of which was of particular interest, a call to the Palace of Westminster made within a half hour of last year's incident in the Blackwall Tunnel.

The call, made by Harrington purporting to be a Mrs Hamilton, was to the office of Akram Murad, MP for Southampton Itchen and newly appointed Secretary of State for Immigration. As with all such calls, it was recorded and would otherwise have appeared innocuous were it not for this discovery. The subsequent forensic analysis of Murad's life went on to raise further areas of concern including one of particular interest to me, his visit to Hampshire's Force Control Room on the night of Bronagh's death.

Setting that that to one side for the moment, further enquiries discovered several bogus email accounts on which messages were left in draft folders. Once read, those messages could then be deleted without ever having been sent. This meant they were not being picked up by GCHQ's listening stations. That didn't mean however, once you knew what to look for or rather once Charlie knew what to look for, those deleted messages couldn't be retrieved.

The first of these accounts confirmed Murad's link to the leader of the group responsible for the attack on the cruise ship, his presence in the control room no doubt having been to monitor the operation.

The second was to a series of coded messages offering times and dates for meetings with Behdad Khadem, the Leicester Square suicide bomber.

The third, simply referred to as 'S,' had an additional encryption capability on which Charlie was still working and finally, the fourth was our reason for being in Turkey, one Mehmet Ali, a Lebanese arms dealer responsible for supplying the Semtex explosives used during the Portsmouth bombing.

*

Operating as a legitimate arms dealer across Europe and the Middle East, while Ali's centre of operations was a villa in the mountains above Kas, much of his business was done on board his six berth, thirty five metre gulet moored in the harbour. Found primarily across the eastern Mediterranean, these wooden hulled schooners evoke images of the Ottoman Empire and are popular as charter vessels for tourists seeking a holiday beyond the beaches and hotels on the mainland. Not that any tourist would be setting foot on this one as it swayed gently in the warm afternoon breeze.

'Right on cue,' I said to the girls as a white Humvee pulled up onto the quay.

The driver's door opened and a typical bodyguard, all bulk with no neck, emerged in shades, blue shorts and a Hawaiian shirt. After a swift look round, he opened the rear doors of the vehicle from which two men stepped onto the quay. Ali certainly looked the part in a white suit, panama hat and to complete the ensemble, white shoes. His guest, less like Al Capone, was conservatively dressed in khaki trousers, white short sleeved shirt and what looked like a linen jacket slung over his arm.

Picking up a pair of binoculars from the table I scanned the quayside for signs of any additional players then focused on the bodyguard, the tell-tale bulge of a sidearm apparent beneath his untucked shirt. Taking a moment to do another recce, the guard ushered his charges to a waiting tender which would take them out to the gulet.

'All set?' I asked the girls.

With a wink from Jill who was clearing enjoying this new role, perhaps a little too much, they finished their drinks, pulled out a pair of brightly coloured rucksacks from under the table and much to the disappointment of several onlookers, sashayed off towards a set of wooden stairs at the far end of the terrace.

To say I wasn't anxious as I watched them leave would be a lie for although I had every faith in the two of them, not being in direct contact was something that made me nervous. Add to that, this was our first operation together and while planned meticulously, there were always the 'unknown, unknowns,' as Donald Rumsfeld once referred to in a speech about the lack of evidence linking Iraq to the possession of weapons of mass destruction.

For now though and with little more to do than wait for my cue, I reflected on the remainder of the meeting with Sir Henry on my return from Austria.

It seemed that Geraldine Taylor's response to the events of last year and more recently, the bombing in Leicester Square was to exercise her prerogative as Prime Minister and effectively *'declare war'* on those persons who, as Sir Henry put it, 'chose to threaten the lives of others by means of terrorism.' More commonly known as the royal prerogative, such powers date back to the time of Henry VIII and although strictly speaking belong to the Monarch, by convention they are, in practical terms, exercised by the PM or in some instances by cabinet members. That said, given the need for absolute secrecy, her decision had been made without consultation with her Cabinet. *'Leaky fucking sieve,'* were apparently the words used when Sir Henry broached the subject.

Despite this directive, the PM was under no illusions that one day this decision would leak and she needed to be sure that a lawful procedure was in place for dealing with these individuals, hence the inclusion of the Attorney General and one James Kirby QC.

Appealing to Gentleman Jim's sense of fair play, Sir Henry had persuaded him to take on the role of 'Special Advocate' in a quasi-judicial process known as the 'Hillary Courts.' Named after the incumbent Home Secretary, this was a variation on the trial without jury, 'Diplock Courts,' introduced in the 70s for dealing with internees during the troubles in Northern Ireland. In this instance, intelligence gathered on terror suspects deemed to pose a threat to life would now, in closed session, be presented to a panel of three Supreme Court Judges. In much the same way as one who argued against the canonisation or sainthood of a candidate within the Catholic church, Jim's role as *advocatus diaboli* would be to act as devil's advocate on behalf of the defence by exposing any flaws in the evidence presented by the Attorney General on behalf of the Crown, both positions being of equal importance given the ultimate sanction for the subject was to be terminated without prejudice.

My thoughts were interrupted as a waitress approached the table and picked up my empty coffee cup.

'Enas allos espreso?' she asked.

Glancing down to the quay, I could see the girls had arrived and were waiting on the tender to return from the gulet.

'They are beautiful,' said the waitress, switching to English.

'Excuse me,' I replied.

'Your friends.'

'Yes, yes they are,' I said, feeling a touch of rouge creeping up the back of my neck.

'Perhaps one for you more than the other?' she smiled.

You could be right was an instinctive thought that left me a little shocked as I quickly changed the subject, 'Evet, baska bir kahve guzel olurdu, tesekkurler' (Yes, another coffee would be

71

lovely, thank you).

There was no specific intel on the guard as he returned with the tender, other than Ali preferring to recruit former Spetsnaz, Russian Special Forces, operatives as bodyguards. Perhaps this accounted for the crescent shaped scar around his left eye, thought Matthews as they took the short flight of steps down from the quay and stepped carefully into the tender. Saying nothing on the short journey back to the gulet, he chose instead to leer at the girls as they lounged on the plush leather bench in the bow.

Although this was a first for both of them, they'd both worked vice at different times during their respective careers. So with plenty of experience dealing with 'call girls,' high class or otherwise, in this role they knew that smiles were for the paying customer and not the hired help hence, 'In your dreams, big boy,' said Dennison as both, very much in character, gave him the middle finger.

Not that it made any difference as he continued to leer at them until the tender pulled up alongside a wooden slatted rope ladder that would take them up and amidships to an open gate in the gunwale.

Swapping stilettos for flats from their rucksacks and with a backward glare of her own as the guard tried to put his hand on her arse, Dennison scurried up the ladder, closely followed by Matthews.

'Listen fuckhead,' said Matthews as the guard joined them on deck. 'Anymore of that shit and we'll be having a chat with your Boss.'

Raising a hand in apparent surrender, he took a step back and directed them into the main salon. Pointing to their rucksacks, he indicated for them to be placed on an oblong glass topped table surrounded by eight cream leather dining chairs. At its centre stood a huge silver terrine filled to the brim with white powder.

'Doesn't say much, does he,' said Dennison.

'All hands, no balls,' replied Matthews.

As the guard rummaged through their rucksacks, both women looked round the salon. Matching sofas and rosewood paneling, punctuated at intervals by chrome framed portholes, extended the length of the room. Towards the bow were two sets of stairs, one leading up to the bridge and the other down, presumably to the staterooms. To the stern, double smoked glass doors led out onto the aft sundeck where Ali could be seen entertaining his guest.

'What is this?' demanded the guard, holding up a box containing a set of handcuffs.

'Tools of the trade, love,' responded Matthews. 'Now be a good boy and put them back or…' she looked out towards the sundeck.

Throwing the cuffs back into the rucksack, he scowled and said, 'Leave here and follow me.'

'Not a happy bunny,' laughed Dennison as the girls linked arms and followed the guard through the double doors.

It hadn't taken Charlie long to do a preliminary work up on Mehmet Ali. Born during the mid-70s amidst the emerging chaos of civil war in Lebanon, a Shia Muslim, he'd spent much of his early childhood living with his parents in the town of Baalbek to the north of the Beqaa Valley. A Shia stronghold, his early years were heavily influenced by the teachings of Ayatollah Khomeini. By fifteen, he'd joined the ranks of Hezbollah as they waged an Iran funded guerilla campaign against the Israeli occupation in south Lebanon. By the time the Israelis withdrew in May 2000, he was a seasoned veteran with established links to Iran thanks to their provision of weapons and military training during the campaign. With little interest in Hezbollah's emerging influence as a political entity across the region, Ali chose to put his skills to work elsewhere and if a little cash followed on then that, so far as he was concerned, was Allah's will.

*

Shaded from the sun's glare by a canvas bimini top draped from the boom of the main mast to poles that extended beyond the gunwale, Ali and his guest looked relaxed as they reclined on more cream leather cushions scattered across a wide semi-circular sofa that followed the contours of the stern of the gulet. To one side, a table, covered in white linen, paid host to an array of silver platters that overflowed with olives, tomatoes, breads, fried vegetables, cheeses and kebabs unlike anything Dennison had seen in your average kebab house at home. Ali was clearly out to impress his guest, she thought. Let's hope he's not disappointed with what we have to offer.

With sleeves rolled up over thick hairy forearms Ali pointed at Matthews. 'You, sit here,' he commanded, slapping the cushions alongside him, then flicked his hand at Dennison, 'and you, join my friend.'

A half hour later, the gulet's anchor chain rose and a puff of exhaust smoke belched from the engine at the stern. It was time for me to settle the bill.

I left a generous, but not too generous tip for the waitress and returned to a hired jeep left in an alley near to the bar. A few minutes later I'd wormed my way through a series of narrow cobbled streets and was on the way out of town.

It was still early in the season so little more than twenty minutes later, I pulled into a graveled car park overlooking a deserted bay that in high season would be teeming with holidaymakers. Hewn out of the rockface, I made my way down a steep winding staircase and crunched across a pebbled beach towards a rickety old jetty. Used by local fishermen and bleached by the sun, the wooden structure extended out into the clear blue waters of the Med and on another day would have made for a perfect diving platform. At the far end, a less ostentatious mode of transport than Ali's was bobbing gently in the breeze. That said, the fifteen foot Waverider 450 was more than sufficient for my needs. Gripping the edge of the canopy that covered the wheelhouse, I stepped down into the stern and eased my way between two waist high cushioned seats in front of the centre console. Firing up the sixty horse power Suzuki outboard, I set the engine to idle, then went fore and aft to unhook the dock lines and pull the fenders on board. Returning to the wheelhouse, I eased forward on the throttle and carefully maneuvered clear of the jetty.

My final task before getting fully underway was to place my iPhone in a cradle mounted on the console and activate the tracker app. Almost instantly, the tiny unit sewn into the handle of Nici's leather whip was chirping nicely.

According to Charlie, when not peddling arms across the

globe Ali was an enthusiastic member of the dominatrix scene. I'm not sure what Allah thought about that, but perhaps he couldn't wait for his share of virgins in the afterlife. Mind you nobody ever says how old the virgins are meant to be, so who knows, perhaps he was hedging his bets by getting in some extra action before his time came.

Once clear of the harbour, the gulet hugged the Lycian coastline as it motored north towards Kalkan. An important port during the 19th century, cargo ships loaded with charcoal, silk, olive oil, wine and cotton sailed from Kalkan to the far reaches of the Ottoman Empire. In September 1941, it became a staging post for nine U-boats of the 23rd flotilla. Ordered south from its base on the Greek Island of Salamis the objective was to intercept coastal shipping sustaining Allied forces during the siege of Tobruk. However, by the time the flotilla reached its destination, only eight of the nine U-boats remained. With no explanation as to this loss, it wasn't until June 1987 that the U-boat was discovered in one hundred and eighty feet of water, two miles off the Kalkan coast. With no discernible damage to the superstructure and no obvious explanation for its demise, the decision by the Greek government was to allow the U-boat to become a war grave. That was, until Mehmet Ali heard about the story and having greased the palm of Kalkan's Mayor with silver, the U-boat became a war grave no more.

*

The sun was dipping below the horizon as the gulet arrived at its destination. Ali turned to his guest, a concerned look on his face. 'Are you not pleased with her?' he asked, nodding towards Dennison. 'Or would you prefer this one?'

Despite being highly recommended by their mutual friend in London and told they had similar tastes when it came to certain preferences, Ali hadn't thought to clarify whether this included his guest's sexual orientation. Keen to keep the man happy or more importantly the million dollar deal on the table, he wondered whether he should have included a boy on the trip.

His concerns however, were short lived as the guest turned to Dennison and lifted her chin between his thumb and forefinger. 'She is beautiful Mehmet and grateful as I am for your hospitality, I would prefer not to mix business with pleasure, at least not until I have checked the merchandise.'

'As you wish,' he shrugged, turning his attention to the main salon as the guard appeared carrying two sets of scuba gear. 'I understand you are an accomplished diver?'

'You could say that,' the guest responded.

'Good,' he said, slapping Matthew's thigh so hard she squealed, a red welt appearing instantly on her exposed skin. 'Dragan, take them to our quarters and make sure they're ready for our return.'

The guard nodded and indicated for the girls to follow him back into the main salon.

Setting the Waverider's engine to idle, I let her drift gently on the breeze and retrieved a pair of rods from a locker in the stern. Fishing on a river bank was never my thing, nor was deep sea fishing to be honest. I'd given it a go when visiting, my half-sister in Key West so knew the basics, but that was as far as it would go as I cast the first bait-less line out over the gunwale. Once both rods were set up, I checked the iPhone once more. The signal was still strong so I sat back in the swivel chair and propped my feet up on a coolbox. Sipping from a bottle of water, I picked up the binoculars and scanned the horizon. Satisfied, I put them back down and settled in to wait.

Both men dropped backwards off the bathing platform at the stern of the gulet. Once below the surface, they illuminated powerful dive torches attached to their wrists and descended to the seabed. Ali indicated to his guest to hold his position by extending his fist, palm side up. When the guest responded in kind, Ali checked his bearings on a compass attached to his other wrist. With five finger tips of a flattened hand showing their direction of travel, he turned and set off towards their objective.

On the surface, Dennison and Matthews had collected their bags and followed the guard downstairs from the main salon and along a corridor at the end of which two sets of double doors bisected the bow and led to their respective staterooms.

Given what they knew of Ali's sexual appetites, Matthew's suite was pretty much what she'd expected. Circular bed, black satin sheets, mirror on the ceiling and garish neon lighting, all of which did little to detract from their intel on the subject. Although she'd experimented with sex toys in the past, they weren't really her thing, not that those in her bag had come from any Ann Summers store on the High Street. With the PVC catsuit laid out on the bed alongside the leather whip, she picked up a pair of love balls and jiggled them in her hand before setting them to one side. The next item out of the bag was a black gimp mask and butt plug. Detaching the metal bit from the mask, she grasped both ends and twisted. The bit came apart to reveal an electrode which she inserted into the base of the butt plug. *Someone from 'Q' Branch must have had fun coming up with this idea*, she giggled as the device began to beep quietly.

On the cusp of the dysphotic zone where sunlight penetration turns to twilight, the vague outline of the U-boat's 88mm deck gun began to emerge. With the recommended maximum depth for recreational divers being one hundred and thirty feet, the U-boats depth at one hundred and eighty feet, coupled with its, still official declaration as a war grave meant that visits to the site were rare. This suited Ali's needs well as he indicated for his guest to follow him beyond the conning tower to a spot midway along the aft deck.

Hovering above what had once been one of two escape hatches built into the submarine's deck, Ali flipped the lid off a small control panel and punched a series of numbers into an electronic keypad. Grasping the access wheel in both hands, he turned it anti-clockwise until lugs at all four points on the outer rim were aligned. With the water pressure on the outside equal to the already flooded inner chamber, the hatch lifted easily back on itself. Adapted to accommodate a far greater capacity than was its original design, the chamber was of sufficient size to allow both men to comfortably enter the U-boat. Once inside, Ali resecured the hatch and pulled down on a handle attached to the chamber wall. Almost immediately, water began to drain from the airlock equalising the pressure with the inside of the U-boat.

There was an amusing irony that the device was directing Matthews towards a painting by *Gustave Courbet* entitled, according to the plaque beneath, *L'Origine du monde,* a the nineteenth century depiction of female genitalia. Setting the device to one side, she ran her fingers around the edge of the frame until she found a catch which allowed the painting to swing out from the wall at right angles. Exposing a safe recessed into the wall, she returned to her bag of goodies and retrieved a box containing the handcuffs the guard was so enamoured with earlier. Smiling as she set the contents to one side, she took the box and clamped it over a digital keypad on the front of the safe. Standing back, she waited patiently as the box lit up and began working its way through several million possible combinations.

The sound of a generator hummed quietly in the background as the divers stepped through into the main body of the U-boat. Providing fresh air and lighting throughout the cramped interior, the once pride of Hitler's wolf pack was now stripped bare of all but essential equipment, effectively creating a tubular storage facility of five water-tight bulkheads and an arsenal of weaponry sufficient to mount a third world coup.

'Very impressive,' commented the guest, as they made their way towards the forward torpedo room. Crates upon crates stacked either side of the central walkway were neatly compartmentalised into specific weapon types. Assault rifles, machine guns, sniper rifles, handguns and last but not least the subject of this transaction, explosives. 'You seem to have your fingers in lots of pies, Mehmet,' said the guest recognising the insignia of various countries from which the weapons originated.

'Yes indeed, my friend,' he agreed. 'My sources are diverse, but all of excellent quality,' he qualified, as his guest focused his attention on the crates marked Semtex-H.

'Do you mind?' he asked.

'Of course,' he replied. 'You must, as you say, check the merchandise.'

Concentrating on the contents of the safe, Matthews failed to notice the door to the stateroom swing silently open.

Standing in the doorway, a tray of delicacies in one hand, a bottle of Dom Perignon and silver ice bucket in the other, the guard watched Matthews for a few moments until, with a satisfied grin, he set the items to one side.

Matthews spun round as she heard the clunk of the tray being placed, none too delicately, on a credenza at the entrance to the stateroom.

The guard paused for a moment then stepped forward and lashed out with the open palm of his right hand. Turning away at the last second, Matthews managed to deflect the blow onto her shoulder, but such was its force she flew across the stateroom, landing in a heap at the foot of the bed. Stunned by the speed and ferocity of the attack, she scrabbled backwards as the guard advanced towards her.

'Get the fuck away from me!' she screamed as he reached down, grabbed Matthews by the hair, hauled her to her feet and threw her on the bed.

With the transaction's devil in the detail concluded, both men made their way back to the chamber.

'What happened to the crew?' asked the guest as the door opened.

'Argh!' Ali replied dismissively. 'Fish food. Who cares.'

'I see,' replied the guest. 'Well, it's been a pleasure doing business with you, Mehmet,' and offered his hand.

'At a million dollars, I am happy to be of service my friend,' replied Ali and gripped the hand of his guest.

'By the way,' said the guest. 'How do you propose to make the delivery?'

'The chamber doubles as a docking station for a submersible, so once the funds arrive your goods will be delivered as promised.'

The guest nodded and both men entered the chamber.

Distracted momentarily as the guard reached into the front of his pants, Matthews drew back her right leg and rammed the heel of her foot into the bridge of the his nose. She knew she'd hit the mark, the crack was unmistakable, but instead of backing off, he just smiled and with blood dripping from his nose, grabbed hold of her legs, forced them apart and yanked her towards him.

As soon as the chamber was flooded, Ali released the outer hatch and indicated for his guest to go ahead. Once clear, the guest hovered above the deck and waited for Ali to follow. Having re-secured the hatch, Ali gave the thumbs up signal to end the dive and they began to ascend towards the surface.

Dennison was returning to the sundeck, the buffet at the forefront of her mind, when she heard Matthews scream. Spinning round, she raced back through the salon, down the stairs, along the corridor and barged into her own stateroom.

Grabbing her rucksack, she delved inside and pulled out the reason for the detour. Detaching the ears, she charged back out into the corridor and burst through the open door to the adjoining stateroom where, for the merest second, she stopped to take in the scene. The guard's backside and bloated penis were on full view as he wrestled with her friend's writhing body. Flipping the device on its end, Dennison stepped forward and in one fluid movement rammed two exposed electrodes into the base of the guard's scrotum. As twelve hundred volts surged through his nether regions, he let out a primeval scream, reared back off the bed and crashed down on top of Dennison. Pinning her to the floor and despite the guard's rigid body making it virtually impossible to move, Dennison remembered her training and kept both electrodes firmly in place for the full five seconds needed for the adapted taser to complete its task.

Adding an extra seconds few for good measure, Dennison wriggled out from under the deadweight and looked up to see her friend sitting on the edge.

'You alright, Hun?' she asked.

Matthews nodded, remnants of mascara staining her cheeks as she slid off the edge of the bed and stood over the still rigid body of her potential rapist. She knew that contrary to popular belief, often promulgated by the movies, tasers are incapable of rendering a person unconscious. Instead, they operate on the principle of electrical muscular incapacitation, which accounted for the guard's eyes being wide open and fully aware of what was going on as she knelt down alongside him. Holding out her hand,

Matthews took the device from her friend and aware the effects only last for a few seconds, lifted his now flaccid penis with her thumb and forefinger, studied his shriveled scrotum for a second longer then jammed the electrodes into his testicles.

Ali felt the contact. It was only slight, but enough to make him look round. Below him at the beginning of the ascent, his guest was now hovering parallel to him, only a few metres away.

Monitoring Ali's movements carefully, the guest noted the puzzled expression in his eyes as he began to suck on thin air. With a half full cylinder on his back, it was fair to say the arms dealer would, as an experienced diver, think he had a blocked air hose. So with any residual oxygen in the pipe having been swiftly exhausted, the guest watched Ali spit out his primary regulator and clamp the secondary between his teeth.

Unsure as to why he was still unable to breath, Ali swiped the flat of his hand across his throat, a gesture designed to indicate his oxygen supply was cut off and for his fellow diver to come to his aide by offering his own secondary regulator.

The guest didn't move, instead he fixed his gaze on the widening eyes of his counterpart as confusion was followed swiftly by panic then desperation as the build-up of carbon dioxide in his lungs moved the harbinger of death inexorably towards asphyxiation.

In a last ditch attempt at survival, Ali kicked for the surface. Or at least he thought he did. Instead, his oxygen depleted brain failed to register the vice like grip on his ankle until, after what felt to him like an eternity, but in reality was only a few more seconds, the secondary regulator slipped from his mouth and saltwater flooded into his lungs.

Unlike freshwater where it's the water itself which causes a person to drown, the guest knew that in saltwater it's the build-up of liquid in the air sacs that stops oxygen from reaching the blood, effectively causing the person to drown in his own fluids. While not a pleasant experience either way, it was nothing Mehmet Ali didn't deserve thought the guest as he waited patiently for him to die. With just the one task remaining, he swam around the lifeless body, reopened the valve on top of the cylinder and with no small degree of satisfaction, watched Ali drift away to become, in his own words, 'fish food.'

*

On receiving the all clear signal, I stowed away the fishing gear, fired up the motor and a few minutes later brought the Waverider alongside the gulet. Climbing on board, I made my way along the gunwale towards the stern where I found the girls sprawled out on cream leather cushions, tucking into a delicious looking buffet.

'We earned it,' said Jill, explaining what had happened in between mouthfuls of shish kebab.

Laying on his side on the far side of the deck, the guard's wrists and ankles were hogtied behind his back. Grunting like a stuffed pig, probably something to do with what Jill told me was the bar of a gimp mask keeping his jaws apart, he glared at me, clearly recognising I was not the cavalry.

'Nothing he doesn't deserve,' said Nici.

'No argument there, Nici,' I said. 'Are you okay?'

'I'm okay,' she replied, not altogether convincingly.

'Do you still have it?' I asked.

'Here,' said Jill lobbing the taser at me.

'Ingenious,' I said. Needless to say, MI6 had its team of specialists, although when I'd first heard of a *Rampant Rabbit* being adapted in this way, even I was surprised.

'Any left for me?' said a voice from the rear of the gulet.

With fins in one hand and cylinder in the other, the dripping figure of Ali's guest appeared on deck.

'Job done,' he said, with a satisfied grin as he stripped out of his wetsuit and with a wink to the girls gawping at his ripped physique, dropped the kit on the floor and made straight for the buffet.

Taking up Sir Henry's offer came with a list of jobs, top of which was to find someone with the specialist skills needed for this operation. With that in mind, my first port of call was to touch base with Colonel Phil Truman of the Special Boat Service who, as part of a reciprocal arrangement with the SAS, was officer in charge of the Special Forces joint training and recruitment programme based at 22 SAS HQ, Hereford.

With police services across the UK required to periodically take part in live counter terrorism exercises, this invariably brings together a host of other agencies including Special Forces. Known as 'Remount' it was at one of these exercises I'd met Col. Truman. Over a beer in the officers mess he suggested a certain Marty Farrow might fit the bill. There was however, a small problem which required a trip to south east London and the Governor's office of HMP Belmarsh, one of the UK's most notorious Category A prisons.

*

It's no secret that organised crime within the prison community forms part of a complex, illicit economy that spawns a ruthless chain of command. Factions headed by some of the most violent criminals effectively rule the highways and byways of each wing or in the case of Belmarsh, Housing Blocks A though to D and HSU, the High Security Unit.

Since day one of his arrival from the Old Bailey, the Governor explained that Harry Jardine had used his connections with organised crime groups across the country to formulate a lucrative drug trade which, when combined with a reputation for brutal retribution against those who crossed him, swiftly moved him to the top of the food chain. Obviously the Governor didn't like it, but was brutally honest in his assessment that he was powerless to do anything about it, such was the evolutionary nature of life inside a prison whereby shipping Jardine out would simply have resulted in another stepping into his shoes. But, no man is an island and with the transitory nature of such facilities, the need for Jardine to constantly bring on board new recruits was essential, hence his interest in one of the latest arrivals.

So from a bank of monitors in the Governor's office, I'd watched with interest as a scene unfolded from which I was able to see, first hand, Col. Truman's recommendation in action.

Looking down through the suicide nets to the recreation area below, Jardine watched his potential recruit play a solo game of chess.

Knight to King 3.

'He wants to see you.'

This was the second approach of the day. The first in the exercise yard and now during association hour.

'I told you, I'm not interested.'

Rook to Bishop 5.

All eyes looked towards the table on which a new game was about to be played out. The behemoth, known as the Beast of 'B' Block loomed over Marty Farrow. At seven feet something, his sleeveless grey sweatshirt revealed muscles the size of bowling balls and tattoos depicting all manner of neo Nazi paraphernalia. He was not used to getting 'no' for an answer.

'He won't ask you again.'

'And, I won't tell you again.

As the huge fist smashed down into the centre of the board, Farrow asked himself, *How the fuck did I get myself into this…?*

The barrister stood, adjusted his robes and addressed the witness box.

'*So Mr Farrow. Let me get this straight. You're a former member of the Special Boat Service?*'

'*Yes, Sir.*'

'*The waterborne equivalent to the SAS?*'

'*You could say that, Sir, yes.*'

'*Which makes you a highly trained killing machine…*'

'*My Lord, please,*' *objected defence counsel from the other end of the bench.*

'*Sustained,*' *frowned the Judge then turned to his left.* '*Ladies and gentlemen of the jury, please disregard Mr Powell's last comment.*'

'*My apologies, My Lord,*' *said the barrister, with no discernible hint of apology in his voice.* '*So, having left the service, Mr Farrow,*' *he continued, '*you went on to become a cab driver?*'

'*I did the knowledge, Sir, yes.*'

'*But instead of getting a Hackney license, you joined Uber?*'

'*Yes, Sir. There was a waiting list and I needed to earn some money in the meantime.*'

'Now let me see,' he said, scrutinising his notes unnecessarily. 'You say you picked up a fare in Clapham. Three men you say?'

'Yes, Sir.'

'And those three men tried to rob you?'

'Yes, Sir.'

'And yet there's no evidence to suggest there were three men at all, is there Mr Farrow?'

He remained silent.

'Is there, Mr Farrow?'

'No, Sir.'

'In fact,' he raised his voice. 'Only the body of a single man who YOU say tried to rob YOU, a highly trained...' he glanced at his colleague, 'former member of the SBS with more than sufficient skills to deal with such a situation?'

He didn't wait for an answer.

'My esteemed colleague for the defence suggests that your actions were those of self defence, yet... I put it to you this is a lie.'

'I don't lie, Sir.'

'But you have, Mr Farrow,' he raised his voice again, 'and

instead of using restraint when the victim took you on, you hit him
so hard, he FLEW across the pavement, SLAMMED into a wall
and broke his neck...'

Even from my location, the stench of pending violence was palpable as I watched the board fly in the air and chess pieces clatter on the floor. Pockets of Blacks, Muslims and other ethnic groups that normally kept themselves to themselves edged forward in anticipation of something more exciting than the movie playing in the background.

Staring at the empty board in front of him, Farrow knew this was the last thing he wanted, but he also knew that if he didn't deal with it there and then it would never go away, even if that meant a spell in the HSU.

With a deep sigh, Farrow's hand shot forward, his thumb digging deep into the Beast's radial nerve at the base of his thumb and forefinger. As the fist sprung open, Farrow leapt to his feet. Keeping his thumb in place he wrapped his fingers around the back of the Beast's hand, rotated the wrist and in one fluid movement swung the him off his feet. The whole thing took less than a second. It had to. Speed was of the essence when dealing with a bigger guy. It also meant he had to finish it. Rotating the arm he kept the Beast off balance, pulling him around until his own momentum sent him crashing to the floor.

Extending the arm straight, Farrow was about to strike down on the point of the elbow, a crippling blow that would shatter bones and rupture tendons, when a voice bellowed out, 'Farrow! Put him down!'

Farrow paused. The voice had come from the command and control hub that fed each of the four wings attached to HB B, 'The Guvnor wants you.'

Marty entered the office a few minutes later and close up it was easy to see he was one of those people who simply looked the part. Not the tallest, maybe five ten, shaved head, stubby fingers, each akin to individual bolts of iron. I'd no idea what form of martial arts he'd studied, but seeing him in action, I was not surprised at the outcome of the confrontation. Even in prison scrubs, there was no denying his muscular physique, so in civvies, I'd found it hard to understand how the jury could have believed there was only one person involved in the so called attempted robbery, an assertion with which Col. Truman had evidently agreed, hence his recommendation.

Leaving puddles of water in his wake, Marty picked up a plate and helped himself to some food from the buffet as I walked over to the guard.

As much as I would have liked to send a message to others of Mehmet Ali's ilk by hanging him and the guard from the yardarm, the need for this operation to remain secret was of paramount importance. Too many difficult questions would be asked of the PM should her decision to deal with scum like this become public and besides, the last thing we wanted was for other prospective targets to go underground.

So with some regret, I walked over to the guard and pulled him up by the collar of his colourful shirt. 'Not so much of a big man now, are you?' I said, looking at the fear in his eyes as I jammed the twin electrodes into his exposed neck.

I didn't want him dead, at least not just yet. Should wind and tide bring his body to shore, like Ali, his death needed to look like a diving accident. So once the thrashing stopped, I removed the gimp mask, replaced his clothes with Marty's discarded dive gear, gave him a final twelve hundred volts for good measure, opened the valve on the cylinder and with Marty's help hauled him up and dropped him over the side.

CHAPTER 9

Back on home soil, I'd arranged to meet Jill at *Le Pain Quotidien*, a Belgian bakery come café in Covent Garden. At the heart of London's theatre district, the Garden has come a long way since the mid sixteen hundreds when it was a simple fruit and veg market. Nowadays, with that side of things relocated to south of the Thames at Nine Elms Lane, its neo-classical architecture is home to a thriving industry of cafes, pubs, designer shops, craft markets and street entertainers.

We'd travelled up separately that morning. Jill from her home in the New Forest and me from Portsmouth. Despite being an overcast day we opted for a table on the terrace opposite Jubilee Hall, a bustling market in its own right selling everything from clothing, textiles, arts and crafts to antiques and collectibles. Jill being Jill meant she'd already had a fry up that morning – how she managed to fit so much in such a tiny frame beat the hell out of me – but apparently she was still 'peckish,' so we ordered a Lebanese Platter to share and a large bottle of still spring water.

Covent Garden has always been a favourite of mine, made all the more special by daily live music filtering up from the courtyard of the Crusting Pie Pub in the South Hall where youngsters, often from the Royal Academy of Music come together as string quartets to earn a 'crust' or two of their own while entertaining the tourists. That it was also handily placed, only a stones-throw from Trafalgar Square and Sir Henry's office was an additional bonus.

'So what did the Chief have to say about losing you?' I asked, making reference to Jill's boss, Hampshire's Chief Constable.

'Devastated, of course,' she replied with a grin. 'God! This is good,' she purred as a piece of flatbread smeared in organic hummus and sundried tomatoes disappeared from view. 'No, she was fine and apparently I'm welcome back if things don't pan out this end.'

'Well let's hope it doesn't come to that,' I said, tearing off a piece of flatbread before it went the same way – it was good.

'Mind you,' she ventured after a moment. 'By all accounts,

the compensation package was pretty good too, so either way, a win-win for the job.'

It was clear from the start, this operation would have deep pockets, not to mention some considerable influence as evidenced by Marty's early release from Belmarsh. I'm not sure what the Probation Service would have thought of his first outing though, but as they say, *what the mind doesn't know...*

'Ah! That's better,' said Jill, as she eventually sat back and contentedly patted her stomach. 'So how long do you think this will last?'

'What, your secondment?'

'No us, you doughnut,' she said, laughing at my startled expression. 'Of course, the secondment.'

'Who knows,' I said, trying to recover my composure. 'But one things for sure, I doubt they'll be a shortage of customers, at least in the foreseeable future.'

'Today, being a case in point I guess,' she replied, popping the final piece of flatbread in her mouth.

With time to spare and Sir Henry being one for punctuality, after a stroll through the hustle and bustle of the covered market place, we stopped briefly alongside the cobbled West Piazza to watch a couple of guys on unicycles juggling flaming machetes before worming our way down to Trafalgar Square.

This was Jill's first visit to Sir Henry's office and although she'd known of him when he was an Assistant Chief in Hampshire, I could tell she was getting nervous at meeting him officially for the first time.

'Don't worry,' I said as we entered the building via a nondescript door to the side of the bank. 'He's not as intimidating as he looks and you'll love, Di, his PA.' It was clear that the foyer had been adapted from its original purpose as a staff entrance to the bank. Whatever corridors there had been were now blocked off leaving only a single elevator to the side of which was a buttonless panel set at a slight angle away from the wall. Placing my hand on the opaque surface, the doors to the elevator slid open. 'Come into my parlour,' I said as I invited her to step inside and punched the button for the top floor.

'How's life in the not so fast lane?' I asked, as the doors opened directly into Di's office.

'Not as exciting as yours by all accounts,' she replied, jumping up from behind her desk from where she sidestepped Jill's outstretched hand to give her a big hug. 'Welcome to the fold, Jill, and my sincere condolences to you for having to look after this reprobate.'

'Thank you,' replied Jill, nodding sagely at the wisdom of

the tanned, spikey haired one.

'I guess not being married helps though,' she said, glancing down at Jill's left hand.

I rolled my eyes. 'Has Charlie arrived yet?'

'Yes, he's in there,' said Di, as she leaned over her desk to press the intercom button. 'Sir Henry... Alex is here with Jill Dennison.'

'Ah good,' responded the disembodied voice over the speaker. 'Send them in.'

'Come in, come in,' said Sir Henry, as we entered the office.

Waving us over to a, new since my last visit, highly polished cherrywood, at a guess, conference table on the far side of the room, I could see Charlie was well away, engrossed in something on his laptop. With seating for twelve, Sir Henry rose from his chair at the head of the table. In full battle dress with shirt sleeves rolled back and braces bulging against his girth, he extended a huge paw that envelope Jill's outstretched hand. 'Welcome to my humble abode,' he smiled warmly. 'I understand your part in the operation went well, even if the methods used were a tad unusual.'

'You could say that, Sir,' she replied, her cheeks flushing.

'They both did a great job,' I said, quick to cover her embarrassment as we took our seats. 'And Marty of course.'

'Yes, yes, of course. How is he?'

'All good, but meeting with his probation officer today.'

'I'd like to be a fly on that wall,' said Sir Henry with a chuckle, as he returned to his chair.

'Hi Jill,' said Charlie as he pressed the 'enter' button with a flourish and looked up. 'Nici not coming?'

'Sorry Charlie,' I said. 'She's gone back to the NCA, but don't worry, she's on the books now and will be back if we need her in the future.'

He grinned with approval, as I noticed a circular piece of smoked glass recessed into the centre of the table. Maybe ten centimetres or so in diameter, I leant across and could see that beneath the glass was what could best be described as a multi-coloured globe rotating on an invisible axis.

'What on earth is that?' I asked.

'All in good time, Alex,' said Sir Henry, as he rubbed his hands together. 'Let's get down to business.'

The debrief went pretty much as expected. Once it was known

there was to be a rendezvous at sea and scuba gear involved, HMS
Intrepid had been put on stand-by. Already on patrol in the Med as
part of Operation Sophia, the EU's response to the migrant
problems in the region, the Echo Class survey ship – don't be
fooled by the term *survey ship* – was a fully equipped war ship
capable of among other things, the support of submarine
operations. Once Marty explained how the U-boat's airlock was
able to accommodate a submersible, it was a relatively straight
forward job to send down a team of divers to recover the weapons
and explosives from the submarine. No longer a war grave, a
controlled explosion was then considered, but discarded in favour
of leaving her in-tact thus giving greater credence to the scenario
of a diving accident should the bodies of Ali and his bodyguard
eventually be washed up.

As for Akram Murad, MP for Southampton Itchen and
Secretary of State for Immigration, his personal and professional
life continued to be covertly turned upside down. This included
24/7 surveillance by watchers from MI5, intensive scrutiny of his
financial records, family history and of course the now *not so*
secret email accounts which, among other things, had uncovered
his association with Mehmet Ali. This discovery allowed Charlie
to set up a ghost programme from which he was able to pose as
Murad and introduce Marty as a fellow arms dealer. The next
question had been to decide at what stage to bring Murad in for
questioning, a decision put on hold off the back of the information

recovered from the safe on board Ali's gulet.

With a nod from Sir Henry, Charlie reached forward and tapped the screen on his tablet. The globe at the centre of the conference table began to spin faster and a hologram of a seventy something man rose from the centre. Rotating slowly on its axis, the grey overcoat and trilby made him look like a character from a John Le Carre novel.

'Nikolay Kamenev,' announced Sir Henry. 'Former head of Russia's SVR and trusted confidant of President Vasily Ulyanov.

Known to be one with few such alliances, I asked, 'What made him so important to Ulyanov?'

'Something he picked up from his predecessor by all accounts,' said Sir Henry. 'Back in 2008 when the constitution prevented Putin from being reelected as Russian President for a third term, it's suspected he struck up a deal with his successor, Dmitry Medvedev, the idea being for him to be made Prime Minister until such time as he could stand again in 2012. But Putin wasn't prepared to completely let go of the reins, so as PM he retained control of the security service from where he was able to *keep an eye* on his successor until such time as he could resume his role as President.'

'So what you're saying, Sir,' said Jill, 'Kamenev was Ulyanov's eyes in the Kremlin?'

'Precisely,' said Sir Henry. 'Ulyanov had learnt from his predecessor which is why, when Kamenev's name came up on Mehmet Ali's flashdrive, he quickly became a person of interest.'

'In what capacity?' I asked.

'It's not entirely clear, but it seems that having moved on from his position as head of SVR, Kamenev set up a private security company with a sideline in the arms business.'

'Hardly surprising I suppose, given what's been going on over there since the collapse of the Soviet Union.'

'Indeed,' agreed Sir Henry. 'But what's of particular significance is Kamenev's arrival in the UK tomorrow as part of an advance party for President Ulyanov's attendance at next month's World Energy Summit at the Merchant Taylors Hall.'

'So still part of the inner circle.'

'It would appear so, yes. His company are security consultants to Gazprom, currently the largest exporter of oil and natural gas to the European Union which, as a state-owned company suggests he is, as you say, very much part of Ulyanov's inner circle.'

I was familiar with the Merchant Taylors Hall from my days in the Met. On Threadneedle Street, literally a stone's throw from the Bank of England, MTH is generally regarded as one of the more exclusive conference venues in the City of London and a fitting venue for such a prestigious event.

'I'm guessing that given our proposed alliance with the US and Canada, the issue of renewable energy will be on the table?' I said, looking towards Charlie as Kamenev's hologram disappeared, replaced instead by the Summit timetable on a widescreen TV mounted on the wall at the head of the table.

'Absolutely,' he said as a smorgasbord of keynote speakers appeared.

Looking at the list of names and photos, one stood out above all others. Professor Alistair Bird, the world's foremost authority on renewable energy. By no means my area of expertise, it was nonetheless impossible to miss the gathering momentum towards climate change and the need for non-fossil fuel alternatives as sources of energy. How that would go down with Ulyanov and Nord Stream AG, the majority shareholder in Gazprom, remained to be seen. Already a political hot potato with some EU countries feeling sidelined or threatened by the pipeline that flows directly into Germany, one thing for sure was that the estimated fifteen billion Euros it cost to complete the project was nothing compared to the trillions likely to be generated once fully on line.

'When you say "currently" the largest exporter of oil and natural gas to the European Union, Sir, what do you mean?' asked

Jill.

'Well spotted,' said Sir Henry. 'With the US having brought their east coast LNG (Liquified Natural Gas) plants on line, the liquified shale gas from fracking fields across the US is now being shipped to Europe.' He let that digest a moment then continued. 'According to the International Energy Agency (IEA), come 2022 the US will be producing more than a fifth of the World's natural gas, effectively putting it on the same level as Russia and Norway, but without the need for any pipelines.'

'Which represents a direct threat to Russia's domination of the European market,' said Jill.

'Exactly, but not just from the US,' continued Sir Henry. 'With Canada's LNG plants on the west coast also on line in British Columbia, the threat to Russia's *global* aspirations is also a big concern for them.'

'Okay, I get that,' she said, clearly warming to the occasion. 'But surely LNG is a fossil fuel, so how does that fit with the move towards climate change and alternative sources of renewable energy?'

'Good question and yes you're right. LNG does come from fossil fuels, but it is considered to be the cleanest of all such fuels and widely regarded as a complementary solution for what's called an energy mix with those of a renewable nature such as solar, wind or biomass.'

'And that's where we come into play,' I said, picking up the narrative. 'As part of an alliance with the US and Canada, not only are we a good fit geographically, but thanks to the likes of Professor Bird, we are at the forefront of developing our own natural resources to further complement those LNG exports arriving from the States and Canada.'

'In what way?' Jill persisted, clearly not leaving any stone unturned.

'Everything from wind farms in the North Sea to wave and tidal plants along the Atlantic coast. The energy from these alone have the potential to power not only our own national grid, but also fuel a proposed super grid of renewable energy between ourselves and Europe.'

'Christ!' she said. 'Ulyanov really is getting it from all directions?'

'Which is why we must pay special attention to Kamenev while he's in town,' said, Sir Henry.'

'So where's he staying?' I asked.

'They've booked the entire top floor of the Savoy for between now and the three days of the Summit.'

'That's interesting,' said Jill.

All heads turned back towards her.

'Why do you say that?' asked Sir Henry.

'A Saudi owned hotel in the heart of the West End playing host to a competitor in the oil market. Just seems a little strange that's all.'

'Dare say they're paying through the nose for it, but good point.' said Sir Henry, his whiskers switching slightly. 'Charlie, will you look into that please and while you're at it, breakdown a few firewalls or whatever it is you do and see if this trip has a hidden agenda.'

'Sure thing,' replied Charlie, his eyes lighting up at the chance of doing what he does best.

'Okay, good,' said Sir Henry. 'Let's move onto something more pressing with regard to the Leicester Square bombing.'

Seven miles or so north and direct from the assembly lines in Louisville, Kentucky, the distinctive rumble of the SUV's fourth generation Ecoboost 3.5L V6 engine drew envious glances from bystanders as the Ruby Black Lincoln Navigator cruised along White Hart Lane. Unlike others in his line of work, Bedri al-Ghazi had little time for using his own product. He considered those who chose to do so as fools. His was the business of making money to support his lavish lifestyle and not to blow it away by abusing his good fortune. But in this game, presence was also what mattered and besides, if the *booliska* ever decided to turn him over, then they'd never find anything. Sucking his teeth and nodding his head in time to the deep base of *No Woman No Cry* he spun the wheel right into Tottenham High Street and pulled up alongside the kerb.

Serhans Barber Shop had been a fixture on the High Street for many years. Derived from the Turkish *ser* meaning *head* and *han* meaning *leader*, the Barbers was aptly regarded by the locals as *the* place to go for a Turkish hot towel shave. It was also Bedri al-Ghazi's secret pleasure and despite being some miles from his home in Tower Hamlets, was part of a weekly ritual he'd undertaken since arriving in London from Somalia several years ago.

'Salaam alaykum,' greeted the owner, as al-Ghazi entered the Barber's.

'Wa alaykum salaam,' responded al-Ghazi as both men embraced.

'It is good to see you my friend,' said the owner as he guided him to a table set back from the line of barber chairs.

'It is always too long,' responded al-Ghazi as he took the seat proffered by the owner.

As was their custom both men exchanged pleasantries until

an assistant dressed in white robes appeared carrying a silver tray on which sat a double tea pot, strainer, tulip shaped glasses and pot of sugar cubes. Despite his chosen trade, al-Ghazi considered himself a cultured man and appreciated the care taken by the owner's attention to detail as he poured the crimson liquid into the glass, added two lumps of sugar and sat back to allow his guest a moment to savour the aroma of his offering. As much a part of the shave itself, it was engaging in this ceremony, an intrinsic part of Turkish society since the eighteen hundreds, that brought al-Ghazi to this barber shop week after week.

'What is wrong, my friend?' asked al-Ghazi noticing beads of sweat on the owners forehead. This reaction to his presence was something he was used to, but not generally in these surroundings and especially not when he was about to expose his neck to the edge of a ustura, the sharp open blade used for the primary purpose of his visit.

'I am sorry,' the owner replied, his hand trembling slightly as he poured more tea into al-Ghazi's cup. 'Omer has been taken ill and is unable to look after you today, but,' he hurried on, 'I am pleased to say, Hammad, has kindly offered to take his place.'

'And who is this, Hammad,' demanded al-Ghazi, clearly annoyed at this change in routine.

As if on cue, a second man, also dressed in white robes, stepped from behind the curtain and bowed his head to al-Ghazi.

'Hammad is Omer's cousin,' the owner explained, 'and by our good fortune, praise be to Allah,' he raised his hands and looked to the heavens, 'he is visiting Omer from one of the finest *berber dukkani's* in Istanbul.'

Rubbing a soft hand over the stubble on his chin, al-Ghazi frowned, then rose from his seat at the table and walked over to the waiting barber chair. 'Very well,' he said, looking at Hammad. 'Let us hope you are as good as Omer,' the veiled threat not lost on the owner.

It had been little more than a month since the attack in Leicester Square and was still fresh in the minds of all round the table. Although Isil had claimed responsibility, that was hardly surprising given they'd claim responsibility for a cat getting run over if they thought it would help their cause. What was unusual, was the lack of progress in rounding up the British based Jihadi network believed to be behind the atrocity. It seemed that two associates of the suicide bomber had literally disappeared overnight from their homes in Bradford, something which sparked of greater sophistication in the planning process than was historically the norm.

There was however, the issue of the bomber himself and the findings of a JTAC report commissioned by Sir Henry.

The Joint Terrorism Analysis Centre, based at MI5s Millbank headquarters in Thames House, works in conjunction with the police, government departments and other intelligence agencies to analyse and disseminate information from investigations into terrorist activity. In this instance, toxicology reports showed the bomber as having high levels of tramadol in his bloodstream.

Sir Henry went on to explain, 'While the use of synthetic opioids to calm the nerves of would be suicide bombers is not unusual in itself, what is interesting is the unique chemical composition of the plug retrieved from the head of the bomber...'

'Excuse me?' questioned Jill.

Sir Henry smiled then continued, 'If you think about it, there's not a lot connecting the head to the torso, so when a vest detonates, nine times out of ten it's blown clean off and by clean off I mean it's not unusual for the head to be found intact several hundred metres away, often as not with a half chewed opioid plug stuck in the mouth. In this case, the unique nature of the tramadol in the plug links to a batch from south east Asia. According to our friends at Mossad, after a series of suicide bombings in Tel Aviv and more recently the coastal resort of Eilat, the source of the drug is has been linked to a supplier in Somalia, one Suleymaan al-Farouki, a crime lord with only one known supplier in the UK.'

'Family member?' I asked.

'His cousin, Bedri al-Ghazi, who,' he glanced at his watch, 'is about to find out what it means to peddle drugs for use in suicide bombings in the UK.'

Leaning his head back in the chair, al-Ghazi closed his eyes as Hammad applied a facial wash scrub followed by a hot towel across his mouth and chin, the ends folded up and diagonally over each eye so that only the nose was left exposed. The purpose of the towel, enhanced with a few drops of essential oil, is to open the pores of the beard, allowing for a closer shave with less irritation. After a few minutes, Hammad removed the towel and applied shaving oil. Next came the shaving cream, applied using a soft brush made from the finest badger bristles and finally the ustura. During a hot towel shave, up to seven layers of skin can be removed so having made sure he followed the tradition of two shaves, one with the grain and the other against, Hammad quietly blessed his father for having shown him this traditional method as he finished by applying an aftershave cooling gel and moisturiser.

The whole process took less than thirty minutes after which Hammad stepped back from the chair, bowed to his client who acknowledged his obsequious gesture with a nod and disappeared behind the curtain to the rear of the shop.

Carefully removing the transparent, synthetic gloves used to apply the aftershave cooling gel, Hammad placed them in a small plastic box, along with the bottle containing the gel.

Removing his robe, he listened for the owner to bid farewell to his al-Ghazi then opened the back door to the shop and stepped out into an alley where a man in overalls was cleaning the windscreen of an old pick-up truck.

No words were exchanged, none were necessary as Hammad climbed up into the passenger side of the cab and waited for the man to join him. Nor would there be the need for an autopsy, the amendment to al-Ghazi's medical records clearly showing that his heart failure, later that evening, would be attributed to natural causes.

CHAPTER 10

Resting his forearms on the lectern, Professor Alistair Bird looked round the lecture theatre. Packed with postgraduates hoping to complete their MSc/MPhil in *Environmental Change and Management*, the course was widely regarded as one of Oxford University's most topical and popular science degrees. The icing on the cake for the 'Environmental Change Institute' (formerly Unit) had been the appointment of Professor Bird as academic lead for the course. A former Royal Navy medic and world authority on renewable energy, Bird, was of average height and build with a shock of sandy hair, clear blue eyes and a ruddy complexion from summers spent on his catamaran in the Solent. Diametrically opposite to so many of his dry academic contemporaries, he was a veritable 'Indiana Jones,' combining incisive wit and charm with an energetic outdoor lifestyle that allowed him to relate to young and old alike. Passionate about protecting the environment and all things alternate to the need for fossil fuels, his enthusiasm was infectious, hence and despite nearing the end of a Friday afternoon, the lecture theatre being full.

Picking up a remote clicker from the lectern in front of him Bird addressed his audience of eager young under graduates. 'Okay ladies and gentlemen,' he said, as the image of a *Samsung Galaxy Note 7* appeared on the screen behind him. 'We've previously talked about the benefits of lithium ion batteries and their ability to hold a charge, but who can tell me what led to Samsung permanently discontinuing this particular smartphone back in October 2016?'

A show of hands saw him point toward a female student with long blonde hair towards the rear of the lecture theatre. 'Yes, Ally,' said Professor Bird.

'Didn't they keep catching fire?'

'That's right, but what caused the fires?'

She stayed quiet as another show of hands appeared.

Keen for a specific answer Bird pointed to one of his go to students. 'Yes Jordi,' he said.

'Lithium ion contains a flammable electrolyte, Professor, so any design flaws in the batteries, like those found in the Note 7, can result in fires and in some instances explosions.'

'Exactly and that's not funny,' responded Bird, 'especially if it happens to be in your pocket at the time or worse still in the cargo hold of a plane.'

That drew a collective intake of breath as the image of a *Delta 757 airliner* replaced the *Galaxy Note 7* on the screen.

'Which is exactly what happened on a Sky West flight 4449 from Salt Lake City into Bozeman, Montana in 2018. Luckily, the crew smelt smoke *before* the plane took off and a search of the hold found a toilet bag in a passenger's checked in luggage had exploded. So if you've ever wondered why electrical items such as laptops and smartphones must stay in hand luggage when boarding a flight then now you know.'

He paused for a moment to let that sink in then continued, 'Okay, now staying with the airline theme, you may also remember that not so long ago, five separate incidents in five days led to Boeing's entire fleet of 787 Dreamliners being grounded.'

A few heads nodded.

'In each instance, faulty electrical systems linked to the use of lithium ion batteries were identified as being to blame. Kind of makes you wonder why we seem so insistent on using these types of batteries doesn't it – any ideas?'

'Because they're an efficient way of storing energy,' said Ally.

'True, but what about hydrogen?' suggested Bird. 'Surely that's safer and in some respects a more efficient way of storing energy?'

'But Professor,' said Jordi, 'The primary sources for hydrogen are fossil fuels which defeats the object of the exercise if we want to meet our environmental objectives.'

'And without lithium, the electric car market wouldn't exist,' came back Ally.

'Both good points,' said Bird with a smile, enjoying the developing duel between two of his favourite students. 'There's no question that without lithium ion there would be no electric cars, bikes or any number of electrically powered vehicles in the future.'

The image of *Nissan Leaf hatchback* replaced the *Delta 757* on the screen.

'Imagine though,' he continued. 'Instead of batteries in electric cars such as this Nissan extending the entire length of the chassis, the same amount of energy could be stored in something as small as one of these.' He reached into his pocket and pulled out a Triple A battery. 'Now, how amazing would that be!'

'But that still doesn't solve the issue of flammable

electrolytes,' said Ally.

'No, you're right, Ally, it doesn't,' he replied, 'and that's exactly why research is looking to address that issue, along with a whole host of other objectives such as longevity, energy density and of course safety.' Glancing up at the clock at the back of the theatre, he took a step back from the lectern. 'But for now ladies and gentlemen, in readiness for when we next meet, I want you to consider ways in which the miniaturisation and storage of energy in this way could benefit the wider global community and of course, as importantly, Jordi, the environment. But till then, have a great weekend, don't drink too much and I'll look forward to seeing what you come up with.'

Amidst the usual buzz as the students filtered out of the lecture theatre, the Dean of the faculty appeared at the top of the stairs and eased his way through the throng. Late sixties, wayward mop of grey hair, matching beard, often with leftover crumbs around the edges, beige and white gingham shirt, red bow tie, green wool blazer, plaid waistcoat and brown corduroy trousers, George Thompson was typecast for his role as he made his way down the steps to the side of the theatre.

'Dickie, old boy. Another good turn out,' he announced with gusto.

Bird looked up from packing his briefcase and smiled. 'Yes, George, couldn't be happier and a great bunch to work with.'

'Well you're going to have another audience to impress at the Energy Summit,' he said as he reached the lectern. 'Talking of which, I've just received another call from the Immigration Minister.'

Bird scowled for the first time that afternoon. He'd been dodging calls from Akram Murad for the last few days. Not that he minded keeping the Government in the loop, but due to the sensitivity of the project, only senior members of the Cabinet, along with the Energy Minister, were permitted to attend the official briefing he'd given earlier in the week.

'I'm afraid he's just going to have to wait for the Summit like everyone else,' he said.

'He's not going to be happy.'

'I can't help that, George. Look, I need to do a spot check on the facility and make sure everything is going to be ready for the big reveal and I just don't have time to talk to another bloody politician trying to get ahead of the game. Look, will you do me a favour and put him off and I promise I'll give him a bells and whistles briefing afterwards.'

'Okay, but please make sure you do or he'll be on the blower to the Vice-Chancellor next.'

'Will do, George, and thank you.'

With that, Bird scooped up his briefcase, tucked it under his arm and headed for the exit.

CHAPTER 11

Despite the enthusiasm of his audience, it had been a frustrating day for the Professor. There was so much more he wanted to tell his students. Never before had he been so excited about the future of the UK's renewable energy programme. But for now, as he drove north along the A44, he was enjoying the thrill of being behind the wheel of his BMW i8. Yes it was a hybrid and something of a compromise given his area of expertise, but he knew that one day this sports convertible would become as much of a classic as the Aston Martin DB5 and E-type Jaguar. So *what the hell,* he'd thought when signing on the dotted line, *why not!*

Turning off the main arterial road onto the B4022, Bird took advantage of oncoming headlights to put his foot down and enjoy the thrill of taking country lanes at speeds designed to test the traction of the nineteen inch alloys. Only too soon though, he reached the right hand turn for home from where he dropped down a narrow lane until the tiniest of chocolate box villages appeared up ahead. Illuminated by the soft amber glow of ye olde street lamps, Great Tew, is a traditional mix of honey stone thatched cottages, typical of the Cotswolds, and much to Bird's delight, comprised of little more than a church, a pub, a primary school and the former post office he now called home. The property came complete with a safe, handily left behind by the Royal Mail, into which Bird placed his briefcase before answering the call of his rumbling stomach and heading for the pub.

'Long day, Doc,' said the bartender, as he walked into the busy public bar.

'You could say that, Cheryl,' he replied, not bothering to correct his demotion from Professor to Doctor. 'Got anything exciting for me on the menu? I'm starving.'

'For you sweetie, how does stew and homemade dumplings sound?'

'Perfect,' he said. 'You're a star.'

With that sorted, he ordered a pint of 6X and with a nod here and there, found himself a spot at a small table alongside a cosy inglenook fireplace.

A traditional sixteenth century pub of flagstone floors, oak beams and a ceiling festooned with countless numbers of Toby Jugs, the clientele offered an eclectic mix of locals he normally found invigorating. Some from the smoke, having had enough of the city life, others who'd been in the village from birth, and all with fascinating tales to tell. But not tonight for the Professor. He was knackered and had a long week ahead. So once his dinner arrived, a huge bowlful with chunks of warm bread and butter on the side, he tucked in and looked forward to a good night's sleep.

It had been late by the time he'd got to the pub and even later by the time he finished his meal. So with Cheryl calling last orders, he left the warmth of the fireplace behind and headed home. He'd left a porch light on, but as he turned the key in the lock he realised he must have left it open. Not that it was a problem as half the doors in the village are left unlocked, but he could have sworn… *Oh well, never mind*, he thought, putting it down to tiredness as he went through to the kitchen and reached for the kettle.

'Turn round slowly.'

The instant Bird heard the mish mash of Asian and Cockney, a cascade of catecholamines flooded from the adrenal glands around his kidneys. Entering his central nervous system, the fight or flight response known as *Hyperarousal* or the *Crumbles*, told him to either *get the hell out of Dodge* or *confront the threat*.

This physiological reaction to perceived danger was one with which Bird was all too familiar from his time as a medic in the Gulf War, but with the flight option evidently out of the question, instead he tightened his grip on the kettle, spun round and hurled the improvised weapon in the direction of the voice. Glancing off the side of a balaclava head, Bird maintained his momentum and launched himself forward.

Taken off guard, this was the last thing the intruder expected from a university Professor, he took the full force of the charge in his midriff as both men fell backwards into a Welsh dresser. Hitting the deck simultaneously, bone china crockery and glass flew off the shelves as a handgun spilled from the intruder's hand and skidded across the flagstone floor. First to his feet, Bird lunged for the weapon as the winded intruder kicked out in desperation at his trailing leg. Catching the back of Bird's heel, no sooner had the fight started it was over as the Professor fell sideways, cracked his head on the edge of the kitchen table and blacked out.

Breathing heavily the intruder got to his feet and retrieved the handgun. Checking the safety was on, he tucked it into his waistband and rolled the unconsciousness Professor over onto his front. Ripping out the flex from a table lamp, remarkably still upright on the dresser, he tied the Professor's hands behind his back. Taking a moment to catch his breath, he tested the knot then walked over to the sink where he filled a washing up bowl with water from the cold tap. Finally, he pulled a chair out from under the kitchen table, sat down and dumped the bowl of water on the Professor's head.

Spluttering awake, Bird looked up and awkwardly rolled over onto his side then back so he could sit up and face his assailant. 'What the devil do you think you're doing!' he exclaimed, as he slid backwards across the floor until his back was pushed up against the wall.

The intruder glared at Bird as he touched the side of his head above the ear then looked down at his fingers. Blood had seeped through the balaclava. 'Where's the safe key?'

'Go to hell!'

Instead of answering, the intruder reached for a mobile phone in his pocket and tapped out a message.

Five minutes ticked by in silence until the back door opened and the bartender, her head covered in a hood, was shoved through the opening by a second person, his features also hidden beneath a balaclava. Hands tied behind her back, Bird could hear Cheryl's sobs from under the cloth as she was forced down onto her knees.

'Last chance,' said the intruder as he walked over to her, flipped the safety and pointed the gun at the back of her head. 'Where is the key to the safe?'

'The bureau in the lounge,' Bird replied without hesitation. 'Taped to the back of the second drawer down.'

Handing the gun to his accomplice, the intruder pulled a drying up cloth from a rack beside the sink, soaked it under the cold tap and walked back over to Bird.

'Open,' he said.

'Why?' replied Bird. 'You've got what you want.'

The intruder said nothing. Instead, he looked over to his accomplice who again pointed the gun at the hooded figure.

Bird opened his mouth.

With the gag firmly in place, the intruder went through to the lounge, reappearing a few minutes later with Bird's briefcase in his hand. Taking the gun back from his accomplice he took a suppressor out of his coat pocket, screwed it into place, placed the barrel to the back of Cheryl's head and pulled the trigger.

The muted sound of the gun's discharge did nothing to diminish the horror of the scene or Bird's strangled roars as the round tore out through the front of the hood and buried itself in the wall. Remaining upright for a second, as if failing to recognise its own mortality, the body toppled slowly forward, hitting the unforgiving flagstone floor with a grotesque thud.

Tearing at his restraints, but unable to free his hands, Bird pushed himself up against the wall. Gaining sufficient purchase to rear up off the floor, he threw himself head first at the gunman. For the second time that evening the intruder was taken off guard. Unable to raise the gun in time, Bird stopped at the last second, planted his feet and swung his head forward. The headbutt hit home, the crack unmistakable as Bird felt the bridge of the nose explode beneath the balaclava. As the intruder staggered back, Bird followed up with a kick to the side of the knee that flipped him up in the air and sent him crashing to the floor.

Teeth now bared and snarling behind the gag like an enraged animal, a primeval, visceral reaction to what he had just witnessed, Bird stamped on the intruder's head and spun round to face the accomplice. Rooted to the spot, wide eyed fear registered in the eyes behind the mask as Bird advanced. Stumbling backwards, he fell over the discarded kettle and landed on his backside as Bird jammed the heel of his boot into his face.

Sensing movement behind, Bird swirled round, cursing himself for not having kicked the gun away. Sat propped up against the kitchen table, the weapon was back in the intruder's hand. Resting it on his knee, he removed the balaclava and gingerly examined his damaged face.

So young were Bird's final thought as the gun spat out its lethal contents.

PART 3

'Big Brother is Watching You'

George Orwell

1984

CHAPTER 12

There were several potential exit points for the *subject*, the term *target* having been outlawed years ago. Each were covered by MI5 watchers and as with all such operations it was a ball ache for Dougie Palmer as he monitored the bank of screens in front of him. Never the easiest of venues on which to set up a surveillance operation, the good news was that since Brexit, the plethora of media attention around Parliament had not dropped off which meant no one took any notice of an additional Sky News van.

'Look, I know there's a need for compartmentalisation,' grumped Pam Dibben, Palmer's partner for the last two years, 'but, for goodness sake, Dougie, how much longer is this going on?'

'Take a chill pill, Pam,' responded Palmer. 'He'll make a mistake eventually. They always do and we'll be here to catch him.'

Both in their late forties, Palmer and Dibben were members of Alpha team. Chosen, as is so often the case, for their nondescript appearance and the ability to blend into the crowd, at five eight and three respectively, both wore street clothes to complement their role should static surveillance require some unexpected footwork. Not that any such thing had happened since this duty had suddenly become a priority.

'Yes, I know that, but what about lunch?' she said, shaking an empty flask and looking forlornly at an equally empty doughnut box, crunched up and all alone in a makeshift bin alongside the bank of monitors.

Making sure to arrive with the early morning news crews, they'd been on plot since five that morning, so stomachs were rumbling. 'Doggy bags'll be here soon, Pam, so don't panic.'

'It's alright for you Tubs,' she laughed, leaning over his shoulder and poking his paunch, 'but a girl's gotta eat you know.'

Palmer shook his head and returned his attention to the monitors while Dibben took her mind off her hunger pangs by running through a series of radio checks with the rest of the team.

*

The *subject's* day had and was likely to continue to be a busy one. Beginning with a Cabinet meeting at number ten first thing, Akram Murad, had gone on to Chair a meeting of the 'Immigration Audit Committee,' before heading back to his office in the Palace of Westminster from where, according to his schedule, he'd be tucked up in a series of meetings for much of the rest of the day.

Not that it mattered too much. Thanks to the Surveillance Commissioners having taken the unprecedented step of authorising directed and intrusive surveillance on a Cabinet Minister, Murad, as Palmer put it, was 'bugged to buggery' at work, in his vehicle and at home. The only testing time came at lunchtime when Murad, as was the case today, would forego the Parliamentary dining room in favour of a brisk walk to a Lebanese café in Maiden Lane, just off the Strand.

From there, he collected his meal, an easy to eat wrap and a coffee, bought a copy of the Times from a stall on the corner of Northumberland Avenue and wandered down to Whitehall Gardens alongside the Victoria Embankment. He then spent a half hour or so eating his lunch and doing the crossword before returning to the Palace of Westminster. Always the same bench, always the same time – unless his presence was required in the House or the weather was inclement – and always the same bin to deposit the trash. As both Palmer and Dibben could attest, this almost OCD behaviour was either exactly that or classic tradecraft in lieu of a brush pass or dead drop. But so far, subsequent sweeps of the route by different members of Alpha Team, including the bin, had yielded nothing. Likewise, countless reviews of CCTV footage along the route picked up nothing unusual in his behaviour.

In the lexicon of tradecraft adopted by intelligence agencies across the world, Murad also showed no signs of engaging in anti-surveillance tactics. Standing still for a moment, doing something inconsequential while scanning the street for any sign of surveillance, stopping to look in a shop window or to tie a shoelace. In essence, anything that would give him the opportunity to spot a tail. Not that it would have done him any good for 'Five's' watchers were the best in the business. Nor was there any indication of counter surveillance whereby others working on his behalf would be tasked to ensure he wasn't being followed. It was therefore assumed that Murad had no idea he was on the 'Watch List,' MI5's compendium of known terror suspects.

Not that any of this was foolproof of course, thought Dibben as she plonked herself down in a chair alongside Palmer. There were so many ways in which a trained operative could pass on information which was why, when Palmer sat bolt upright in his chair, Dibben took note and watched carefully as his fingers flew furiously back and forth across the keyboard in front of him.

'What's up?' she asked.

'There,' said Palmer pointing to a split screen on one of the larger monitors.

Each image showed Murad leaving No 10 and turning left towards the security gates that separated Downing Street from Whitehall.

'What is it?' asked Dibben again as she squinted at the monitor.

'It may be nothing,' said Palmer as he reached for the digitally encrypted radio. 'Alpha 2 to Alpha 1, over.'

'Go ahead, Alpha 2, over,' came the instant reply.

'Need you back here ASAP, Frankie, over.'

'Roger that, Dougie. In five.'

'In less than three, the inner door, which screened onlookers from what was really going on inside the van, swung open.

'What've you got for me?' asked Frankie Cervera, as she pulled the door shut behind her.

A raven haired beauty, dumbed down for the occasion, Cervera was brought up in Akram Murad's constituency of Southampton Itchen and like so many others was as surprised as the rest of the team when her local MP became the focus of such intense scrutiny. Not that it was for her to question the reasons why, but given the time and resources devoted to this operation it was clear he was a *mala persona* and therefore from her perspective, she would do anything needed to help bring him down.

'See for yourself,' said Palmer, pushing his chair back so Cervera could get a good look at the split screen.

'Shit!' she exclaimed a moment later. 'Dougie, bring up the CCTV footage from lunch.'

Palmer's fingers again flew over the keyboard. 'There you go,' he said, pointing to a second monitor. Also in split screen mode, this one showed each of the CCTV cameras on the route taken by Murad that day. 'What do you need?'

'Just scroll through slowly, please Dougie,' she said, at the same time pressing the mike button on her wrist. 'Alpha 1 to Alpha 3, over.'

'Yes, Frankie, what's up?' responded the cultured voice of her deputy, Tony Ellis.

With Murad confirmed as being firmly ensconced in his office, the rest of her team were taking a break, but not for long. 'Tony, I think we may have something,' said Cervera. 'Get everyone out on the ground. Key locations on the subject's lunchtime route – more to follow.'

'Roger that,' replied Ellis. 'Standing by.'

For the next few minutes Cervera scoured the CCTV footage 'There!' she exclaimed. 'How the fuck did we miss that!'

Cervera pressed her wrist mike again. 'Tony, all units to cover access and egress points to Whitehall Gardens on Victoria Embankment.'

'What are we looking for?' he responded.

'Anyone that approaches the bench is to be picked up.' By *picked up*, this meant they would be followed away from the scene until such time as it was safe to detain them for questioning. Like as not, this would take place on the street with no need for a fuss or trip to the nearest police station, unless of course there was a reason.

'All received, Frankie.'

'Right Dibber's, you're up,' said Cervera, giving Pam Dibben a wink, as she tucked her shoulder length hair under a baseball cap and zipped up a reversible green puffa jacket.

Grabbing her own coat and a Selfridges shopping bag, Dibben followed Cervera out of the van and hustled along to Westminster Bridge where, arm in arm like two forty somethings on a shopping trip in the big City, they took the flight of stairs down from street level onto the Victoria Embankment.

*

Working from home, I was finishing off the report on the Turkey gig, when I got the call from Sir Henry. It seemed that things were moving at last and he wanted me back in the office.

Despite Jill offering to look after Scrumpy from time to time, this was never going to be a permanent arrangement, at least I didn't think it was, which meant I'd had to make alternative arrangements for my new housemate. Luckily, Mervyn and Francis, a retired couple who live in a town house just along Bath Square, offered to look after him whenever needed. They'd had a Springer of their own up until a year ago when he'd taken his tennis ball to doggy heaven and I guess they missed the company only a four legged friend can bring to a home.

So with the lad in safe hands, I took the opportunity for some fresh air and wandered down to the Hard where I hopped on the next fast train from Portsmouth Harbour to Waterloo. I'd always found the hour and half journey a good time for reflection and today was no exception as I mulled over the events of the last few months, the latest developments being ones I could hardly have imagined when I stood in the lecture theatre at Hendon and swore allegiance to the Queen.

The oath or attestation all police officers are required to take at the point of becoming a constable is one that has always and will always be the reason for my doing this job. That my role had changed exponentially in recent times and stretched the boundaries of the oath somewhat was not lost on me. Indeed, while some may consider the 'eye for an eye' approach to the revised judicial system to be unlawful, from my perspective, so long as we had a robust process in place, supported by the likes of Jim Kirby to ensure fairness on behalf of the accused, I felt no pangs of guilt that the likes of Mehmet Ali and Badri al-Ghazi could no longer ply their trade across the world.

'Excuse me, is this seat taken?'

Lost in thought I looked up at the attractive woman behind the voice who was indicating the seat opposite me.

'All yours,' I said, with a smile.

We'd just stopped at Haslemere which accounted for the influx of passengers keen to get a seat before reaching Guildford. That it was lunchtime didn't seem to matter much on this line. Possibly something to do with the move towards flexible working, a concept which I was more than accustomed with or perhaps it was simply the pull of the big city and cheaper fares at this time of day. Who knows.

Mid to late forties, shoulder length dark hair, my new companion was power dressed, no doubt for the male dominated city environment, in a dark blue pin stripe pencil skirt, matching jacket, cream blouse and a Gucci shoulder bag which she placed on the seat next to her. Taking out a laptop she placed it on the table between us and was about to open the lid.

'Do you mind?' she asked.

'No, of course not,' I replied.

'It's just that some people are funny about personal space,' she said.

'Not me,' I replied. 'Please go ahead.'

'You looked like you were miles away,' she said as she opened the lid and keyed in what I assume was her password.

'Yes, I was rather. Just thinking.'

'Anything exciting?' she raised her eyebrows.

'No such luck, unless you're into politics.'

'Yuk!' she grimaced, 'you don't look the type.'

And what was the type, I thought as the image of Akram Murad floated through my mind. Sixth sense, coppers nose, call it what you will, I couldn't help but feel events surrounding the Immigration Minister were coming to a head. How that would turn out was anyone's guess, but for now, I was more than happy to turn my back on that for the next hour or so and sit back and relax while my travelling companion tapped away on the keys in front of her.

*

Although *dead-drops* are more commonly associated with the cold war, Cervera recognised that in the absence of electronic communications, there were occasions when the old ways for passing on information were the best, hence briefing her team to be extra vigilant for this type of methodology. To this end and in much the same way as the CIA rely heavily on CNN and other networks to provide them with invaluable intelligence, the same could be said for the British media keeping the UK Intelligence Services up to date on matters that might otherwise slip through the net.

In this instance and with Cabinet meetings taking place on an almost daily basis, it was Murad's departure from No 10 that morning which caught Palmer's eye. His red Ministerial folder, always tucked under his left arm and away from the cameras camped on the kerb opposite the UK's seat of power, was for once clearly on view under his right arm. Were it not for the microscope under which he was being surveilled nothing would be thought of such an innocent change to his daily routine, but for both Palmer and Cervera it set the alarm bells ringing.

Known as a *Marker* in the trade, something as innocent as a chalk mark left on a lamp post, a scuff mark on a kerb or a light in a window where curtains would otherwise be drawn could all indicate a dead-drop had taken place. For Murad, it was this simple change of routine that set alarm bells ringing. Captured on film by the media and subsequently confirmed by Cervera's review of the

CCTV footage covering Whitehall Gardens, she was able to verify that a drop had indeed taken place. A mix of emotions had flooded through her as she'd sat back from the monitor. *Anger* at missing it first time round, tempered by *relief* there was an opportunity to rectify the mistake and finally *satisfaction* that any residual doubts she may have had as to the Minister's treachery were dispelled by the skill with which he made the drop.

He was definitely a player and the key was the newspaper. Used as a distractor in much the same way as a magician uses sleight of hand to perform an illusion, once you knew what to look for, it could be seen clear as day.

With all eyes now on the bench, Cervera and Dibben entered the park, stopping briefly to buy a couple of coffees from a street vendor before wandering over to the bench where they sat down alongside a tall, thickset guy reading a copy of the Telegraph.

At six five, Tony Ellis wasn't your typical watcher, but when there was the need for a city gent type persona, his pin stripe suit, pigskin leather briefcase, umbrella and gaberdine raincoat, folded neatly on the bench between him and Cervera, made him the perfect fit for this aspect of the operation.

'Anything, Tony?' asked Cervera as if talking to Dibben who was looking through her shopping bag.

A master of the dark arts himself, Ellis used the newspaper as cover to slide a small magnetised metal box, about a centimeter thick, into Cervera's hand.

'Attached to a metal strut under the bench,' he said.

'Sneaky bastard,' said Dibben, joining in the conversation as if responding to Cervera's comment.

Waiting a few minutes to finish their coffee, Cervera stood up, air kissed Dibben and both women set off in different directions as Ellis pulled a Tupperware container and thermos from his briefcase.

Arriving on time I bade farewell to my travelling companion under the clock and headed for the exit at the far end of the concourse. Dropping down onto Belvedere Road, I strolled through Jubilee Gardens under the watchful eye or should I say thirty two watchful eyes of the London Eye and across Westminster Bridge from where it was a short hop up Whitehall to Trafalgar Square and my rendezvous with Sir Henry.

Pouring himself a coffee from his flask, Ellis, mused to himself as to the Darwinian world of counter terrorism. That those of limited intelligence who cross swords with the Security Services or worse still, Special Forces, are already dead, juxtaposed by those who learn from their mistakes and remain a threat. Wondering in which category those involved in this plot would fall, he put the cup down and took a bite from his favourite cheese, cucumber, tomato, spring onion, pepper and mayo sandwich.

Lunch had been a precautionary measure designed to keep the collection of the box at bay, but not one which could be left too long. They needed to know the other half of the equation which meant getting the container back in place as quickly as possible. So on returning to the news van, Cervera handed over the container to Palmer and watched carefully as he checked for booby trap devices or anything which may give away signs of tampering. Luckily, it had been a relatively simple lock to unpick, for Palmer anyway, and within a couple of minutes the metal container was opened.

Inside was a single strip of paper on which a series of numbers and letters were printed gcp19vyvh4k0jz11q/237/171. Once photographed and sent off to Thames House for the techies to pore over and hopefully decipher, the container was resealed and returned to the bench, relieving Ellis of his immediate duty. It was then simply a matter of waiting.

By late afternoon there had been several false alarms. Adults reading papers, lovers holding hands, kids messing about, each requiring the box to be checked for movement or disturbance, but all to no avail until an Asian male in his mid to late twenties sporting a tasty looking black eye, stopped alongside the bench to tie a lace on his trainer.

As might be expected, the reach of MI5 extends far and wide across the capital including to the many ex-service personnel who have taken up roles as concierges in the more security conscious hotels. Not that knowing the right person was necessary in this instance, for having previously been the home of the first chief of Britain's Secret Intelligence Service, MI5 were always welcome at the Royal Horseguard's Hotel, no questions asked. From her new OP (Observation Post) in a vacant suite overlooking the Whitehall Gardens, Cervera watched the retrieval through a pair of military grade zeiss binoculars, while Dibben adjusted the Sigma 600m super telephoto zoom lens and clicked away rapidly on her Sony A7R III. Not the best pick up by any means thought Cervera, but enough to suggest a basic level of training which could also extend to the new subject being surveillance aware. This was something she would need to take into account during the next phase of the operation as they watched him leave Whitehall Gardens and head east along the Victoria Embankment.

With Bravo team keeping tabs on the Minister and Alpha team on the new subject, Cervera and Dibben left the OP and rushed downstairs to the underground car park. Waiting patiently behind the wheel of a Skoda Octavia, Mike Stannard was one of a group of advanced drivers recruited from the Met Police Traffic

Operations Unit.

'Time to rock 'n roll,' said Cervera, as she jumped into the shotgun seat and Dibben dove in the back.

In the meantime, Paul Bright and Nyree Mills, followed on foot as the rest of Alpha team went mobile. Posing as lovers out for a romantic stroll, Mills held on to Bright's arm keeping pace with the subject as he made his way along the embankment towards Cleopatra's Needle where he took advantage of a break in traffic to skip across the road and hop over a set of low railings into Victoria Embankment Gardens. Whether this was a deliberate attempt at anti-surveillance or simply the route he was planning to take anyway, only the subject would know, but for Dougie Palmer, monitoring his progress on CCTV from the Sky News van, it made little difference. Using the same gap in traffic, Bright and Mills crossed the road, entering the Gardens by the main entrance alongside the Embankment Café from where, under Palmer's guidance, they quickly pick up the subject's trail.

Approaching the north east corner, the subject turned left into a circular seating area from where he exited the Gardens. Stopping to admire the statue of a distraught, half-naked muse gazing up at a bust of Arthur Sullivan, Mills pretended to read from the plaque at its base as Bright watched the subject approach a white catering van parked outside the rear entrance to the Savoy Hotel.

'Looks like they're going mobile,' said Bright, radioing in the location as a second Asian male, with his head under the bonnet, looked up as the subject approached the van.

'Ouch! That must have hurt,' said Mills, noting the black eyes and bandage across the bridge of his nose.

Wiping his hands on a rag, he reached up, slammed the bonnet shut and limped round to the driver's side of the van as the subject climbed in the passenger side.

'We have two subjects, I repeat two subjects mobile and heading west on Victoria Embankment from Savoy Place,' said Bright, following up with a description of the second male and registration number of the van.

Reaching for the radio mike in the glovebox as the Skoda pulled out into Whitehall Place just ahead of the van, Cervera pressed the transmit button. 'Alpha 1 to all units,' she said. 'Subjects are mobile,' and with that became one of three vehicles designated to handle the mobile surveillance.

While she would have liked a motorbike as well, following the van turned out to be easier than expected. Cervera knew that spotting one car would not have been difficult. Even two could be tricky for a surveillance team, but with three shadow cars in play, this broke up the pattern nicely. With the first tail car behind the subject vehicle, the second back from that and available to rotate at a moment's notice this left the third, occupied by Cervera, Dibben and the driver, in front, a combination that even a fully trained operative would struggle to spot.

It also was to this vehicle that fell the most difficult part of any such surveillance tactic. With the best will in the world it was impossible to know what the subjects were thinking, which was exactly what happened a moment later when the van cut across three lanes from Trafalgar Square into Cockspur Street. Immediately turning left into Spring Gardens the van came back round on itself into Cockspur Court and Warwick House Street before ending up back in Cockspur Street. This meant the lead car had to scurry around under the guidance of the trail cars until it or the third shadow car was able to assume the lead position. In this instance though, thanks to the plethora of one way streets in this part of the city, coupled with Dougie Palmer making the most of several of the five thousand plus CCTV cameras dotted across London, no harm was done.

'Well if that's all they've got,' said Cervera, as the van reappeared in their rearview mirror, 'this could be an easy ride.'

'Don't tempt fate,' said Dibben, from the backseat, as they turned off, allowing for the third vehicle, a Ford Mondeo, to take up position ahead of the van.

The next hour or so saw the trail cars switch in and out of visual coverage as the catering van wormed its way through the streets of central London before eventually heading out of the city on the West Cromwell Road. A PNC check came back *not* lost or stolen to a catering company in Yorkshire which inferred the plates had been changed, an assumption later confirmed by local units who attended the registered company address in Leeds. In the meantime, the convoy passed through Hammersmith and Chiswick and turned south west onto the A316 through Twickenham and Sunbury-on-Thames. From there, they went southbound on the M3 then west onto the A303 heading for Salisbury Plain and the Neolithic World Heritage Site of Stonehenge.

At the same time, Palmer had again been hard at work using images captured from CCTV to identify the Asian males as Khalid Hassan and Syed Wazir, members of the Jihadi group which had disappeared in the aftermath of the Leicester Square bombing. It turned out that both men had been subjects of interest to MI5 for some time, but in much the same way as was the case for the 2017 London Bridge terrorists, a lack of any direct intelligence, coupled with the Security Services high caseload, meant that the investigation into their activities had been similarly suspended.

Frustrating as it was, Cervera knew that while the UK has suffered more than its fair share of terrorist incidents in recent times, the reality is that MI5 are responsible for preventing numerous such instances each year, even though nine times out of ten no one would ever know. That this success is largely due to the viciousness of the average terrorist being matched only by their stupidity, she also recognised, that far from being two-dimensional movie villains, often they are gormless, naïve individuals lacking in basic training and common sense, as evidenced by Hassan and Wazir's lackadaisical efforts at detecting a tail. What makes it all the more maddening then, is when something out of the blue happens to conspire against an operation of this kind, a sentiment she expressed to Dibben as fat droplets of rain began to splatter on the windscreen.

CHAPTER 13

They call it a perfect storm, the rare confluence of coincidence that so often begins normally, yet ends in disaster.

Pete Carr stood back from packing up the Range Rover in readiness for the trip to Longleat. Never the easiest of tasks, especially when it involves strapping two excited youngsters into their child seats.

'Daddy!' cried Tabatha, as ominous grey clouds delivered the first drops of rain. 'Are you sure the monkeys will come out?'

'Yes of course, Tabs,' said her father. 'They're out in all weathers and yes, Freddy,' he grinned as a small head popped up in the rearview mirror, 'the lions too.'

That seemed to calm them down as he hoisted the last of

the luggage into the back of the 4x4.

'All set Pete?' asked his wife, as she returned from handing the keys in to reception.

It was half-term and the family had driven down from Ipswich in Suffolk to stay the night at a B&B in the tiny Wiltshire village of Chilmark. In truth, Pete and Jenny were as excited as the children about the visit. It was something they'd spoken about on their first date and were now, at last, able to do. Not that they needed the children as an excuse to visit the Safari Park, but like so many such plans, time had slipped by and once Freddy came along, closely followed by Tabatha, it seemed the right thing to do was to wait and enjoy the whole thing together as a family.

'All done,' replied Pete, as he held the door open for his wife.

'Thank you my good man,' she said as she pecked him on the cheek and slid into the passenger seat.

'Oh yuk!' squealed both children.

'Get a room,' said Freddy.

'Frederick!' exclaimed Jenny, in mock amusement. 'Where did you get that from?'

'Sorry, Mum,' he replied, head down, looking at his hands. 'Billy, heard his big sister say it to her Mum and Dad.'

'All set?' asked Pete as he got in behind the wheel. 'What?' he asked, as Jenny burst out laughing.

'Nothing Hun,' she said, winking at Freddy. 'Come on, let's get going or we'll miss the gates opening.

The combination of increasingly poor weather and half-term hadn't helped the holiday traffic. Not that it would stop Paul Murtan from making his usual visit to Starbuck's on the way to work. He also needed a pee, so rather than taking the usual drive-thru lane he pulled up in a space out front.

Having sorted out his immediate priority, Murtan was stood in line when a voice called out. 'Anyone own the Citroen out front?'

He hadn't seen any other Citroens in the car park when he'd pulled in so turned and waved to a man in brown UPS overalls stood in the doorway.

'I'm sorry, mate,' was the first thing the UPS guy said as Murtan walked up to him. 'It was in my blind spot.'

'What do you mean?' asked Murtan, already wondering how bad the damage was going to be.

'Think it's probably easier if I show you,' he replied, looking extremely sheepish.

With that, they went outside to see the UPS truck parked on the bonnet of the Citroen. The first thing Murtan thought, was that his wife was going to go kill him when she found out. He'd only borrowed her pride and joy that morning, a classic cream and maroon 2CV Dolly, because his car was in for an MOT.

'I'm really sorry, mate,' said the driver again as he noticed Murtan's epaulettes tucked inside his civvy jacket.

'Not half as sorry as I'm going to be when my old lady finds out,' he said, resigned to a serious bollocking when he got home after his shift. Assuming of course, he *could* get home or to his shift for that matter.

With twenty years in the job as a Thames Valley police officer Murtan knew there was no point getting angry about the inevitable so, ten minutes later and having sheltered from the rain in the cab of the UPS truck, they'd exchanged names, addresses and insurance details and the lorry driver was on his way. What was left was a sorry sight. The customary domed bonnet of the 2CV had been crushed into an ugly V shape with a sizable gash down the middle. Lifting the bonnet, before calling the breakdown service, Murtan checked out the engine compartment which, incredibly, appeared to have come through the experience unscathed. Perhaps there was a chance for him to get to work on time after all. Despite the rain now funneling down through the gash in the bonnet, Murtan's hopes were confirmed as the engine turning over first time. So deciding to put off the bollocking until he got home later that night he pulled back out onto the main road, heading east on the A303.

With visibility getting worse by the second, the mood in the Range Rover was becoming as gloomy as the rain was getting harder. Creating huge pools of water in the road, Pete Carr was wary of aquaplaning so kept the Range Rover in four wheel drive and wipers on full as the family ploughed through the country lanes until they were reached the main road and turned west onto the equally sodden A303.

'Don't worry guys, the forecast is good for later,' said Pete reassuringly, even though the App on his smartphone had shown it was going to be pretty awful all day. Not that it mattered too much he thought as they had a two day pass which meant they could at least do the house tour today and the safari tomorrow.

What Paul Murtan hadn't been able to see when he checked under what was left of the bonnet was the damage caused to the sump when it was squashed down onto the tarmac. A tiny fracture in the drain plug had resulted in an equally tiny oil leak that remained unnoticed until the engine started coughing, spluttering and doing its impression of a wallaby from the nearby safari park. Murtan knew he would need to pull over and call for an emergency breakdown service, but with this part of the A303 only a single lane in each direction and no verge in sight, he was resigned to plodding along until reaching a lay-by.

Maintaining a good hundred metres from the car in front, Pete checked his rearview mirror for the white van which had been tailgating them since joining the A303.

'What's wrong?' asked Jenny, noticing Pete gripping the steering wheel.

Quietly, so as not to upset the kids, he replied, 'Just some idiot who doesn't know how to drive in the wet.'

No matter how many times he dabbed his brakes, the van, why is it always a white van, continued to nudge closer. Get back you idiot, he thought as Freddy leant forward against the straps in his child seat. 'Daddy,' he said, squinting through the windscreen. 'Look at that funny little car.'

Taking his eyes off the mirror, Pete looked ahead. In the oncoming lane, maybe a couple of hundred metres or so away, he could see an old Citroen 2CV chugging slowly towards them.

'Oh Daddy! What's happened to that poor car?' asked Freddy. He loved cars as much as lions. 'It looks like an elephant's sat on his tummy!'

'He's had a bit of a prang,' Pete replied, the calmness in his voice belying a growing sense of anxiety in his stomach. Flicking on his hazard lights, he again dabbed the brakes, rechecked the rearview mirror, then cursed under his breath as the van moved even closer before pulling out and surging past the Range Rover.

Notorious for congestion at the best of times, the A303, which runs from Exeter in Devon through to Andover in Hampshire, is a combination of dual and single lane carriageways with the latter, as Paul Murtan was experiencing, having few lay-bys.

It was for this reason that most commercial drivers, including Bill Mason, tended to avoid this route when heading for London, even though on a good day it was quicker than taking the M5 North and M4 East. That is unless the market town of Salisbury is one of the driver's delivery stops or he has a daughter who'd been badgering him for weeks to drop in and see her new addition to the family. Such was the case for Bill Mason, but as his twenty six ton Volvo approached the end of the Mere Bypass and the dual carriageway merged into yet another single lane, he grumped to himself as the not unexpected steady stream of traffic reduced to a crawl.

From high up in his cab, Mason peered ahead and saw the

reason for the delay. But it wasn't the back end of the old 2CV chugging slowly up Chaddenwick Hill that caused him to hit the clutch and start downshifting gears.

About to breathe a sigh of relief as the van looked to have cleared the overtake instead, Pete watched in horror as the tail end of the van twitched on the wet road surface, skidded and clipped the front offside wing of the oncoming 2CV. Sending the lighter vehicle into a spin, the out of control 2CV swerved across the white lines and into the path of the Range Rover.

As Murtan fought to control the skid and bring the 2CV back into the correct lane, unbeknown to him, the impact with the van had caused the already damaged drain plug on the sump to break off, spilling its entire contents onto the road.

From an almost detached perspective Mason watched the entire scene unfold. The oil spilling out onto the road. The driver of the 2CV desperately trying to control the skid. The front of the Range Rover dipping as the driver cadence braked in an equally desperate attempt to slow down until, in a last ditch attempt to avoid a collision, the 4x4 pulled out into the oncoming lane. His lane.

Were it not for the combination of oil and water on the road surface, Pete might well have made it back into his own lane, but instead, even in 4x4 mode, there was nothing for the tires to grip as the Range Rover hit the slick and slid inexorably forward towards the oncoming HGV.

Mason was only too aware of the differences between thinking times, reaction times and braking distances in the wet and dry. Add to that the oil then despite his efforts to reduce speed, it was like stopping a tanker on the high seas as the two vehicles converged. Unable to do anything but brace himself, Mason could only imagine the horror for the poor family as the Range Rover disappeared from view, followed instantly by a sickening crunch as the tractor unit was rocked back on its suspension.

Amidst the stench of fumes and burning rubber, there was an eerie moment of silence as Mason jumped down from his cab. Fully expecting to see the Range Rover buried under the front wheels of his HGV, instead, he was surprised to see the 4x4 had careened off to the side of the road from where it had nosedived into a drainage ditch alongside the carriageway. But then, as smoke began to billow out from under the bonnet, closely followed by orange licks of flame, he was faced with an impossible decision. To return to his cab for a fire extinguisher and risk the flames taking hold or try and get the family out? In the fraction of a second it took for him to think, the decision was made for him as the flames grew stronger and began to travel back along the underside of the chassis towards the fuel tank. Rushing forward, Mason reached the rear door nearest to him and yanked it open. A boy and girl were trapped screaming in their child seats as Mum and Dad, he presumed, were slumped against seatbelts, their heads enveloped in airbags. 'It's okay guys,' he said to the children as he quickly unbuckled the straps on the girl's seat nearest to him.

Scooping her up in his arms, he stepped back onto the verge. 'There you go Honey, I've got you,' he said as a woman's voice called out from behind him.

'Here, give her to me!'

Mason turned to see two women running towards him, the first reaching out for the girl while the other leapt across the trench to the far side of the stricken vehicle. At the same time, a man appeared with a red fire extinguisher tucked under his arm like a rugby ball and jumped into the ditch. A second later, Mason breathed a sigh of relief as the familiar whoosh of CO_2 could be heard and seen as it billowed out from under chassis.

But the moment of relief was short lived. 'We're going to need more!' yelled the man as the extinguisher began to splutter.

With no time to wonder where they'd come from, Mason handed the girl over as instructed and ran back to his vehicle. Clambering up into his cab he fumbled with the metal clasps that held the CO_2 canister in the footwell, at the same time cursing himself for not having taken it with him in the first place. An oversight that would ultimately save his life, he eventually freed the extinguisher from its housing and jumped back down onto the road as the fuel tank on the Range Rover erupted. Throwing him back off his feet and slamming him into the grill of his HGV, Mason could only stare in abject horror as the 4x4 was engulfed in an impenetrable ball of flame.

CHAPTER 14

Looking up at the arrivals board the Sheik noted British Airways flight BA 236 from Moscow had landed. In a light grey suit, complete with chauffeurs peaked cap, he blended in well with the other drivers waiting patiently for their respective charges to make their way through to the arrivals hall from baggage reclaim. Resting his elbows on the barrier in front of him he held up a white plastic card on which the name Mikola Virastyuk was written in bold black marker pen.

The advent of Brexit had resulted in many changes across the UK, none more so than for arrivals at International Airports, including Heathrow. With upwards of eighty five million passengers travelling between the UK and EU each year, delays at passport control were inevitable, as was the need for UKBA, the UK Border Agency, to increase staffing levels. To help manage this period of change, UKBA turned to the Ministry of Defence Police to provide additional resources while a raft of new officers were recruited and trained.

One of those MOD police officers was Constable Steve Beard, a veteran cop with thirty years behind him in the Met who, on retirement, transferred to the MOD where he'd spent the last nine years leading a relatively stress free life compared to his time in the smoke. Not that age or time in the job had dulled his senses. Quite the contrary, for Beard was as keen as ever to give one hundred percent to whatever role came his way, including today, which was spent monitoring the queues of arrivals as they painstakingly made their way through passport control.

On the street, the ability to recognise a *tell* was something Beard had used on countless occasions in the past to ensure he always had reasonable grounds to conduct legitimate *stops and searches* on potential suspects. But as he watched the passengers shuffle forward until it was their turn to be summoned, it was more than one *tell* which drew his attention to the diminutive white male in his fifties.

From his position behind the dozen or so booths welcoming non-UK nationals to Britain, Beard nudged his colleague. 'Lane six, Al,' he said and nodded in the direction of the guy who had a bad case of the fidgets. Constantly checking his watch and looking beyond the control booths towards the signs for baggage reclaim, it was obvious his anxiety levels were getting the better of him.

Chalk and cheese in terms of stature and looks, Beard, at six three, buzz cut, silver grey hair and rugged features, towered over Al Stamp who, at five eight, had a red beard his wife told him had slid of his head once they were married. Not that passengers took much notice of looks when approached by a couple of cops cradling H&K semi-automatic carbines in their arms. Such was the case for this arrival as he cleared passport control only to come face to face with the two officers.

'Come with us please, Sir,' said Beard, in a manner not to be reckoned with.

A red flush instantly appeared on the passenger's neck as, in heavily accented, broken English, he replied, 'W…w…what have I done wrong,'

Not another *tell* in itself, as most passengers would have a similar reaction to being stopped in this way, but the tremor of the passport clutched in his right hand and the appearance of damp patches under the armpits of his beige jacket suggested to Beard this was one on which further enquiries would be necessary.

'It's nothing to be worried about, Sir,' said Beard calmly, nodding towards the passport. 'Can I see that please?'

The man handed the passport over. 'Please,' he said. 'I am in a hurry...'

'Ah, from Russia, I see. Mr Virastyuk, is that right?' asked Beard, ignoring the man's somewhat insipid plea.

'Yes, yes, from Moscow. I here on business.'

'Well, as I said, Sir. If we could have a few minutes of your time please, I'm sure we'll soon have you on your way.'

Broaching no further discussion, Constables Beard and Stamp ushered Virastyuk through an unobtrusive service door and away from several curious onlookers.

The Sheik had been noting the DME baggage labels for Moscow's Domodedovo Airport as passengers from flight BA 236 filtered through into the arrivals hall. But as the steady stream of passengers reduced to a trickle and the message for the flight dropped off the arrivals screen, he frowned, tugged on the peak of his cap, tucked the card under his arm and made his way over to Café Nero. One of several concessions in the arrivals hall, he joined the queue of weary passengers waiting for a caffeine fix before moving on to their respective destinations.

'Can I help you?' asked the girl as he reached the counter.

'An Americano, please,' he replied. 'Black and nothing to

eat, thank you.'

Paying for his coffee in cash, he helped himself to sugar and stood at one of the tall bar tables waiting a few extra minutes before heading for the exit and signs for the short stay car park.

As the Sheik returned to his car, Viktor Zhukov and Svetlana Ivanov were arriving at a farmhouse on Bodmin Moor. Rented through a shell company, the isolated property near to the granite outcrop of Garrow Tor, offered panoramic views towards Caradon Hill, Rough Tor, Brown Willy and Butter's Tor. Popular with hikers, the area provided the perfect cover for two city slickers looking for adventure in the relative wilderness of one of Cornwall's more infamous locations, home, according to local folklore, to the mythical 'Beast of Bodmin.'

Graduates of the 'Charm School,' a euphemism for Russia's infamous spy school on the outskirts of Moscow, Zhukov and Ivanov were GRU colonels who spoke perfectly accented English commensurate to their cover as Daniel Saunders and Stephanie Green, corporate executives for a Venture Capital firm in the City of London. The farmhouse also provided them with the opportunity to explore the nearby fishing port of Padstow on the northern coast of Cornwall from where, under the auspices of extending their adventure, they planned to hire a cruiser for a trip round the peninsular to St Mawes on the south east corner of the county.

Careful not to make the same mistakes as Anatoily Chepiga and Alexander Mishkin, the alleged, former GRU operatives responsible for the Novichok poisoning of Sergei Skripal and his daughter Yulia, they'd entered the UK independently, Zhukov via Felixstowe on a DFDS ferry from the Hook of Holland, Ivanov on a freighter into Southampton and with the third member of the team due to arrive soon via Heathrow, they felt that on this occasion all bases were covered.

Whether it had been supreme arrogance on the part of the then President Putin that travelling to the UK on genuine Russian passports and bona fide visas, albeit under the aliases of Ruslan Boshirov and Alexander Petrov, would result in Chepiga and Mishkin avoiding detection was unknown. Perhaps, it was speculated, Putin wanted them to be identified and in so doing send a message to other would be double agents that such treachery would not escape punishment. Again nobody knew for sure and now with Ulyanov as President, nobody would. What was known, by both Zhukov and Ivanov, was that should the architect of *this* operation be discovered, the consequences would extend far beyond the expulsion of a few 'legal' spies operating under the guise of being so called diplomats from various Russian Embassies around the world.

Even the use of current rather than former GRU operatives

was a factor in this equation. Unlike Russia's other security and intelligence services, all of which have heads that report direct to the Russian President, the GRU Director is subordinate only to the Russian military command. So if evidence ever led back to Dzerzhinsky Square, this would provide President Ulyanov with an additional layer of deniability should it be necessary. How that would play out for the GRU Director remained to be seen, but suffice it to say, they knew it wouldn't be a healthy one.

CHAPTER 15

Frankie pushed the empty whisky glass across the counter and nodded to the bartender as I perched on the stool next to her. Hair pulled back in a tight ponytail, cuts and scrapes on her face and arms made her look like she'd been dragged through a hedge backwards which wasn't far from the truth. Having pulled the little boy from the Range Rover, the explosion had thrown the two of them clear and into a gorse bush on the far side of the ditch.

'I'll get that,' I said, as the bartender reached behind him for the half empty bottle of *Tequila*. 'And I'll have a Coroner please.'

I'd known Francesca Cervera off and on for a number of years. First as a rising star in Hampshire, from where she was poached by MI5 and since at the occasional social, usually around

Christmas time. A single Mum with two great kids of her own, how she managed to juggle her lifestyle between home and work was a mystery to me, but one thing was for sure, I knew she would be hurting, hence wanting to keep an eye on her and hopefully give her something positive to focus on.

She looked at me as the bartender put our drinks on the counter. It obviously hadn't been her first as she raised the glass and glugged it back in one. 'Thanks,' she said and indicated for another.

Tucked away beneath the arches of London Bridge, the Mug House on Tooley Street is a favorite watering hole for local businesses, including those working at Thames House.

'It wasn't your fault you know.'

'You don't know that.'

'Yes I do. We've reviewed the footage from the viewcam in your vehicle and it's clear what happened.'

'Try telling that to Mike's family,' she said, as another shot followed. 'And what about those poor kids?'

'I'm told the grandparents are looking after them.'

'Some consolation.'

'I know, but it would have been worse without you guys being there.'

'*You* may think so?' she snapped.

'I do and look, they didn't know they were being tailed and the fact that the driver was a fucking idiot for making the overtake in the first place was not your fault. Nobody could have seen that coming, least of all you, so stop feeling sorry for yourself as I need you to focus on the investigation or Mike's sacrifice will be for nothing.'

At first I thought she was going to take a swing at me, but then her face softened. 'Okay, I get that,' she said. 'I'm sorry. It's just so fucking sad and on top of that we lost the bastards.'

'We did, but not all was lost.'

'What do you mean?'

She put her shot glass, untouched, back on the bar counter.

'After the van hit the Citroen, they took the next exit off the A303 and dumped the van in a country lane on the outskirts of a village called Stourton.'

'I know it,' said Frankie. 'I've got friends living in Bourton, just down the road from there.'

'In which case you'll know it's pretty rural, so it was only by luck it was found by a local farmer who rang it in.'

'No sign of the driver and his passenger, I suppose?'

'No and nothing from GCHQ either, so we're assuming they had burner phones to arrange a pick up.'

'Okay, so why are you here, Alex?'

'Aside from stopping you falling off that bar stool, to let you know that the van was picked up on ANPR last week.'

Of the eleven thousand Automated Number Plate Recognition cameras across the UK road network, approximately fifty million *reads* are registered at Hendon's NADC (National ANPR Data Centre) each day. So when a number plate is fed into the system, such as from outside the Savoy, a simple search will ping up any previous *reads* on that vehicle.

'And?' she asked, looking increasingly interested.

'Southbound on the M5 in the early hours, from where it pulled into Strensham Service Station.'

'Please tell me it was covered by CCTV?'

'It was. We've got footage of three males, Hassan and Wazir, by the looks of it, although the images are quite grainy and one other.'

'And the other one?'

'Unknown, but older and also Asian or at least from that part of the world.'

'Cleanskin?'

'Looks like it. Nothing on facial recognition or any of the databases.'

'So what were they up to?'

'Breaking into a container on the back of a trailer in the lorry park.'

'What did they take?'

'Typical tea chest style packing case. Not too heavy, but easy enough for Hassan and Wazir to transfer into the back of the van.'

'And from there?'

'Back south on the M5, where it came off at junction 25 for Taunton.'

'So the West Country then?'

'Perhaps.'

'And no more ANPR, I guess?

'No, too rural.'

'What about CCTV in or around Taunton?'

'No, nothing, which tends to suggest they were heading for the West Country, but nothing to confirm it either way.'

'What about the driver of the lorry? Did he have any idea what was going on?'

Frankie was on a role now and I was pleased to see her eyes clearing as she seemed to have forgotten about the still full shot glass on the bar counter in front of her. 'Interviewed at home,' I said. 'Says he knew nothing of the transfer.'

'Do we believe him?'

'We do. There's nothing on him apart from a few mishaps as a youngster. No affiliations of any kind other than his Trade Union and no reason to have known what was in the container.'

'Really?'

'Yes. It was loaded onto his trailer in Grangemouth from Latvia and was later offloaded in Port Talbot.'

'Minus one packing case.'

'Presumably.'

'But surely there must have been a manifest or something showing what he was carrying?'

'There was, but apparently they are notoriously short on detail and in this instance, the contents were listed simply as refractory materials.'

'Huh?'

'Apparently they're heat resistant materials for kilns, furnaces, that type of thing.'

'So a dead end?'

'Not necessarily. At least we know who we are looking for now, well two out of three anyway and we've got Charlie updating *Atelier* to make sure if anything comes our way then it will get picked up.'

In the aftermath of the Portsmouth bombing, Charlie introduced me to his new toy, a state of the art computer called *Atelier*. Based on the echelon system used by the NSA to gather and assimilate intelligence from across the 'Five Eyes' network, *Atelier* goes one step further by incorporating previously autonomous intelligence and crime databases from all UK police services. Intuitively interrogating this data 24/7, *Atelier* cross references literally trillions of pieces of information, looking for anything which may be relevant to an ongoing investigation or terrorist activity. It also channels footage from the six million plus CCTV cameras around the UK into the same hub, so if our suspects are recognised off the back of facial or gait recognition, then one way or another we should be alerted. So, when I said to Frankie, 'not necessarily,' I meant it.

'Talking of Charlie,' said Frankie, 'how's he getting on with Nici Matthews?'

'Still trying,' I said, more than a little concerned where this conversation might now be going.

'Can't blame him,' she smiled for the first time since I arrived. 'And what about you and Jill?'

And there it was, 'What do you mean, me and Jill?'

'Word on the grapevine has it you two are getting quite close.'

'Just friends,' I said, perhaps a little too quickly.

'With benefits?'

'Come on,' I cringed. 'It's time to get you home!'

'No need, I'm fine with getting the train,' she said sliding of her stool then staggering slightly as she grabbed my arm. 'Oops!'

'Have you moved or something?'

'No.'

'In which case it's only a slight detour off the A3 for me, so makes sense to drop you off.'

'Thought you used the train?'

'Borrowed a pool car in anticipation of you being the worse for wear, so don't look a gift horse in the mouth.'

'I suppose you're right,' she said, doing her best to suppress a hiccup.

'Good, now write that down!'

'Eh?'

'It's not everyday a woman tells me I'm right!'

That got me a slap on the arm.

'They'll be a reason for that,' she said as with a backward glance towards the still full shot glass, we left the bar.

CHAPTER 16

By the time I got home, it was getting late for picking up Scrumpy, but as I pulled up on the cobbled drive, I could see lights still on in Mervyn and Francis's second floor bay window. I decided to take a chance and knock, but needn't have worried as Francis came to the door with a very excited Scrumpy.

'Oh my,' she said, smiling down at the lad as he did his usual impression of a fairground Waltzer. 'He must have known you were on your way as he's been a proper fidget for the last half hour or so.'

'I'm sorry,' I said. 'I'd hoped to be home earlier...'

'Don't worry,' she stopped me. 'You know how much we love having him.'

'Well, thank you so much,' I said, clipping on his lead.

'He's no trouble,' said Francis. 'Same time tomorrow?'

'I'm working from home tomorrow so we should be fine, thank you, unless of course I get called in.' Francis still thought I was a police officer which meant her 'any time' offer to help out was invaluable.

'Well you know where we are,' she said and handed me a carrier bag. 'Just some left over supper,' she said with a wink. 'Goodnight, Alex.'

'Looks like we've done rather well here,' I said to Scrump's as the door closed and crouched down so he could get a look in the bag of goodies, equally proportioned between one man and his dog.

It was a mild evening with clear skies so I lifted his nose up to get his attention. 'How do you fancy a midnight picnic?' Okay, it wasn't midnight and I knew the lad couldn't hear me, but then we weren't exactly George and Timmy from the Famous Five either and besides I could do with a leg stretch and was sure he wouldn't object. So with that joint decision made, we set off along the cobbled back streets of Old Portsmouth until we reached a stone staircase that took us up onto the battlements, known locally as the Hot Walls. Connecting two of the city's most iconic fortifications, the Square and Round Towers were, like

Palmerston's Follies out in the Solent, built to repel potential invaders during the Napoleonic wars. Nowadays though, they offer a far more tranquil purpose as excellent vantage points for watching the comings and goings of a busy harbour.

As we reached the top of the stone steps, I looked back across the rooftops. A couple of hundred metres or so away, another more recent, yet equally iconic structure, could be seen illuminated alongside the old Camber Docks. Dominating the skyline, the giant tugboat shape of Ben Ainsley Racing (BAR) HQ was home to Great Britain's bid to win the Americas Cup. It had also been part of an elaborate act of duplicity on the part of the terrorists responsible for the attack on the Blackwall Tunnel, something which Sun Tzu himself would have appreciated were it to have been successful.

I'd never read 'The Art of War,' but I was aware of the basic principle that all warfare is based on deception, every battle being one or lost before it's ever fought. His advice was quite simple. *Defeat the enemy where he is unprepared and appear where you are not expected.* That could so easily have been the case last summer and as we found a bench that looked out across the harbour to the lights of Gosport, I couldn't help but feel we may well be heading down a similar path.

Having missed the debrief on the Turkey operation Nici Matthews was keen for a catch up with her friend and if that meant an excuse for a girlie night out then all was good in her world. A toss-up between her home on the Isle of Wight or Jill Dennison's in Fordingbridge resulted in them having just polished off a steak meal at The George, an 18th century pub on the edge of the New Forest.

'So how are things going between you and Alex?' Nici asked, as she circled her finger round the rim of an empty wine glass.

'Oh you know, good from a work perspective, but it's obvious he's still not over Bronagh, so I don't want to push things, assuming of course there's something to push.'

'Come on,' laughed Nici. 'Of course there is. You only have to see the way he looks at you.'

'Really?'

Nici shook her head. 'Yes really! It's obvious to everyone, but you two. Not that I was miffed or anything, but who do you think was the first person he looked to when he joined us on the gulet?'

'Don't be silly, that's just him looking out for everyone as usual.'

'If you say so,' she sighed. But honestly, I think he's still hurting and I don't want to jump in feet first and find the water's too deep.'

'Okay, but don't hang around too long in case someone else swims up from the shallow end.'

'What, like Scrump's you mean? He loves the water.'

Both girls laughed. 'My round,' said Nici, getting up from the table. 'Same again?'

'Yes please,' said Jill, as her mobile pinged.

Fishing it out of her rucksack on the back of her chair – she wasn't much of a handbag type of girl – Jill grinned as she opened the WhatsApp message and a picture of Scrumpy appeared on what she guessed were the hot walls.

Perhaps it was time to take a risk after all, she thought, as Nici returned with the drinks.

CHAPTER 17

It was a recurring nightmare.

The stomach churning excitement of the proposal mixed with the terrifying prospect of a refusal then, as is so often the case in this twilight world, the inexplicable, heartrending anguish of holding B's lifeless body in my arms, her life blood seeping through my fingers.

Quite what was happening beyond the nightmare I would of course never know, but each time I'd wake to a soft whimper and a wet nose gently urging me back to the real world. Kindred spirits perhaps. After all, it was only a short time after B's murder that Scrumpy lost his handler. One thing was for sure though and whatever the psychology of it, I was grateful for the new friend in my life as I swung my legs out of bed and we padded downstairs to put the kettle on.

A half hour later, we were back up on the Hot Walls and jogging across the wooden bridge that spanned a moat in front of ramparts that overlooked the harbour and out towards the Isle of Wight. Scooting through the fairground on Clarence Pier, too early for the customary smells of fish, chips and candy floss, we dropped down onto the shingle beach for Scrumpy's first wee mail check of the day. I'd read somewhere this routine was akin to us reading the newspapers, so who was I to deprive my friend of his daily fix as I waited for him to finish the article. It didn't take long and after leaving his own views on the subject we set off again.

With three miles of uninterrupted promenade ahead, not to mention the return leg, we picked up the pace, the familiar sense of euphoria flooding through my veins as the endorphins, natures very own opiate, kicked in. Much like the intent behind my trip to Austria and occasional use of the train, running was also a perfect time for reflection.

Despite knowing our actions were legal and we now had something in place which allowed us to fight fire with fire, I still struggled with my own motives behind accepting the role offered by Sir Henry. Was I simply after *vengeance* for Bronagh's death and therefore a glorified *vigilante* or as I recalled from Des Horne's history lessons at school, was I simply a variation on the true meaning of the term, *vigile*, one who kept watch for fires in ancient Rome or as in our case, part of a group who take action by putting out those metaphorical fires.

Sufficient justification or not, I'd made my bed and who knows I thought, as we passed the War Memorial on the edge of Southsea Common, how many lives could have been saved if Archduke Franz Ferdinand hadn't been assassinated in Sarajevo or conversely Claus von Stauffenberg, chief conspirator in Operation Valkyrie, had been successful in the plot to bring down Hitler. Rhetorical questions I know, but perhaps by getting ahead of the game we can in some small way, quell those fires before they start.

Anyway, swinging right and down to the side of the Aquarium we picked up the pace and with a refreshing sea breeze at our backs passed the bandstand, nestled in a natural amphitheatre created from the battlements surrounding Southsea Castle. Racing up a small incline that took us round the back of the old artillery fort constructed by Henry VIII in 1544, we dropped down the far side of Castle Fields and back onto the prom.

South Parade Pier came next after which we stopped for Scrumpy to deliver another message as I looked out across the water to the beginnings of an old anti-submarine barrier built during the second World War to protect the harbour from German U-boats. Each year, this series of concrete blocks that stretch out to Horsesands Fort, some two miles in the distance, sit just below the surface, maybe six feet or so and catch out many an amateur sailor who fail to head for the dredged, 'deep water pass' or 'small boat passage' nearer to the shore. That this location brought an end to the incident on the cruise ship last year was never far from my thoughts whenever I was in this neck of the woods, but today those thoughts were interrupted by the sound of crunching footfalls and rhythmic grunting of someone pounding along the shingle behind us. Looking back, we watched as the figure of what can best be described as your archetypical PTI approached. White vest, cargo pants, boots and Bergen rucksack all complemented the bald head, barrel chest, bulging biceps and enviable tan.

'Looking good,' I said, as Marty Farrow stepped off the shingle and joined us on the promenade.

'Thought you guys might like some company,' he said. 'Sorry I missed the debrief.'

'How did the meeting with your probation officer go?'

'Told her the truth of course. Isn't that what I'm supposed to do now I'm an ex con?'

'You did?'

'Yep! Went on a nice sailing trip, took in a bit of scuba diving then killed an international arms dealer. All pretty much, run of the mill stuff really. Funny though, she didn't seem to believe a word of it. Mind you, got me an invite to dinner and a tick in the box which means I'm ready to rock n' roll whenever needed.'

I didn't like to ask what the 'tick in the box' was for as I tugged at the rucksack on his back. Yep, it was heavy. 'What've you got in there?'

'Bricks of course, what else?'

'You're mad,' I said, shaking my head. 'And not getting any younger.'

'Can't argue with that,' he said with a grin. 'But come on, are we just going to stand here all day?'

'Good point well made,' I said, as all three of us set off again towards Eastney and the far end of the seafront.

Up ahead, the Yomper statue, unveiled by Baroness Thatcher in 1992 to commemorate the Royal Marines who served in the Falklands War, gazed out across the Solent as if on guard outside what was once the Royal Marine Barracks. It also marked the point at which dogs were allowed back on the beach. So, letting Scrump's off to do his own thing, we jogged down to the low water mark where the shingle gave way to sand and continued along the water's edge. The soft sand did little to impact on Marty's pace, but what was clear by his body language, he was itching to ask me something.

'Go on,' I said, 'what is it?'

'I was just wondering, why me?'

'Why what?' I teased, knowing full well the meaning behind the question.

'Oh come on. You don't or rather didn't know me from Adam and yet you plucked me out of the clutches of Belmarsh and gave me a dream job of dispatching the bad guys.'

'Well it wasn't by luck, Marty,' I said and with that went on to explain how, courtesy of Col. Truman, his particular skills had come to my notice.

By the time I'd finished, we were back up on the promenade and with Scrump's retethered were making our way home.

'Okay,' said Marty. 'Now that makes sense.'

'What do you mean?'

'Colonel Truman has invited me down to Hereford.'

'Well I guess that explains the backpack and running boots. I take it the *Fan Dance* will be on the menu?'

'Apparently so, yes.'

'What about the *Killing Room*?'

'That and everything else the Regiment has to offer,' Marty replied, with a grin. 'To be honest, I'm a bit nervous as it's been a while.'

'You'll do fine,' I said. 'When are you planning on going?'

'I was rather hoping tomorrow would be okay with you?'

With the operation on Akram Murad outside of Marty's remit, there was no reason why he shouldn't take up Col. Truman's offer and from a purely selfish perspective, given what we might need from him in the future, I was delighted he had been offered the opportunity to brush up on some old skills.

'Fill your boots my friend and good luck,' I said as we slowed to a warm down pace and arrived back at Clarence Pier. 'You're going to need it!'

CHAPTER 18

With 'Five' unable to make head nor tail of the coded message retrieved from Whitehall Gardens, the breakthrough on the dead drop came down to Charlie. In addition to being a keen triathlete, he was also into orienteering, a hobby which proved to be the key to the puzzle. It was also the reason I was stood on the balcony of an executive suite at the Rosebowl Hilton Hotel overlooking the lush green turf of Hampshire's County Cricket Club.

Having got home from seeing Marty, I'd taken a quick shower, changed into a pair of jeans, polo shirt and deck shoes then raided the fridge. Loading up *Trinidad* with a stash of essentials, bread, cheese, half a bottle of white wine, water for my companion and a rawhide chew which would at least allow me to eat half my lunch in peace, the plan was to take a leisurely run along the coast to Hayling Island. But, as Robbie Burns once said, 'the best laid plans of mice and men...' and in this case dog, were put on hold by a call from Charlie on my encrypted mobile.

Without preamble he'd launched into one of his typical openings that required an interpreter, 'Once I realised the first set of digits were a geohash code...'

'Whoa Tiger!' I'd said, take a breath. 'What on earth is a geohash code?'

'Sorry, Alex. I keep forgetting you're a dinosaur.'

'Careful lad, I resemble that remark!' I laughed, mainly because he was right.

'Geocoding is a simple methodology for encoding geographic coordinates.'

Simple my eye, but I got the gist, 'Latitude and longitude you mean?'

'Exactly! The first string of letters and numbers on the strip of paper from the dead drop, "gcp19vyvh4k0jz11q" delineate an area on a map called a cell.'

'How precise an area?'

'Depends on the varying resolution. The more characters in the string, the more precise the location.'

'And in this case?'

'The Rosebowl, Hampshire's County Cricket ground just outside Southampton,' he'd paused, 'but, that only accounts for the first seventeen digits.'

'Keep going.'

'Once I isolated those digits, I went on line and looked at the map of the ground. At first, I couldn't find anything relating to the penultimate three digits, 237. Seat numbers, rows, that kind of thing, but then I looked at the fixture list and saw the Club are hosting the first of a series of five One Day Internationals against Pakistan this summer and the first match is a day/night game due to be played on the 23rd of July.'

Judging by the tone of his voice, I knew there was more so resisted the temptation to interrupt.

'So,' he'd continued, 'I hacked into the ground's database and it turns out Akram Murad is an Honorary member of the Cricket Club, which if you think about it, kind of makes sense seeing as he's the local MP. Anyway, last summer, I went to the Rosebowl with some mates to watch an Ashes Test and we all said that if we did it again we'd book a couple of suites at the on-site Hilton Hotel. Mind you, you'd need to win the lottery to do that on match day as the back of the Hotel is in pole position for watching the cricket. It literally takes up a quarter of the boundary with balconies that look directly out onto the Ground. So with that in mind, I took a look at the Hotel's database and there were the final three digits, an executive suite on the top floor, booked in Murad's name.'

Pete Curly came through the patio doors and joined me on the balcony. As one of 'Five's' tech services team, he'd checked into suite 171 earlier in the afternoon, purportedly in readiness for an economic forum due to be held in the Hotel's main Conference Room tomorrow morning. That he knew nothing about economics was kind of irrelevant. Nor that he would actually be attending. What *was* important was that this suite was magically made available thanks again to Charlie's wizardry, as were two others on the same floor. One for Jill and one for me. As for Frankie and her team, they would again be using the cover of the media from their pitch outside the ground while posting her team at strategic choke points throughout the Hotel. As for Jill and I, we'd checked in independently that afternoon for a two night stay. Apparently, it was only the likes of the local MP who could get away with a one night stay around match day. Anyway, having stowed our gear, I'd left Jill to settle into her suite while I checked on Pete's progress.

'Thanks Pete, you're a star,' I said as we stepped back into the suite and looked round. Not that I expected any different, there were no signs of any of the gadgetry he'd spent the last couple of hours installing, but most importantly, when he checked out the following morning, the Member of Parliament who seemed to think it was okay to betray his country, wouldn't, as Pete put it, 'be able to fart without us knowing about it.'

CHAPTER 19

With the Rosebowl operation gearing up nicely, Marty Farrow drove through the gates to Stirling Lines, Garrison HQ for 22 SAS.

Named in honour of Lieutenant Colonel Sir Archibald David Stirling, founder of the SAS, Stirling was dubbed *'The Phantom Major'* by Rommel and referred to by Monty as *'mad, quite mad.'* His heroic exploits during the second World War were the stuff of legends. Over a fifteen month period, he used the element of surprise and a small team of highly trained soldiers to wreak havoc among the enemy, destroying hundreds of Rommel's aircraft, munitions dumps, railways and telecommunications systems across North Africa. That he was eventually captured and ultimately saw out the war in Colditz, did nothing to diminish his reputation or the aura which surrounds the Regiment to this day, something of which Farrow was mindful as Col. Truman, from his office adjacent to the parade ground, handed a glass of single malt to another legend of the Regiment, Major Jim Keeble.

Maj. Keeble had seen active service in both Iraq conflicts, Afghanistan and several other less well known hostile regions around the world where the specialist skills of UK Special Forces were required. Never wanting to become, as the Americans put it, a REMF (Rear Echelon Mother Fucker), but with his operational days coming to an end, he was offered the position as Commander for 'E' Squadron, an opportunity he grabbed with both hands.

Considered the most shadowy of UKSF units, 'E' Squadron comprises a small band of hand-picked operators from the SAS, SBS and SRR, the Special Reconnaissance Regiment. Their role is to work on clandestine operations with MI6, the Secret Intelligence Service, or as some members of the unit prefer to think of themselves, 'Minders' for the suits. It therefore fell naturally into 'E' Squadron's remit for this arrangement with the SIS to extend to Sir Henry's team and with that, the opportunity for Marty Farrow to revisit some of his old skills.

'So, what do you think, Jim. Happy to put Marty through his paces?'

'Definitely, Sir,' Keeble replied, taking a sip from the glass. 'We all know he was well and truly fucked over by the courts and deserves to be back in the fold.'

'That he does, but don't molly coddle him. According to, Alex Lendon, he's going to be a key member of this new unit, so needs to be fully up to speed.'

'No chance of that,' responded Keeble as he looked down at the thick file on his lap. 'If his service record is anything to go by, then I don't think we'll have any problems.'

'Good,' Col. Truman replied as there was a light tap on the door. 'Come in Radders.'

Stephen Radley stepped into the room. Slim, forties, fair hair, receding, he was conservatively dressed in an off the peg grey suit, white shirt and blue tie. One of several civilian employees working for the Regiment, 'Radders' had come with the job when the Colonel took over from his predecessor. 'Mr Farrow is here to see you, Sir.'

'Excellent,' replied Col. Truman. Standing up from behind his desk. 'Send him in please.'

CHAPTER 20

With Bravo Team monitoring Murad's activities in London, we decided to take advantage of a night off and book a table at BEEFY'S. Part of the Hilton Hotel and with panoramic views of the action on match day, the Steak and Seafood restaurant was, as you might expect, very much in the mould of England's finest all-rounder. Not that you could miss the connection, with life size murals of Sir Ian Botham at either end of the restaurant, one appealing a dodgy decision and the other propelling a Duke ball into the stratosphere.

'So what do you think?' I asked, as Jill took a sip of Argentine Malbec.

'Good,' she replied. 'How about you?'

'Perfect,' I said, setting my vintage bottle of Corona on the bar. As might be expected on a night before an International, the restaurant was buzzing which meant there was a good half hour wait on our table. Taking advantage of the delay I suggested, 'Come on, let's take a wander out onto the terrace.'

Much like in Turkey, eyes followed us across the room as we weaved our way across the restaurant and out through sliding doors into the warm evening air.

'Just because we're working,' she'd said earlier on answering my knock on the door to her suite. 'There's no reason why I can't take advantage of staying in a posh hotel once in a while, even if it is on company time.' With her blond hair up, Breakfast at Tiffany's, Audrey Hepburn style, light make up and understated black three quarter sleeve jersey dress, she'd looked stunning and it was all I could do not to stare as we'd walked to the lift that would take us down to the restaurant. Smelt great too.

'You know, it's okay,' she said, as she hooked her arm through mine.

'What is?' I asked, a little apprehensively.

'To move on...' she paused, as if sensing my anxiety and weighing up whether or not to continue.

I didn't know what to say. I did know what she meant or at least I think I did and if so I wanted her to continue.

'Bronagh would want you to,' she said, lightly squeezing my arm. 'No matter who it's with, she would want you to move on.'

I knew she was right and there was only one person I wanted that to be with so, taking a deep breath, I looked back at the crowded restaurant.

'How do you feel about room service?'

CHAPTER 21

Marty Farrow rose at 0630 for PT followed by a five mile run with three of his new colleagues. With the bulk of 'E' Squadron's troopers engaged alongside MI6 on other operations, Tony Barber, Mark Scanes and Mike Allen had been held back by Major Keeble to provide Farrow with some competition during his re-indoctrination into the world of UK Special Forces. All sergeants and weapons experts in their own right, each man brought something different to the table. Barber, a sniper, unparalleled across each of the three services, Scanes, explosives and Allen, the eldest, multi skilled and natural leader of the team. What was pretty much equal across the board, was their fitness, attested to by them having barely broken sweat during the run. That Farrow had been SBS while the others were SAS added some good natured spice to this challenge which ended forty minutes later outside the weapons range. Grateful for time spent over the last few weeks pounding up hill and down dale, Farrow was quietly pleased to see the look of respect on the faces of his new team members as they warmed down. How that would translate to the range, he thought, remained to be seen, but for now, it was a good start.

Walking into the armoury, Farrow pulled up short as he recognised the familiar face across the counter.

'How's it going, Marty?'

'All good my friend,' Farrow replied, reaching forward to grip the outstretched hand of Regimental Sergeant Major, Archibald 'Archie' Banks.

RSM Banks had been in charge of the Regiment's toys for the best part of two decades and although he'd seen many 'Marty's' come and go, he always remembered their names. As one of only three unidentified officers to receive the Military Cross for gallantry during the Persian Gulf War, this was a trick Banks had developed by way of thanks for never having to buy a drink in the NCO's Mess.

'So what's your poison, young fella?' Banks asked.

Perhaps one of the lesser known facts about the Regiment is the opportunity for troopers and officers, aka Ruperts, to choose their preferred weapons. In Farrow's case it was a step back in time for him as he selected the Glock 17 pistol and Hechler &

Koch MP5A3 submachine gun. Once the preferred weapon for hostage rescue operations, the MP5 was made famous during Operation Nimrod, the Iranian Embassy siege in 1980. With its 9x19mm Parabellum rounds being less likely to pass through the target and strike a hostage, this was something Farrow felt might be useful given his new line of work. That the MP5A3 had a retractable stock was also part of his thinking, lending itself to concealment under a jacket and therefore ideal for undercover work.

'Good choice, but you might like to give this a go instead,' suggested Banks, handing over a weapon, not dissimilar in size or shape, but one which Banks went on to explain had some distinct advantages over the MP5.

Introduced to the regiment specifically for close protection and covert reconnaissance assignments, the readily concealable UCIW or Ultra Compact Individual Weapon had a custom shortened buffer tube which reduced the overall length of the weapon from just over twenty seven inches to twenty two inches, yet packs the punch of a 5.56x45mm NATO round.'

Farrow took the proffered weapon, balanced it in his hands, then grinned as he looked down the barrel. Immediately recognising the UCIW complemented his muscle memory, he nodded to the RSM. 'Thank you, Sir,' he said, and walked through into the range where the others were waiting to see what he had to offer.

First off, Farrow set aside the UCIW and without saying anything, donned his ear protectors and glasses, chambered a seventeen round magazine in the Glock and set his sights on the five metre silhouette target. *That'll do for starters* he thought, noting the cluster of holes just above the heart. That was, until he looked to his right at Allen's grouped headshots around a single ragged hole and Barber's not so ragged hole right between the eyes. *Oh well, something to work on.*

Next came the c8 carbine assault rifles. In response to the advent of body armour, the c8 had been in general use by UKSFs since the late 1900s and early 2000s. Featuring a flat top receiver with a rail system for mounting scopes, along with another set of rails for other accessories such as lasers, torches and grenade launchers, it was the preferred choice of the other three troopers, unless Barber was required to engage in his speciality. In that instance his Accuracy International AX50 snipers rifle, combined with a Schmidt and Bender scope-sight, would take centre stage.

For now though, Farrow retrieved the UCIW, extended the retractable stock and nestled the butt into his shoulder. With his right thumb floating over the three position fire mode selector on the pistol grip, he actuated the SEF trigger group to 'E', single fire, and alongside the others, engaged pop-up steel plates the size and shape of human heads. Like shooting ducks at a fairground, no sooner were the targets driven up by compressed air, they were dispatched with a satisfying clang. What made this whole exercise even more spectacular was that it was being done off the back of a five mile run designed to simulate the stress of a real combat situation. Not that the reality of combat can be truly simulated, it was nonetheless an impressive performance and provided Farrow with a degree of reassurance that he could still hold his own as and when the occasion required.

CHAPTER 22

I woke early expecting to feel guilty, but instead felt something quite different. No, not that. Okay, maybe that, but more so there'd been no nightmare and no wet nose. Instead, a sense of… oh I don't know, it just felt good as I carefully slid out from under the duvet and sat on the edge of the bed.

'Where do you think you're going?' said Jill, opening one eye as she reached up and gently ran her nails down my back.

'Room service?' I suggested.

'I think we did that last night, didn't we?' she said. 'You okay?'

For once, I didn't need to think about the answer. 'Yes, I'm good,' I said. 'Really good in fact.'

'Good,' she smiled. 'Now get back in here.'

An hour later, two full English's with coffee and orange juice had been dispatched. *An army marches on its stomach* seemed to be one of Jill's adages I'd have to get used to if this relationship was to last. Not that I minded, I thought as Frankie appeared with an update and two carry on style suitcases on wheels. With a 'told you so' look as Jill emerged from the bathroom wrapped in a toweling robe, she explained that Murad had travelled down from London to his constituency the night before and according to his schedule was conducting surgeries this morning prior to making his way to the hotel later in the day.

'Anything to note?' I asked, pouring an extra cup for her.

'Nope,' she replied. 'According to Mick...' Mick Leebek was Frankie's opposite number and Bravo Team leader. '...he's got an open plan office and staff to take minutes so it's unlikely he'll get up to anything until he gets here. That said, we're running checks on who comes and goes, but so far nothing to get excited about.'

'Okay, good,' I said. 'We all set this end?'

'Yep. Dougie and Pam have run signal checks on the kit installed by Pete yesterday, who by the way, checked out a half hour ago.'

'Nothing to keep him in bed, I guess,' piped up Jill from in front of the dressing table.

I shook my head as Frankie opened the suitcases. Inside, a thick layer of foam protected a variety of goodies from which we'd be able to keep an eye on Murad's room once he arrived. For now though, once the monitors and speaker were set up on a sideboard, all we could see was the chambermaid making up the suite for the next guest. Obviously happy in her work, she sang her way through the bathroom routine – not sure that would be my favourite task of the day – and with the skill of a thousand hospital corners, made up the new bed in barely two minutes.

With that, Frankie bade us farewell and with a wink at Jill – incorrigible – left us to go and brief the rest of her team.

CHAPTER 23

Dispensing with his dedicated close protection officer from the Met Police Protection Command, Murad travelled alone from his surgery to the ground in his personal car, a metallic green Lexus SUV. Arriving just after 2pm he had plenty of time to make his way to his suite and unpack his overnight bag in readiness for the start of the match at 2.30pm. According to Mike Leebek, Bravo Team leader, the usual list of runners and riders looking for support in one capacity or another had attended during the morning. All had been checked and double checked against 'Five's' watchlist with nothing untoward showing up.

From my perspective and as surveillances went, I'd certainly had worse. Thanks to the contours of the hotel which followed the perimeter of boundary, my suite offered a birds eye view of the MP's balcony on the far side of the building. Leaning on the handrail, I watched as Murad joined the crowd in applauding Pakistan onto the field of play, followed by a chorus of Jerusalem from the Barmy Army as the England openers strode out onto the square. Looking back though the patio doors, I could see Jill keeping half an eye on the wide screen TV as Sky Sports showed a list of forthcoming ODI's, the next scheduled for Lords the following Tuesday. Catching my eye, she winked as she turned back to the monitors on the dressing table and donned a pair of earphones. All set, she did a final radio check with Frankie's team and settled back to see how the day and evening would unfold.

As the first ball was hit straight down the ground for four by Jonny Bairstow, Nikolay Kamenev looked out across the Thames from his penthouse suite at the Savoy and reflected on the last few weeks.

The meeting in the desert with the man known as the Sheik, an affectation which Kamenev thought unnecessary, had nonetheless gone well. That their interests were mutual did nothing to detract from what he believed would be a profitable relationship. The $500,000 US Dollars nestling in his Swiss bank account certainly supported this assertion. Not that his loyalty to President Ulyanov was in question, but if history and past experience had taught him anything, it was not to depend on the status quo. Indeed, many of his countrymen had fallen foul of successive

Russian leaders and not just the well-publicised likes of Alexander Litvinenko and Sergei Skripal. Numerous Diplomats, Ambassadors and former agents within the security services have met mysterious and unexplained deaths over time. So as the English would say, he was not prepared to *count his chickens* just yet, but if things went according to plan, he would be able to live a long and prosperous life – hopefully.

Four and a half thousand miles to the south, Prince Ali bin-Sayed stepped back from the television. A cricket fan since his days at Oxford where he studied for an MBA, he hoped that one day, his country would be able to host a World Cup. For now though, his immediate thoughts were focused on the speed at which events were progressing and whether he was now having regrets? Surely not, he thought, as he sipped his tea. His actions, known only to those within his inner circle, were such that if successful would springboard him to power. After all, which of his sycophantic cousins, fawning at the feet of the King, would be able to step forward as the saviour of their Kingdom and most importantly, its wealth?

It seemed that it was only he who recognised the threat posed by the burgeoning relationship between the US and Canada. Their liquification of natural gas to transport energy around the world and now, with the UK on the threshold of not only producing vast reservoirs of energy from its own coastline, they would soon have the capacity to harness that energy in such a way as to virtually eliminate the need for fossil fuels in Europe and beyond. This, as bin-Sayed knew only too well was something which could no longer be ignored or indeed, tolerated. That he had to work with the Bolsheviks to achieve this aim was something he would have to endure, for now at least, but once the threat to his nation's existence had been neutralised, things could return to normal with the Kingdom securing its rightful place as the World's foremost energy producer. Till then, he would have to be patient and trust – that was a difficult thing to accept – in the Sheik's ability to fulfil his promise of success.

CHAPTER 24

The afternoon brought a fresh challenge for Farrow. The half mile, hard run, rather than the fast jog of the daily routine was again designed to stimulate the adrenalin in readiness for the forthcoming exercise.

Taking cover behind a garden wall, Farrow, Scanes and Allen had eyes on the front of the *Killing House* while Barber, as sniper, established an OP in a property to the rear of the detached two storey building. With central doorways to the front and rear and four rooms on each level, each with its own window, the remainder of what would have been a complete strike team of up to sixteen troopers were virtually covering the rest of the building.

According to the briefing for the exercise, police armed response units had responded to an automatic alarm at the home of a Cabinet Minister. Held hostage by a terrorist group purporting to be fighting for the freedom of their leader, negotiations had broken down and threats were being made to kill the hostages so, with the scene cordoned off, the decision had been made to call in the Regiment.

Waiting for the 'Go,' Farrow reminded himself of the SOP (Standard Operating Procedure) used by both the military and police in such situations. A numeric, colour coded system had been introduced several years ago for establishing the location of terrorists, 'Tangos' and hostages, 'Hotels,' within a stronghold. 'White,' represented the front of the building, 'Black' the rear, 'Green' left and 'Red' right, while floor numbers came next followed by window locations counted from the left.

From his location to the front of the building, 'White,' Allen said into his helmet microphone, 'Echo One to Echo Two… Anything to report?'

'Three Tangos, Two Hotels, Black 1:2' Barber replied immediately.

Farrow now knew that from their current perspective, three terrorists and two hostages were holed up on the ground floor in a room to the rear and far right of the building.

'Weapons free, gentlemen,' said Allen as all three raced forward and round to the rear of the building. Moving ahead of

Allen, Scanes released his H&K, allowing it to hang from his shoulder on the sling while he pulled a length of Primacord from a package attached to his body armour. Setting it in place around the doorframe, he pushed the blasting cap into the top right hand corner and rejoined Allen and Farrow.

'Okay. Let's see if you've still got it Marty,' said Allen as Scanes thumbed the switch on the detonator and the door frame disintegrated.

Instinct kicked in instantaneously as Farrow charged through the smoke filled opening with Allen and Scanes right behind him. Inside, the corridor was dark, visibility limited to light from the opening. Positioning himself by the doorway leading into the room to his left Farrow lobbed in a G60 stun grenade. The combination of mercury and magnesium powder resulted in a blinding flash and 160 decibels of sound on detonation, enough to ensure hostages and terrorists alike would be completely disorientated. Running passed Farrow, Allen fired two suppressed rounds into the head of the Tango to his right then traversed left to see Farrow do the same to his Tango while Scanes cleaned up the remaining target.

A moment later the overhead lights came on and Major Keeble appeared from an anti-room. 'Good to see you haven't lost it Marty,' he said, looking round at the three flattened terrorist targets and two hostage dummies left fine and dandy.

'I could have been quicker through the door,' responded Farrow.

'Eight seconds from start to finish is spot on for this exercise, Marty, so don't sweat it,' said the Major, as the extractor fans came on and swiftly cleared away the smoke and fumes. 'Okay, gentlemen. Let's pick up the brass and head for the debrief.'

With no less than six cameras covering the exercise, Marty was sure the debrief would be thorough, after which a few beers in the NCO club would no doubt further cement his relationship with his new friends.

CHAPTER 25

Thanks to centuries by Eoin Morgan and Ben Stokes and a brief, but effective cameo from Jos Buttler, by the end of fifty overs, England had set Pakistan a significant target of 356 to win. The forty minute interval between innings also heralded the arrival of several guests to Murad's suite, from where champagne and canapes were served to a variety of dignitaries from the local community.

'So, Minister,' said Clive Jennings, Southampton's Lord Mayor, 'how do you feel about Portsmouth poaching business from us?'

It was no secret that Portsmouth's International Port, just along the coast, had been making significant inroads into the luxury cruise industry, something which, thanks to the likes of

Carnival and Cunard had, for several decades been largely dominated by Southampton.

'I wouldn't worry, Clive,' replied Murad, 'they've got a long way to go to catch us up.'

'I hope you're right,' said the Lord Mayor, as a man dressed in grey flannels, dark blue blazer and Hampshire Cricket Club tie approached them. 'Oh, by the way, can I introduce you to Asghar Shahidi.'

'By all means,' said Murad, reaching forward to accept the outstretched hand.

'Asghar has recently made a hefty donation to a number of local charities,' continued the Lord Mayor.'

'Ah yes,' said Murad. 'It's good to meet you Asghar. I've heard a lot about you.'

'And I you, Minister.'

'All good, I hope?'

'Of course…'

I leant over Jill's shoulder and said, 'What do you think?'

'Not on our radar,' she replied, pressing the transmit button on the mic stand in front of her. 'Are you getting this, Frankie?'

'We are,' responded Cervera from the Van outside the ground. 'We're running him through our databases, but nothing so far.'

'How does he compare with the three from the lorry park?'

'Difficult to tell. CCTV was not the best, but Dougie's seeing if he can get any better angles on the original footage.'

'Okay,' I said. 'Let's see how this play's out.'

'Roger that,' replied Cervera.

After a further exchange of pleasantries which involved talk of a donation to his Party, Murad excused himself to circulate among his other guests. Tucking in merrily to the food and champagne, they all seemed to be having a good time.

'I say Akram, what a jolly splendid idea of yours,' said a gentleman in Club colours.

'Oh your very welcome, Chairman,' responded Murad with a smile. 'Spur of the moment I know, but seemed like an opportunity not to be missed.'

'Quite right, quite right,' he replied, at the same time glancing at his watch. 'But we mustn't miss the start of the second innings, must we?'

'No, of course not,' Murad replied, 'but you're very welcome to join me on the balcony.'

'That's jolly decent of you, old chap, but I must return to the members stand. Keep up appearances, you know. That sort of thing.'

'Of course.'

'Well let's hope your chaps give a good fist of it. Can't see them turning this one over though, but you never know.'

We both shook our heads. That Murad had no connection whatsoever to Pakistan, other than his skin colour, was clearly lost on the pompous old fool as he simply smiled and reached for a canape from one of the passing waiters.

'Lebanese isn't he?' asked Jill.

'According to his bio, he moved to the UK when he was seventeen where he studied Political Science at Southampton University before going on to become one of the City's youngest Councillors.'

'So how on earth did he get drawn into this business?'

'God knows or should I say, Allah, but it's a good question and one I've have had Charlie working on.'

'Anything so far?'

'Records were a bit sketchy back then, but it seems possible that he wasn't an only child.'

'But was he the only one to come to the UK with his parents?'

'Looks like it, yes.'

'So what's happened to the other sibling?'

'Another good question and one for which we don't have an answer yet.'

'What about his parents?'

'Both killed in a car accident, shortly after he became a Councillor.'

'Surely 'Five' must have run checks on him when he became an MP?'

'You'd think so wouldn't you, but it seems that neither MPs nor Ministers are subject to any form of formal vetting procedure?'

'But that's ridiculous!'

'Can't argue with that. Apparently 'Five' only provide Prime Ministers with information on potential new Cabinet members and then only if that information raises serious national security issues and only if they have access to sensitive information.'

'Which infers they found nothing of interest on, Murad, when he was appointed Immigration Minister?'

'Looks that way.'

'Jesus!' she exclaimed. 'No wonder we're in such a fucking mess with this guy.'

'True, but at least now we know about him. We've just got to hope we can find out what he's up to this time and deal with him accordingly.'

Jill nodded as she reached for the transmit button again. 'It looks like his guests are leaving, Frankie. Spot anything?'

'Not so far,' came back the response.

'Okay, keep looking. He wouldn't have gone to this much trouble without something up his sleeve.'

'Roger that.'

'What do *you* think?' said Jill, as the final guest left and Murad returned to the balcony. 'Alex?'

'Sorry, what did you just say?'

'About what?'

'Something up his sleeve…' I said and pulled up a chair alongside her. The keyboard in front of Jill allowed her to switch between cameras and to rewind footage without affecting the other cameras and… there it was. 'Dammit!'

'What is it?' asked Jill.

As with the dead drop in the park, sometimes the old fashioned methods are the best when it comes to passing on information. 'Christ, he really is good,' I said and zoomed in on the waiter from whom Murad received the last canapé. 'There,' I said, pointing at the screen. 'Frankie, did you get that?'

With the monitors linked via a direct feed into the van, Dougie and Frankie could see exactly what we were looking at *as Murad turned away from the Club Chairman and at the same time as reaching for the canape with his right hand, his left arm dropped to his side and barely brushed the waiter's pocket.*

'Sneaky bastard,' said Jill.

'Frankie?'

'On it,' replied Frankie.

'Dougie,' I said. 'Can you enhance the image of Murad's hand?'

The screen instantly pixelated in front of us, then cleared. 'Looks like a flashdrive or something similar,' said Dougie.

Gone were the days when microdots containing limited amounts of information monopolised the world of espionage. These days, a flashdrive... well, I don't need to say anymore.

'Hang on, Alex,' said Jill, pointing at another monitor. 'Look.'

Back on the balcony, Murad appeared to be searching under the rim of the coffee table, on this occasion clearly not worried about the need for any sleight of hand. Unfortunately, given the time available to us, we'd been unable to install a camera in the railings that surrounded the balcony so all we could see was Murad, side on, as he pulled out something from under the table.

'Looks like a pack of Rizlas,' said Jill.

Peeling off the top paper as if to make a roll up, Murad looked at it for a moment then balanced it carefully on his knee. Next, he reached inside his jacket pocket and took out a thick brown leather wallet and withdrew a large cigar. Well known for enjoying an occasional Cuban, the Immigration Minister was regarded by those in the know as a bit of an afficionado. Like as not, this meant he was about to light up a *Romeo y Julieta,* a favourite of his and Sir Winston Churchill who, I read somewhere, was believed to have smoked a quarter of a million of them during his lifetime. If only intelligence gathering was that easy. Anyway, the process of lighting a cigar was something that could not be rushed and while I very much wanted to rush, in this case, into the suite to grab the piece of paper, the chances of me getting there in time and effectively losing any chance of finding out what he was up to was nil. So, instead, we watched in frustration as he took a silver cutter from a pouch in the wallet, snipped off the end of the cigar then, flipping open the lid of a lighter caressed the end of the cigar with the flames until it took. Once satisfied it was underway, he blew gently on the end, picked up the piece of paper from his knee and with one final look, set it alight and dropped it into the ashtray.

I suppose the only good thing about the casual way in which Murad conducted himself on the balcony was that despite adopting tradecraft for the earlier pass, he clearly had no idea he was being surveilled which meant the same should hopefully apply to the waiter. 'Tell me some good news, Frankie.'

'Sorry, Alex,' came the instant reply. 'Nothing on the ground, but I've got Dibbers heading over to the ground's control room to see if we can pick anything up on their CCTV.'

'Okay, thanks, Frankie.' I said. There was no point in taking out my frustration on her. 'Where are you now?'

'In the lobby downstairs, about to have a chat with the hotel manager.'

'Good. Be straight down.'

By the time, I got to reception, Frankie was already in

conversation with the hotel manager and Head of Security, a guy called George Franks who, as luck would have it, was ex-military. Having shaken hands with both men and explained the need for our presence to be kept under wraps, a principle with which Franks, at least, was familiar, he took us to his office where a bank of monitors covered all the communal areas around the hotel. This included the kitchen where we got our second sight of the waiter.

Five minutes later, a concerned looking catering manager, Manuel of all names, hustled into the office and explained in broken English that the waiter, who had left immediately after the drinks reception, was a last minute replacement for one of his regular team who'd called in sick.

With little else to do, but get the locals to check on the sick waiter's address and for Frankie to capture all the footage in which the waiter appeared for later analysis, I returned to my suite where I explained to Jill what had happened and slumped down on a sofa at the end of the bed.

With Murad appearing to have nodded off on the balcony, Jill looked up at the TV screen. 'Well at 158 for 6 at least it looks like Pakistan are in for a hiding,' she said.

'Small mercies,' I replied as I pulled my mobile from my pocket and keyed in Sir Henry's number.

*

Unaware of the furore created by his recent activity and again careful to avoid traffic cameras, this time on the M27, the Sheik was already heading west on a variety of minor 'B' roads. Reflecting briefly on his disposal of the waiter, he wondered how long it would take for them to discover the body. That he was single and living in rented accommodation would help, but he was becoming increasingly aware of the trail he was leaving behind in order to achieve his objectives. That said, he mused, sacrifices had to be made and now with those objectives in sight, he would soon be able to return to his homeland from where, he'd been told earlier in the day, his next assignment awaited.

CHAPTER 26

Sir Henry placed the phone back in its cradle then slammed his fist down on the desk.

'What the fuck is this country coming to!' he growled.

This unusual outburst reverberated around the walls of his office and took us all by surprise, including Scrumpy who looked up sleepily from his perch in front of the fireplace. With Mervyn and Francis off on a cruise around the Adriatic, he'd travelled up with me that morning and was already a firm favourite with the Boss who, with his own pair of English Setters at home, was very much a dog lover.

It was clear Sir Henry's conversation with the PM had not gone well and in fairness, they both had every right to be pissed.

'We should have seen it,' I said.

'No,' he responded immediately. 'I've looked at the footage and without the close up, anyone could have missed it.' Walking back from his desk, he joined me, Jill and Hammad at the conference table. 'I know there are numerous precedents for this type of thing,' he continued, 'but it never ceases to amaze me how anyone can betray their country in this way.'

He was right of course. Such treachery is etched in history and for any number of reasons. The Americans have a mnemonic for it, MICE as in money, ideology, coercion and ego, of which, arguably, the most common, as attested to by the infamous *Cambridge Five*, is ideology. Known at 'The Centre' (Moscow KGB HQ) as the *Magnificent Five*, Philby, Burgess, Maclean, Cairncross and their recruiter, Anthony Blunt all saw the communist ideology as the best possible, post war, political defence against fascism. Operating as 'illegal' spies as opposed to 'legal,' those who assume positions such as cultural attaches or similar nom-de-guerres, all five and several others if the truth be known, pursued successful careers within British Government passing valuable information across the Iron Curtain. As to why Murad had chosen to turn against his adopted country was yet to be determined and who knows may never be known, but one thing was for sure, his decision to facilitate terrorism in this way was one which he would ultimately regret. For now though, it was a case of gathering more information on the next potential threat and hopefully deal with it before more lives are lost at the hands of this traitor.

'Okay,' said Sir Henry. 'It's no good crying over spilt milk. So what have we been missing?'

'Gaps in surveillance haven't helped,' said Hammad.

'Go on,' he replied.

'A lack of Asian resources in 'Five' for one,' he replied. 'Despite their best efforts, they've been unable to fully monitor his movements during Friday prayers which, happens to be the same Mosque used by both Khalid Hassan and Syed Wazir.'

Okay, that was news to me. 'So what we're surmising then,' I said, 'is Murad has been using the Mosque as cover for passing on information to them.'

'Nothing unusual there,' said Hammad. 'And so long as they continue to invite the likes of Abu Hamza and Anjem Choudary through their doors, this type of thing will continue to happen.'

'But we're not talking about radical Imams within the Mosque, are we?' I asked.

'No, but what we end up doing is focusing those limited resources on Mosques that have welcomed the likes of Hamza and Choudary in the past which allows the likes of Murad to slip though the net and work with relative impunity. On top of that and in much the same way as the more popular Imams attract followers to certain Mosques, the same applies to Murad whose position as a Minister of State and in particular for Immigration, makes him like a magnet every time he attends Prayers and by default provides him with the ideal opportunity to covertly pass on information to the likes of Hassan and Wazir.

'Okay, that makes sense.' I said. 'But why didn't Murad use the same method for passing on the dead drop information that ultimately led to the incident at the Rosebowl?'

'Good question,' said Charlie, entering the room with an open laptop balanced on his arm and Di in tow with something far more interesting, a much needed pot of coffee and tray of sandwiches. 'His schedule as Immigration Minister is seriously busy which means he can't always attend Friday prayers. So I guess, if it's urgent, the alternative is to take advantage of the ever present media scrum outside No 10 to display a marker through which he was able to signal the dead drop.'

'Make sense,' said Sir Henry. 'Thank you Di. So what do we know of our mystery man, Charlie?'

'Progress, but not quite there yet, Sir,' he said. 'As you know, despite the poor quality of the CCTV from the Strensham Services lorry park, we were able to identify Hassan and Wazir, but not, at least at the time, the third male.'

'At the time?' I questioned.

'We're fairly sure the third male and the waiter from the Rosebowl are one and the same.' This stopped me reaching for a sarnie. 'Thanks to Pete's cameras in the suite, we also got an eighty percent match on facial recognition.'

'So do we have a name?'

'We do, but it's not what you'd expect.'

'Come on, Charlie. Spit it out.'

'It's Murad.'

'Yes, we know that. What about the waiter?'

'That is the waiter.'

'Don't be ridiculous. That's impossible.'

'Not necessarily.'

Okay, that took a moment to digest, but Charlie wasn't finished yet as he brought up an image of the arrivals hall at Heathrow on the TV screen at the head of the table.

'You'll remember,' he continued, 'I was digging around into Murad's background and we thought he might not have been an only child. Well it turns out that although his parents *were* Lebanese, he was actually born and raised in Mauritania.'

'West Africa,' I said.

'Correct. So that got me curious and I started looking into the rise of Islamic fundamentalism across the region which, at the time of Murad's birth, was pretty low key. But, as political liberalisation took a foothold across the country, Islamists gradually gained recognition through local elections by inveigling themselves into the moderate Tawassoul party. His parents though, were both professors at Nouakchott University and hardline activists within the Salafi movement, followers of which included Jihadists linked to such groups as Al-Qaeda, ISIS, Boko Haram and the Al- Shabaab. Now while the Salafi movement advocated the need for armed struggle, it appears that Murad's parents looked at the wider picture and recognised the need for both financial backing and political connections if their aims were to be achieved. So for this reason, when the family moved back to Lebanon, a Hamas sympathiser and consultant at Beirut's University Hospital, the Hotel-Dieu de France, was able to doctor the family's hospital records from Mauritania on which Murad was shown as having an identical 'still born' twin brother.'

'The yin and yang of the terrorist world,' said Jill.

'Exactly. So once I had this information,' he continued, 'I was able to adjust the facial recognition algorithm to factor in a combination of other techniques such as the gait analysis used to link Lisbeth Harrington to the Portsmouth bombing and that...' he zoomed in on one specific chauffeur waiting for passengers to pass through the arrivals hall, '…is how I know this guy is Murad's twin brother.'

'How sure?' I asked as we as watched the chauffeur turn away from the arrivals area and walked across the concourse to Café Nero.

'According to *Atelier*, Ninety eight percent.'

'So Murad grew up to become the political arm of the duo,' I surmised, 'presumably leaving his brother to be the money man?'

'Looks that way, yes,' said Charlie.

'That's excellent work, Charlie,' I said. 'But do we know who he was waiting for?'

Charlie kept schtum and let the footage run forward as the unaccompanied chauffeur dumped his coffee in a rubbish bin and left the arrivals hall through the exit for short stay car parking.

'Best guess would be this guy,' he said, switching cameras to show passport control and the arrivals from BA flight 236 from Moscow. 'Mikola Virastyuk, detained by an MOD officer on secondment to UKBA as he cleared passport control.'

'Why was he detained?'

'Sounds like "good old fashioned police work" as you keep telling me, Alex. Lots of reasonable grounds and then once in custody refused to answer any questions.'

'So where is he now?' asked Sir Henry.

'Currently being held at Brook House.'

Jill looked up from her laptop. 'Sorry, what was that, Charlie?'

'One of the secure Immigration Removal Centres near Gatwick. Used by the Home Office for Cat B offenders, sorry, individuals looking to blag their way into the country.'

'Oh, okay, thank you,' she said and returned her attention to her laptop.

Throughout these revelations, Jill had been unusually quiet while studying whatever it was on her screen. 'So what is it that's grabbed your attention?' I asked.

'It may be nothing,' she said, 'but I've been reviewing the transcript of the interview with the driver from the lorry park and it says here the container's contents included 'refractory materials.'

'That's right,' I said. 'What of it?'

'Back in the day I was a CTSECO (Counter Terrorism Security Coordinator) for 'Operation Hydrangea,' the roll out of the first mobile detector portals to be used in Ports across the country. The idea was to identify shipments which may contain radioactive materials. Unfortunately, it didn't get off to a good start. One of the first hits we got was on a container from Italy that was followed to somewhere in the Cotswolds only to find out we'd uncovered a shipment of roofing tiles. It turned out that the tiles and other refractory materials all contain trace elements of naturally occurring chemicals such as uranium and thorium.'

'Harmless though?' I said.

'Yes, unless someone decides to crush them into a fine powder and keep it airborne long enough to be ingested. But where I'm coming from is, more often than not these types of containers set off the radiation monitoring portals when leaving a Port. Consequently they're hardly ever get checked, unless there's some specific intelligence to say a shipment may be a problem.'

'And I take it, this lorry or container wasn't checked?' I asked.

'No.'

'So what we're saying it's possible this cargo was deliberately chosen to hide something radioactive?'

'Could be unless anyone's got any other ideas? Look, if we're talking about shielding radiation, then conventional methods such as Lead can degrade over time. So, if someone is looking for another means to transport, let's say a nuclear device within a Lead lined packing case, then it makes sense to include this type of cargo among a shipment of refractory materials.'

A frosty chill swept over the room as I turned to Charlie. 'Can you bring up the footage from the Strensham Services lorry park, please?'

A moment later, the grainy image of a white van appeared on screen as it reversed up to the back of the lorry. The angle wasn't perfect, but enough to see the rear doors of the container on the back of the lorry and the front of the van from where Hassan and Wazir emerged.

'So where did he come from?' I asked, as Murad's brother appeared.

'No idea,'' said Charlie. 'He must have been camera savvy with his own vehicle and movements up until then.'

'If he's so sharp,' I said, 'why didn't he cover up?'

'Because this camera was covert and not part of the main CCTV set up of the service station. According to West Mercia's database there'd been a spate of thefts from lorries over recent weeks, so the local nick decided to put a camera in to gather intel on potential suspects.'

'What's he got in his hand?' asked Jill, peering intently at the screen, as Murad's brother opened the rear doors of the container and climbed up inside.

Charlie rewound the footage and zoomed in on his left

hand. Although that made the image even grainier, it looked like some form of handheld device and bearing in mind the direction of the conversation we'd just had…

'Geiger counter?' I suggested.

'Could be,' said Charlie. 'It certainly looks like they're in a hurry, so something to confirm the location of whatever it is he was looking for makes sense.'

A moment later, Murad's brother reappeared and indicated for Hassan and Wazir to join him in the back of the container. Almost immediately, all three men reappeared, Hassan and Wazir carrying the tea chest sized wooden transport crate to the edge of the container from where they hopped down and shifted it into the back of the van.

'Doesn't look much like the size of a nuke to me,' remarked Jill.

'It could be,' responded Charlie.

'What do you mean?' I asked.

'During the cold war, it was rumoured the Russians were developing a series of suitcase nukes which could be smuggled across borders for GRU operatives to target NATO leaders in the event of war.'

'Thought that was the stuff of fiction,' I said.

'Not according to... hang on,' said Charlie as he activated the globe in the centre of the conference table. Spinning on its invisible axis for a moment, the hologram of another distinctly Russian looking character out of a sixties spy movie emerged. 'Stanislev Lunev,' he continued. 'A high ranking GRU defector who not only claimed suitcase sized nukes existed, but was able to describe them in such detail that our own scientists were unable to discount the possibility of their existence.' Charlie continued to tap away and the hologram of Lunev was replaced by another equally Russian looking figure. 'There's also Russia's former National Security Advisor, Aleksandr Lebed who openly claimed during an interview on, believe it or not, CBS's Sixty Minutes in 1997, that the Russian Military had lost track of more than a hundred of two hundred and fifty "suitcase sized nuclear bombs" since the cold war.

'Wasn't Lebed favourite to take over from Boris Yeltsin?' I asked.

'He was until Putin came on the scene and miraculously became the favoured child.'

'That's what being head of the KGB does for you I suppose,' I said.

'And probably accounts for Lebed dying in a mysterious helicopter crash only a couple of years later,' responded Charlie.

'Dare I suggest a recurring theme whenever Putin's hold on power came under threat.'

'Until Ulyanov gave him a dose of his own medicine.'

'Indeed,' interjected Sir Henry, who having listened quietly to the debate as it unfolded decided it was time to move things forward.

CHAPTER 27

The Bakerloo Line north from Charing Cross to Oxford Circus, followed by the Victoria Line south to Vauxhall Cross saw Jill Dennison and Charlie Irving arrive ahead of time for their meeting at the HQ for MI6, Britain's Secret Intelligence Service. Deciding to grab a bite to eat, they made their way along Riverside Walk to *The Riverside* an upmarket eatery set within a neighbourhood of high rise, art deco style buildings, dubbed by some as Dubai-on-Thames. This was a bonus for Dennison who having taken a look at the on line menu, decided the triple decker burger had her name written all over it.

A half hour later and with Irving having gone for the pasta option, they strolled back along Riverside Walk towards the imposing structure on the far side of Vauxhall Bridge.

Once likened to a Mayan temple or a piece of clanking art deco machinery, for Jill it was like stepping onto a movie set as they negotiated the imposing three tiered entrance of gates, VBIED (Vehicle Borne Improvised Explosive Device) barriers and body scanning bullet proof portals, all of which did little to detract from this opinion.

This was a first for Dennison who was struggling to hold back her excitement as they entered the outer foyer. Handing over their mobiles, keys and coins to a security guard on the other side of yet another, no doubt bulletproof, glass screen, they were given their visitor passes, duly hung on lanyards round their necks, and directed through one of several other portals into the inner sanctum.

'Lot of glass,' whispered Dennison, as she looked up at a wall of glass that stretched up and up to the zenith of a twelve storey atrium.

'One hundred and thirty thousand square feet worth, by all accounts,' said Irving as a matronly looking woman in her thirties, forties, fifties, it was hard to tell, made her way towards them across the marble floor.

'Charlie. How lovely to see you, darling boy,' she said, stopping to get a good look at his companion. 'And you must be Jill,' she continued. 'My, my, what a beauty.'

'And a taken one,' laughed Irving, as he bent down to peck the woman on the cheek. 'Jill, meet Julie Cloke, Head of 'Q' Department!'

'I hear my toys came in useful,' said Cloke, with a twinkle in her eyes.

Dennison blushed, then laughed. 'They certainly did,' she said.

'Excellent! Right come along you two. No time to waste.'

With that, Cloke turned on her heels and with Irving and Dennison in tow, strode off across the atrium towards a bank of elevators.

Leaving Scrumpy asleep by the fireplace and after a two hour battle through traffic chaos, Hammad and I eventually linked up with the M25 at Leatherhead, from where we turned south onto the M23 and thankfully a relative short hop to Lowfield Heath, just south of Gatwick Airport.

Pulling up outside the gates to Brook House, we were directed to a reserved parking bay by a private security guard. Despite opening in 2009 as a newly built facility capable of housing up to five hundred detainees, the H Block style Immigration Removal Centre, surrounded by high metal fences and topped off with razor wire was, in all but name, a high security prison. Courted in controversy after an undercover Panorama investigation discovered wide spread self-harm and attempted suicides among the inmates, my hope was that our friend, Mikola Virastyuk – if that was his real name then mine was Greta Thunberg – was fit and healthy.

Escorted to the Director's office and having dispensed with the pleasantries, our first order of the day, beyond accepting an offer of tea, had been to view a digital recording of Virastyuk's booking in procedure.

'So what do you make of him?' I asked the Director, Charlie Sinclair, former Wing Commander RAF and veteran of the prison system.

'Strange fish,' he replied. 'Claims to be a muscovite targeted by the FSB (Russia's Federal Security Service and successor to the KGB) on account of a former association with Alexander Litvinenko.'

'The polonium poisoning guy,' said Hammad.

'One and the same, old boy,' said Sinclair. 'Courtesy of the then President, Vladimir Putin.'

'That's not going to be easy to check,' said Hammad. 'He certainly sounds Russian, but in fairness, I wouldn't know a Russian from a Ukrainian.'

'Funny you should say that, ' I said. 'Russian ancestry, perhaps, but the accent is definitely Ukrainian. When we get back we'll need you to get in touch with SBU and send over a photo, prints and the DNA samples taken from him during administration.' A successor to the former Ukrainian Soviet Socialist Republic's branch of the KGB, the *Sluzhba Bezpeky Ukrayiny* is Ukraine's Secret Service with responsibility for, among other things, counter intelligence activity and combatting terrorism. 'I take it that's okay with you, Director?' It pays to be polite, even though we could have insisted.

'Yes of course,' he replied, twirling a slightly affected handlebar moustache around his index finger. 'Anything to help Her Majesty's Government.'

It had been a frustrating wait for Viktor Zhukov and Svetlana Ivanov especially when the Arab turned up empty handed at the cottage. Well, not exactly empty handed, but at least this time he came with news, albeit an unexpected twist which required them to leave the cottage immediately and head east for an overnight stay at a bed and breakfast on the outskirts of Oxford. Neither Zhukov nor Ivanov were keen to be working with a conduit in this way, both preferring to operate without any outside influences, especially one previously unknown. But in this case they had no choice, the orders having come direct from Admiral Miroslav

Chernyshevsky, GRU Director, who briefed them personally and in doing so made it clear the Arab was in charge.

Such were his instructions that the following morning, after a hearty full English and the promise of a five star rating on Trip Advisor, they paid a beaming landlady in cash and made the short drive to a nearby industrial estate. The rental company was of a kind, requiring little more than a driving licence and utility bill as proof of ID, both of which were provided by the Arab and bore scrutiny should it have been necessary.

It wasn't.

With no small hint of envy, the receptionist handed over the keys for the box van to newlyweds. How excited they must be to be moving into their new home, she thought as they left the office. And how lucky she was. Such a handsome man and what a lovely smile. Oh well, my turn one day, she hoped as she slid the paperwork into the out tray and turned to the next customer in line.

As the Director pressed the intercom button on his desk he looked up and asked, 'Is there anything I need to be worried about with this fella?'

'Not that we're aware of,' I replied.

'Yes, Sir?' responded the detached voice of Sinclair's PA.

'Would you be so kind as to arrange for Mr Virastyuk to be taken to,' he looked up at a noticeboard on the wall, 'interview room five, please Janet,' said the Director.

'Yes, of course, Sir,' she replied and with that the line went dead.

'So gentlemen, is there anything else I can do for you while we're waiting?'

The journey was a not unexpected nightmare. The car park, otherwise known as the M25, had lived up to its reputation, while a prang on the M4 turned three lanes to one and then to top it off, the A34 around Oxford at rush hour was a nightmare.

'My old lady's going to give me such a bollocking when I get home,' said Gary Marston from behind the wheel of the prison escort van.

'You and me both, mate,' said Winston Nisbet, his oppo in the shotgun seat. 'She's got one of those three course jobbies with wine and chocolates lined up for our anniversary dinner tonight.'

'And I thought I was in the shit,' laughed Marston, as a box van swept passed them in the outside lane and swung in ahead of the prison van.

'What the fuck's his problem,' said Marston, as he touched

the brakes to avoid running into the back of the van.

As if in response, the shutter door rolled up.

The intercom on the Director's desk buzzed.

'Yes, Janet. Is our guest ready for interview?'

'I'm afraid not, Sir, but James is on his way in.'

'James Gilmanton is my supervisor on B wing,' explained the Director as the office door opened and a burly, forty something guard entered the room, clipboard in hand.

'Virastyuk was transferred to Campsfield this morning, Guvnor,' he said, without preamble.

'On whose authority?' the Director barked.

'It says 'ere...,' he looked at his clipboard and ran his finger down the top sheet, 'some bloke called Murad. Oh yes, looks like he's the Immigration Minister.'

As Marston slammed on the brakes and Nisbet reached for the radio handset on the dashboard, the windscreen exploded.

Both men died instantly as they were flung back in their seats, leaving the prison van to slew left and right across the two lane carriageway before slamming into the central reservation.

Two figures in balaclavas leapt from the box van and ran over to the stricken prison van. Ivanov checked the cab as Zhukov, who'd delivered the fatal blow from the back of the van, made straight for the side door. A box like structure in its own right, the armour piercing rounds that dealt with the bulletproof windscreen soon did the same to the side door as Zhukov stepped up into the vehicle. Left and right of a central aisle, individual cubicles with barely enough room to sit, housed a number of groaning detainees who having been bounced around like popcorn in a microwave, were beginning to voice their outrage as he examined the nameplates alongside each door. Back left he stopped and turned as Ivanov appeared with the keys.

The Director checked the transfer document and shook his head. 'Well I suppose Campsfield makes sense,' he said by way of some explanation. 'Still a Cat B facility, but operates a more relaxed regime suited to detainees considered to be less of a threat than some of the types we have here. Mind you, how this fella came to the attention of the Immigration Minister,' he shrugged, 'is a mystery to me.'

Not to us, I thought as Gilmanton brought his hand up to an earpiece connected to the personal radio on his belt. 'Excuse me,' he said, then pressed the transmit button 'Go ahead, over.'

'Where is Campsfield?' I asked the Director as Gilmanton listened to whatever was being said into his ear.

'Kidlington,' replied the Director. 'Nice spot, just west of Oxford on the Cotswold border.'

PART 4

所有战争都是基于欺骗

Suǒyǒu zhànzhēng dōu shì jīyú qīpiàn

(All warfare is based on deception)

Sun Tzu

CHAPTER 28

With the World Energy Summit only two days away, arrangements were well under way for the arrival of President Ulyanov.

Although the entire top floor of the Savoy was swept regularly for bugs, none were expected to be found by the advance party. Tradecraft being what it is Kamenev knew the planting of listening devices and other forms of covert surveillance were always anticipated, so unless the British Security Service had come up with some new technology unknown to his former agency in the Yasenevo District of Moscow, he was comfortable he had, as the British liked to say, ticked all the boxes.

'Yevgeni,' said Kamenev, to his Chief Security Officer and former Head of Putin's Presidential Security Service. 'Voz'mite vykhodnoy' (Take the afternoon off). Do some shopping. Get something nice for that beautiful wife of yours.' It was true, Yevgeni Kolyakov's wife was indeed a beauty and one known for expensive tastes, courtesy of her husband having travelled the world with Putin. 'Don't worry,' continued Kamenev, anticipating Kolyakov's reply, 'I'll be fine here with Yuri. Besides, I think it is time for a relaxing bath and see if this hotel's famous afternoon tea is as good as they say it is. After all,' he laughed, 'what harm can come from clotted cream and a scone.'

Torn, yet not so torn given the gratitude his wife would show him when he returned home, Kolyakov nodded, 'Spasibo, tovarishch' (Thank you, Comrade). she will be most grateful, even if my pocket is not.'

'Then go, my friend,' said Kamenev, dismissing him with a wave as he reached for the phone and pressed the button for room service.

Having sent the file on Virastyuk to Di before we left Brook House, by the time we got back to the City, Charlie and Jill were back in the office and Sir Henry, had wasted no time in contacting Wladimir Berinchyk, Ukraine's SBU Director of Operations.

'You were right, Alex,' he said as soon as we walked through the door. 'Our friend is one, Oleksandr Kyryukhin, a

Ukrainian scientist formerly attached to Russia's Nuclear Weapons Programme. It looks like he went off the radar a couple of weeks ago, but left behind a wife and three young children.'

'What's happened to the family?' I asked, my thoughts instantly moving towards a Tiger Kidnap scenario whereby a loved one is held captive to ensure cooperation on the part of the third party. It happened last year in London and was a favourite ploy adopted across the world whether it be for the purposes of terrorism, espionage or any number of reasons.

'They've been moved into protective custody.'

Okay, that was a bonus. 'Do they have any idea what happened to him?'

'Apparently he went to meet a friend he plays chess with in the park, but never arrived.'

'Which infers he didn't go willingly.'

'It certainly seems that way.'

'Any thoughts on why they didn't take the family at the same time?'

'According to Wladimir, who has been most helpful by the way...'

'Hardly surprising,' I muttered.

'Quite,' he responded. 'As luck would have it, the son was rushed into hospital with suspected appendicitis shortly after Kyryukhin left to meet his friend. When his wife couldn't get hold of him, she immediately reported him missing. Turns out Kyryukhin's on an SBU watch list so once the report came in, normal Misper procedures were set aside with a guard being placed on the boy while the wife and daughter were scooped up.'

Okay, so that was good news in one respect. Under normal circumstances and unless there are extraneous circumstances, missing person reports are generally left for twenty fours to see if the person returns home, but in this instance it looks like the wheels turned a lot faster and with Kyryukhin's family out of the equation, at least now his family couldn't be used as leverage. But and there's always a but, it also meant that unless he knew they were safe, his role in this affair, whatever that might be, would continue.

'Is there anything Berinchyk can tell us about his time with the nuclear weapons programme?' I asked.

'More your bag than mine, Charlie,' said Sir Henry.

'There is,' said Charlie in response. 'Quite a lot in fact and not good. Not good at all. Apparently he was part of Russia's Status 6 project team, his research focusing on the development of cobalt warheads for use in the development of oceanic multipurpose nuclear torpedoes.'

'I thought that was a ruse put out by Putin to put the gips up the US?' I said.

'Ruse or not,' continued Charlie, 'if it was some form of nuke in the crate from the lorry park and cobalt is involved, we could be looking at a dirty bomb.'

Well that certainly explained the 'not good at all' comment. 'And it looks like we now have two new players to add to the mix,' I said.

'What makes you say that?' asked Jill. 'Couldn't they have been Hassan and Wazir, our Asian pair from the dead drop?'

'Not unless one of them has had a sex change,' I said. 'The viewcam in the cab of the prison van remained in-tact and recorded the whole thing. We viewed it before leaving Brook House and despite the balaclavas, one of them was definitely a woman and the other was taller than the Asians.'

'Any sightings since?' asked Jill.

'No,' said Sir Henry. 'I spoke to West Mercia's Chief Constable and although units were on scene pretty quickly, they were long gone by the time they arrived.'

I had no doubt the box van would turn up at some stage, probably burnt out and if, as was likely, it turned out to be a rental, we might well get descriptions in due course, but right now we needed to firm up on what we did know and try to work out what the hell was going on.

'Okay! Let's leave that for a minute,' I said. 'I think it's fair to say that the signature on the transfer document means that the information passed to Murad at the Rosebowl contained details of Kyryukhin's detention at Heathrow.'

'The rizla paper,' said Jill.

'It looks that way, yes and as Immigration Minister, it wouldn't be difficult for Murad to find out what happened to him after his detention.' Thinking further down the line in terms of the evidence Jim Kirby would expect to see, I followed up with, 'We're going to need a paper trail on that Charlie.'

'On it?' he said, his head down as fingers flew over the keyboard on his laptop.

'So is it time to bring him in?' asked Hammad.

It was a question I'd already considered and discarded. 'We don't have all the pieces of the jigsaw yet and so long as he doesn't realise we're on to him....'

'Continue to keep tabs on him and hope for a break?'

'I'm not sure we've got any choice,' I said, looking to the head of the table.

'Agreed,' said Sir Henry.

*

Kamenev emerged from the bathroom as the doorbell to the suite rang. Yuri eased himself off the sofa and removed a semi-automatic pistol from a shoulder holster under his jacket. Not wanting to frighten the waiter, he held the weapon down to his side as he approached the door.

'*Da*,' he said, as he looked through the peephole.

'Room service, Sir.'

Opening the door, Yuri moved to one side to allow the Asian waiter and trolley to pass. With Yuri's weapon blocked from view, Kamenev stepped forward and said, '*Ya proshu proshcheniya*,' (I am sorry, my friend) as he removed a pistol, fitted with a suppressor from the pocket of his robe. A fleeting look of confusion crossed Yuri's face as the weapon discharged and the hollow point round drilled into his skull just below the temple.

As Yuri slumped to the floor, a second Asian man, dressed casually in jeans, T-shirt and leather jacket appeared in the doorway. Stepping over Yuri's body, he entered the suite as Kamenev unscrewed the suppressor and handed both items to the waiter.

*

Rocking back in his chair, Sir Henry looked to Charlie and Jill. 'So what did you two come up with from our friends at Vauxhall Cross?'

'Quite a woman,' said Jill, as she pulled a sheaf of papers from a folder and placed them on the table in front of her. It looks like the packing case offloaded from the lorry could, at least in terms of size, contain a variation on the US W54 warhead used as part of America's Special Atomic Demolition Munition (SADM) programme.'

'To all intents and purposes,' said Charlie, 'a collection of man-portable nukes for use during the Cold War should the Soviet Union decide to invade.'

'So we're not talking about fiction then,' I said.

'Not at all,' he replied. 'It also lends credence to Aleksander Lubek's claims that the Russian military had developed suitcase sized nukes of its own.'

'Of which several are now missing. So what were the W54s used for?'

'Parachuted into Soviet-occupied western Europe to destroy power plants, bridges, and dams, that type of thing.'

'So not on the scale of Hiroshima or Nagasaki?'

'Not even close,' he said. 'With this type of device, you're looking at a TNT equivalent yield of anything between ten tons and one kiloton which, when compared to 'Little Boy' at fifteen kilotons and the 'Fat Man' at about twenty kilotons, this is relative small fry.'

'So what sort of blast radius are we talking about here?'

'Worst case scenario for an above ground one kiloton nuke would be about half a kilometre. But if you think about Chernobyl, it wasn't so much the size of the blast radius that was the problem, it was the extent of the radiation poisoning. By all accounts this wasn't just detected in Belarus and North Western Ukraine, it spread as far afield as Sweden and even the north of England and Wales, where sheep on the hills were found to have been contaminated.'

'And how long will contamination last for a one kiloton nuke?'

'For a standard thermo nuclear device, about ten years, but bearing in mind Kyryukhin's area of expertise and the possibility of cobalt being used in the construction of such a device then the effects of the blast could be felt for a hundred years and beyond.'

And there lay the crux of the issue, as the phone on Sir Henry's desk rang. Where could such a device be planted to maximum effect?

*

As Sir Henry King was answering the phone, Marty Farrow, along with his colleagues from 'E' Squadron left the NCO mess at Stirling Barracks where they'd been putting the world to rights over an early evening pint or two of the black stuff.

'Looks like the balloon's gone up somewhere,' said Scanes as two Dauphin 2 helicopters were warming up on the parade ground. Liveried to blend into civilian air traffic, the choppers were part of a fleet operated by 658 Squadron Army Air Corp (AAC) in support of 22 SAS. Based nearby at SAS HQ, Credenhill, the pilots are considered the best of the best, their duel role being to covertly transport the SAS around the UK and as necessary deploy them into action during counter terrorism operations.

'Let's hope this is a quick one,' said Col. Truman, as he joined them on the edge of the parade ground. 'Going to leave us thin on the ground if another job comes in.'

'Sir?' queried Farrow.

Of the four operational squadrons based at Hereford, only one was maintained on counter terrorism duty in the UK, such was the case for 'B' squadron. Post the elimination of Major General Qasem Soleimani, 'A' were in Iraq gathering intelligence on Iran's Revolutionary Guard. 'C' were preparing for deployment whilst conducting short term training in Norway and 'G' had recently been shipped out to Djibouti where they were engaged in operations against Islamic terrorists in Somalia.

'Seems like we need a few more letters, Sir.' said Farrow after Col. Truman explained his dilemma.

'You could be right, son,' he replied, standing a little straighter, as several figures emerged from what the Regiment euphemistically call the robing room. Not that robes were the order of the day as a troop of sixteen men, led by Major Keeble and bedecked in coal black nomex, body armour, ballistic helmets and weapons of choice trotted over to the waiting choppers.

Sir Henry replaced the phone in its cradle and with a circumspect look on his face returned to his seat at the conference table.

'That was the Commissioner,' he said. 'It seems our Mr Kamenev has been taken hostage at the Savoy.'

'You sound sceptical,' I said.

'Too much happening all at once,' he replied thoughtfully. 'Never did like coincidences and this one has an aroma all of its own. According to SO15 they're dealing with a group of Chechen Separatists demanding the release of one Aslan Barayev, as in the brother of Mosvar, who led the Moscow theatre debacle back in 2002.'

That brought back memories from my days in SO13 when

this tragedy was used as a case study in how not to deal with a hostage scenario.

A group of forty something Chechens took over the Dubrovka Theatre in downtown Moscow where they held eight hundred plus people captive while demanding the withdrawal of Russian forces from their homeland. After two days of failed negotiations and the murder of two hostages, the decision was made to stage an assault on the theatre. But with the corridors and staircases heavily guarded and the presence of large quantities of explosives placed at key access points, Spetsnaz operators from the FSB, in conjunction with SOBR, the National Guard's, Special Rapid Response Unit, came up with an alternative plan. The idea was to gas the place using the building's ventilation system and although the identity of the chemical used was never disclosed it was believed to have been a derivative of fentanyl. What resulted was not only the death of the Chechens, but also the death of all but two of the two hundred and four hostages.

In true Putin fashion, instead of fronting up to the mistake, he ordered the cleansing of all persons related to or known to the militants, with the exception of Mosvar Barayev's brother, Aslan. Instead and to the best of anyone's knowledge, Aslan, has since been held at one of Russia's more notorious prison camps somewhere in Siberia as a deterrent to other Chechen's considering similar actions.

'And they want his brother released now, after all this time? Why?' queried Jill.

'As I said,' replied Sir Henry. 'It has a strange aroma.'

'Wouldn't be out of place at Billingsgate Market, if you ask me,' said Charlie.

'Quite,' said Sir Henry. 'And they also want a helicopter for transport to Farnborough and a private jet, along with one million US dollars.'

Transferred from the MOD into private ownership in the late 1990's, unlike its larger contemporaries, part of the deal was for Farnborough International Airport to cater only for business aviation purposes. Although since then, this remit has been extended to executive travel and occasional use by the military, this choice of airport made sense as a means to an end, but that didn't stop the whole situation from feeling wrong and very much out of kilter given what else was going on. Having said that, you can only deal with what's in front of you, hence my next question.

'What sort of timeframe are we looking at?'

'They're demanding proof of Barayev's release by 3pm tomorrow and the chopper ready to transport them from the roof of the hotel to the airport.'

'What's the situation on the ground?'

'The Met have got things sewn up for now,' said Sir Henry, 'but a request has come in from the Russian Ambassador, via the FCO, for the Regiment to become involved and the PM's given her provisional approval, subject of course to negotiations breaking down.'

'Is that normal?' asked Charlie.

'No it's not Charlie,' I replied. 'Far from it.'

Things had obviously moved on since the early 80's and the likes of the Iranian Embassy siege when this type of situation would almost certainly have led to the intercession of 22 SAS. But, with the Met now having, Hereford trained, CTSFOs (Counter Terrorism Specialist Firearms Officers) of their own, it struck me as odd that the Russian Ambassador would make such a request when he would be well aware of this capability.

'Who's the lead from the Met?' I asked.

'Dave Pryde,' said Sir Henry. 'On his way to Albany Street Barracks to meet them when they arrive which, he checked his watch, should be anytime now.'

As Hampshire's former Chief Constable, David Pryde's positive action following the bombing in Portsmouth last year got him noticed by the Met Commissioner, hence his promotion to Assistant Commissioner for Specialist Operations. In time, I was sure he would reach the ultimate goal of Commissioner, but for now his role would, subject to negotiations breaking down and final authorisation from the PM, be to hand over control of the operation to the British Army under the provisions of Military Aid to the Civil Power.

No sooner had the D2 helicopters landed, Major Keeble was heading for Major General Ian Walkerdine's office while his men made their way to the briefing room on the far side of the Parade Ground. As Director Special Forces (DSF), Walkerdine's office overlooked the arrival of 'B' squadron, an image of which he never tired, albeit with a tinge of envy that he was no longer operational.

Sometimes referred to by its low profile postal address, 'MoD A Block,' Albany Street Barracks on the outskirts of Regents Park was once home to the *Life Guard's*, the most senior regiment of the British Army and the *Royal Artillery*. Now though, its current occupants comprise the Royal Logistics Corp, Queen's Royal Hussars and 21 SAS, the official HQ for the Special Air Service.

Striding towards Maj. Gen. Walkerdine's office at the end of a long corridor of dull beige painted walls, Major Keeble returned a salute and 'Good morning *Sahr!*' from a Corporal stood outside and stepped through into an ante-room where a female officer was waiting for him.

'Morning Katie,' he said with a smile.

In her late forties, sporting a brunette bob and sparkling smile, Captain Kate Vingoe, stood up on her tip toes and pecked Keeble on the cheek. Her title was Chief Intelligence Officer. Following in her father, Derek's, footsteps, an Oxford Don with a doctorate in quantum physics, Vingoe, as one of several hundred students of Balliol College looking to carve a niche for themselves in society, she'd spent many happy hours in the Bodlein Library, only to find her love of words leading to her being plucked from the bosom of her postgraduate fraternity and thrown into the world of counter espionage. As a fledgling cypher clerk working at Century House, the original home of MI6, she excelled in all things analytical and soon came to the attention of the Regiment where she earned a reputation as an outstanding intelligence analyst, something without which the Regiment could not function.

'Come on, Jim,' she said. 'He's waiting for you.' With that, she opened the door to the adjoining office and they went through.

Kamenev dabbed the sides of his mouth with a linen napkin. It seemed a shame to waste the afternoon tea, which was, as advertised, excellent. Now though, with news of his situation having undoubtedly percolated through to the relevant authorities, it was time to put his game face on. Without question, the Ambassador's request for the SAS to become involved was being processed and while unusual, especially this early in the proceedings – it was after all six days into the Iranian Embassy siege and the death of a hostage, before authorisation was passed to the SAS – he had no doubt preparations were well underway for gathering intelligence ahead of an assault on the suite. The timing, after all, was essential if the overall strategy for the operation were to be successful.

Not that the two Asians knew anything about the *overall strategy*. Khalid Hassan and Syed Wazir had simply been following orders given to them by the man they knew as the Sheik. Any further instructions were to be taken from the Russian. This included taking possession of Kamenev's pistol used to shoot the bodyguard, an AK47, courtesy of the diplomatic pouch that accompanied the advance party and finally, the installation of remote cameras outside the suite and the stairwell at the end of the corridor from where it was possible to access the roof.

With little to be done about the unfolding circumstances at the Savoy, for now at least, and the cloud of a possible nuke in play, I threw the obvious question into the pot.

'How is this likely to impact on the Energy Summit?'

'That's a call for the PM in conjunction with the other World leaders,' said Sir Henry. 'She's already convened a COBR meeting over the Kamenev situation, but so far she is prepared for it to go ahead unless we can come up with something concrete on what's going on with our Ukrainian friend.'

'Is there anything to suggest President Ulyanov will not attend, bearing in mind, if he is behind this, he's hardly likely to blow himself up?' I asked.

'According to the Russian Ambassador, the only change off the back of the Savoy incident is he'll now be staying at the Residence in Kensington Palace Gardens. Why do you ask?'

'Who would benefit most from the Summit being cancelled and why would it be necessary to involve a nuclear device?'

'Russia presumably,' said Jill, 'but that would only be short term as cancelling the event won't prevent the alliance going ahead. That's already in the bag, isn't it?'

'In principle, yes,' said Sir Henry, 'but the formal Treaty is yet to be signed. That's not due to take place until after the Summit when the PM hosts President Thorne and Prime Minister Dubois at Chequers.'

'So is Chequers a target?' asked Jill. 'After all, Ulyanov will be long gone by then.'

'Unlikely,' said Sir Henry. 'It's in the middle of nowhere and buttoned up tighter than a drum at the best of times, let alone in the current climate.'

'Don't forget the Middle East,' said Hammad. 'Both will get their arses spanked if the Treaty gets signed and the alliance goes ahead.'

'True,' I said, 'but again, where does a nuke, assuming it's a nuke of course, come into play? Even by Ulyanov's standards that's a bit rich.'

'Trillions of dollars-worth of rich,' said Jill, 'and not if he can blame it one someone else.

She definitely had a point there. A simple denial without proof would be enough to obviate themselves of responsibility for the detonation of a nuclear device on UK soil. After all, we'd already established the potential for such devices to be out there in the market place, but even so, if Ulyanov sought to hide behind the theory that a terrorist group were to be behind such an attack, decapitating a group of World leaders would be no good to anyone. After all, with Germany and other European countries being key components of the Nord Stream pipeline, it just didn't make sense.

'Well let's hope it doesn't come to that,' said Sir Henry as, yet again, the phone on his desk rang. 'Something tells me it's going to be a busy night.'

*

Maj. Gen. Walkerdine came round his desk and shook Major Keeble's outstretched hand. Both former rugby players, Walkerdine, fly half and Keeble, centre, they dwarfed Capt. Vingoe as she brought them up to speed on the demands made by Kamenev's captors and ushered them over to a developing mind map on a wall at the far side of the office. Various images of Kamenev and Aslan Barayev featured, along with aerial and 3D images of the Savoy, the surrounding area and blueprints of the hotel's interior.

'As you can see, gentlemen,' began Vingoe, 'the topography of the area lends itself ideally to the provision of an inner and outer cordon.' The former, shown in red, reflected the boundary of the hotel, an almost perfect rectangle from its main entrance in Savoy Court, a cul de sac off the Strand, down to Savoy Place on the Victoria Embankment. In turn, the outer cordon, shown in blue, stretched from Trafalgar Square to Waterloo Bridge and north to the southern perimeter of Covent Garden. 'The hotel has been evacuated,' she continued. 'Counter Terrorism Specialist Firearms Officers, shown in green, are posted at strategic locations within and around the hotel. Those officers in yellow are on point to prevent access from the public from Carting Lane to the west and Savoy Street to the east.'

'FCP, Katie?' asked Keeble.

'Kamenev's suite is Black 10:4 on the south side of the

hotel (rear, tenth floor, four windows in from the left) overlooking the Thames so the Met have set up a Forward Control Point on the ground floor of the Strand Palace Hotel, directly opposite the entrance to Savoy Court.'

'Okay good. So other than the apparent Chechnya connection, what else do we know?'

'Very little. They've relayed their demands through Kamenev which seems a bit odd and makes life difficult for the negotiator on the ground.'

'I should say so,' he said. 'Difficult to strike up a rapport if you can't speak to the arseholes... What about mobiles?'

Vingoe shook her head. With crowds gathering a pace around the outer cordon and across the river, there was nothing to stop someone on the outside relaying information to those in the suite. 'The Met have got plain clothes officers on the ground and their covering CCTV, but nothing so far.'

'Jammers?'

By transmitting signals on the same radio frequency as those of mobile phones, communication with the base station could be disrupted and blocked. While effective in preventing the transfer of information should the hostage takers have a partner in the crowd, the downside is the risk that when activated it can alert the terrorists to an impending assault.

'Ready to go if the negotiations break down.'

'Okay, let's keep that under review for now,' said Keeble, turning his attention back to the mind map as Vingoe picked up a baton from a table in front of the display. Pointing towards a building on the south bank of the Thames, she said, 'The Met have got snipers posted here on the roof of the Royal Festival Hall and here on the Queen Elizabeth Concert Hall alongside Waterloo Bridge.'

'Good lines of sight on the suite,' observed Keeble.

'And the stairwell access point onto the roof.'

'Noting the covered, hut like, structure at the western perimeter of the flat roof, Keeble turned his attention to the white art deco façade of Shell Mex House alongside the Savoy. The distinctive clockface had been a feature on the London skyline since the thirties and more significantly towered over its neighbour. 'Have they got anyone here?'

'Not much point,' Vingoe replied. 'No real cover for a sniper. Good for zip lining onto the hotel roof, but according to the Met techies, cameras have been set up in the corridor leading to the suite and stairwell up to the roof, so it's possible they have the same on the roof itself.'

'Can we block the signal?'

'We can, but we'd have the same problem as someone in the crowd tipping them off with a mobile.'

'In which case they *off* the hostage and we piss off the Russians. Anything else?'

'They've drawn the suite curtains which means that so far we've had to rely on the Met snipers infra-red, thermal imaging to figure out what's going on inside.'

Keeble stepped forward and measured the distance from the roof of the Festival Hall to the suite. 'Jetson should help with that,' he observed.

Developed by the Pentagon, the Regiment had recently taken possession of a new toy which uses infra-red lasers to detect a person's unique physiological cardiac signature. Unlike other heart rate sensors which detect changes in how much light is reflected in the blood stream to infer a pulse, Jetson analyses minute vibrations on the surface of the skin to detect a heartbeat based on the size and shape of the heart and orientation of the valves. With an operating capability in excess of 200 metres, Keeble recognised that once they established Kamenev's heart signatures, they could track his movements around the suite without the need to see beyond the drawn curtains.

'So what have we got in there?' he asked.

'Four people. One sat, two moving around and one with a

depleting heat signature on the floor. Probably a bodyguard, like as not shot on entry to the suite,' she said, hesitating slightly.

'What is it, Katie?'

'It's the curtains,' she said. 'The Russian delegation took over the entire top floor of the building in readiness for the President's arrival and yet, it's only that suite where the curtains have been drawn.'

'Go on.'

'Any self-respecting terrorist should know about infra-red technology, but if not, why would they telegraph what suite they're in.'

Keeble looked thoughtfully at the distinctive green tiles that reached down from the flat roof and framed the row of dormer windows. 'And no other signatures anywhere?'

'No. The rest of the advance party are on site at the Merchant Taylors Hall.'

'Why just the one hostage?' mused Keeble. 'Surely, it would have been better to have several bargaining chips to play with?'

'Who knows,' said Vingoe. 'Easier to manage probably and besides, this Kamenev guy is obviously a big cheese otherwise why would the Russian Ambassador get involved?'

'Why indeed,' mused Keeble. 'I wonder what it is about Kamenev that makes him so important?'

With that thought left hanging in the air, Maj. Gen. Walkerdine walked over to the window and looked down onto the parade ground where three long wheel based Land Rovers were waiting patiently with their engines running.

'Time for you to hit the road Jim,' he said. 'Anything else you need, you can sort out from the FCP.'

'Roger that, Sir,' Keeble replied and turned to leave.

Sir Henry replaced the receiver.

'That was Avon and Somerset's Chief,' he said. 'It looks like the heat's off the Summit, for the time being at least. The box van was a rental from Oxford and has been found near an abandoned farm on the outskirts of Bridgewater.'

'Who found it?' asked Jill.

'Not who, Jill, what,' said Sir Henry. 'They activated the on board GPS tracker.'

'Burnt out?'

'Apparently not. Probably didn't want to attract attention to it.'

Jill looked puzzled. 'So why does that take the heat off the Summit?'

'For one, Bridgewater is in Somerset and twenty odd miles west of Kidlington where the hijack took place, but more significantly, tread marks from a second vehicle found alongside the abandoned van were tracked onto the A358 from where they continued west towards Devon and Cornwall.'

'How can they be sure it didn't go the other way? Surely tyre marks wouldn't show up on the road.'

'Tyre marks? No, not unless there were skid marks, but the dogs were brought in and pollen traces embedded in the tyres of the second vehicle meant they were able to track the vehicle for the first few hundred metres or so until it hit the main road and turned west.'

'Clever.'

'Indeed and not as uncommon as you might imagine,' continued Sir Henry. 'If you think about the amount of flowering plants in the world, each with their own unique DNA, if pollen gets transferred to another object, it can tell us a lot about where that object or person has been and in this case, the direction of travel for the second vehicle once it hit the main road. It was also used to trace activity at mass graves such as in Bosnia and Kosovo and even now, the Boffins are looking to use pollen as an additive in the manufacture of bullets to help trace their origin when used in crime.'

Back to the here and now, I turned to Charlie, 'Have Thames Valley been able to get any CCTV of our suspects from the rental office?'

'Looks like it,' he replied. 'But according to RMS, there's an outstanding task on the system for it to be downloaded.'

The Record Management System is used by several police services across England and Wales to record crime and intelligence gathered from any number of sources. Taking in the counties of Berkshire, Buckinghamshire and Oxfordshire, Thames Valley Police is one of those databases which feeds into *Atelier*, hence Charlie's observation.

'Okay, Charlie,' said Sir Henry. 'We need those images ASAP, so let us know as soon as they come in please.'

'Will do, Sir.'

'So what now?' asked Hammad. 'Do we just wait?'

'No,' said Sir Henry. 'I want you and Alex to liaise with the Met down at the FCP. There's no telling how long this thing is going take to play out and I want eyes and ears on the ground. I'll get Di to sort out a room for you to share at the Strand Palace. As for you Jill, I want you with Dave Pryde at Albany Barracks. Same thing. I don't want there to be any chance of a left hand right hand thing going on here.'

'Are you okay looking after Scrumpy?' she asked.

'He can go with you,' he replied. 'Walkerdine's got one of his own, chocolate cocker or something like that. And besides, they're good with animals. Just tell them he's more of a Bear than a dog and you'll be fine.'

Dating back to the late fifties an SAS trooper, ironically from 'B' Squadron, was on patrol in the Malayan jungle when he came across a honey bear cub hiding in an abandoned foxhole. Warned by natives that his mother would kill it after having come into contact with humans, he decided to adopt the bear which soon became a valued member of the Unit. Although the bear died of pneumonia a couple of years later, his memory lives on in the Regiment's archives, including a picture of him which can be found on the wall of the NCO mess at Hereford.

'So,' I said, after a brief explanation. 'If you ever wondered why 'B' Squadron's motif includes a bears paw, then now you know.'

'What about me?' asked Charlie, keen as ever to get his feet on the ground.

'Sorry Charlie,' said Sir Henry. 'You're stuck with me. I need you to keep monitoring *Atelier* to make sure we're on top of anything that comes in, no matter how obscure.'

'Roger that,' he replied with sigh.

'Maybe next time, Charlie,' I said as he stuck his head back into the laptop.

CHAPTER 29

We arrived at the Strand Palace as three Land Rovers pulled up in Exeter Street. To the rear of the Hotel and perhaps most notable for 'Joe Allens,' an American themed Bistro favoured by theatre goers and tourist alike, this quiet side street off the Strand offered the ideal location from which to arrive unobtrusively and away from the attention of the media. As we watched the troopers debus under the dim glow of amber street lighting, there was no mistaking the look of professionalism and confidence in their stride as they towed their wheeled equipment boxes down an alley that connected to the hotel's service entrance.

'How come the Boss isn't coming down?' asked Hammad.

'Stickler for protocol,' I replied.

Hammad looked puzzled.

'He believes in taking strategic control of operations and let the boots on the ground do their thing without interference. No different to the PM's approach to the floods a while back?'

'But she got a lot of stick for that.'

'She did, but once the strategic decisions are made – protect life, use of lethal force, return to normality, that type of thing – what good would it do to keep turning up and effectively getting in the way. Nobody likes to be second guessed, least of tactical commanders looking to make, in some instances, life or death decisions.'

'So how did he get the job? Must have put a few noses out of joint?'

'Probably, but I don't think the PM cared. Obviously he keeps that to himself, but reading between the lines, I think she got fed up with the political infighting between the respective intelligence agencies after the Snowden affair and decided she needed someone she could trust to bang a few heads together and oversee the entire network.'

'But why not appoint a Minister of State?'

'Again too political and also too transient. She was after stability, continuity and someone with sufficient strength of character and reputation to keep them all in line and singing from the same song sheet.'

'Well she certainly got that.'

'She did indeed.'

'And you?'

'Right place, right time or wrong place, wrong time, I guess.' That it took Bronagh's murder to raise my profile and remind Sir Henry I was still around was something I would gladly have turned the clock back for.

'Sorry,' said Hammad, the look on my face clearly betraying my thoughts.

'Don't be,' I said. 'Right come on. Let's see what's the latest on this hostage scenario.'

With that, we took the same route as the troopers into the hotel and walked through to a large conference room on the ground floor where the Metpol Commander was about to start his briefing.

Stood at the back of the room, arms folded across a barrel chest, Jim Keeble was overlooking proceedings.

'Well, well, well,' he said as I quietly introduced him to Hammad. 'It seems you boys have been having some fun lately.'

'Is nothing sacred,' I said as the Met Commander covered

areas already known.

'Not in this game, Alex,' he replied, stepping back further so as not to disturb the briefing. As with so many other specialist units from around the world that trained with the SAS, the FBI's Hostage Rescue Team, Germany's GSG-9 Bundespolizei and now our own CTSFOs, I'd first met Jim when SO13 joined this Hereford fraternity. A hard man, but fair, he was right of course. It was exactly our new line of work that might require some additional muscle from time to time, so it made sense they were in the loop. 'Mind you,' he continued. 'I was a little surprised to be called in on this one.'

I nodded in agreement. 'Political, I suspect. It seems our Mr Kamenev is higher up the food chain than we might otherwise have expected.'

'And difficult to turn down a request from the Russian Ambassador.'

'Agreed. So what are your thoughts?'

'The Met techies have found cameras in the corridor leading to the suite and stairwell to the roof which means we can't go in through the front door or via the roof in case they have them up there as well. On top of that, the negotiator's been told by Kamenev that they "may" be wearing vests.'

'May?' I queried.

'My thoughts too, but I suppose if you've got a gun to your head, you'll say anything they tell you to say.'

'I suppose,' I replied sceptically.

'He was quizzed on it and was vague in his response so whether he did have a gun to his head or not we can't be sure. Bottom line, we can't risk a conventional assault, so we need to come up with another option.'

By 'conventional,' I took this to mean something along the lines of the Iranian Embassy siege when the seventeen minute raid saw a variety of tactics adopted including abseiling down from the roof, blowing out the windows to, in this case, the suite, throw in a couple of flashbangs and it would be all over in a matter of seconds. But, and unlike in 1980 when suicide vest were not the norm, as Jim said, this was not an option.

'Valium margarita?' I suggested.

'If they're using dead switches, no.' he replied. 'Again, cant risk it.'

This tactic for stupefying terrorists with Valium laced pizzas had proved effective in the past, but he was right, in this instance it was too risky. That said, as the cogs began to whirr, another idea sprang to mind. 'We know they've asked for a helicopter, along with everything else, so why not give them one?'

'Go on,' he said, one eyebrow raised.

My suggestion met with a moment or two of thought before Jim nodded slowly. 'But that would need proof of Barayev's release.'

'Yes it would wouldn't it,' I replied as I looked at Barayev's photo on the briefing board, then across to Hammad.

CHAPTER 30

Moira Bingham had lived in the village her entire life. She'd gone to the primary school in the heart of the community, 'a tiny school with big ideas' according to the current headteacher for whom she cleaned once a week. Then onto secondary school in nearby Chipping Norton where she realised she had no aspirations for higher education. Instead, she joined her parents in the family business and for years enjoyed the day to day interactions – aka gossip – with locals wishing to buy stamps, postal orders or perhaps the sending of a mysterious parcel to some foreign land. But when the demise of rural post offices caught up with them Moira's parents had to make the big decision.

That they owned the property was the only thing that had

kept them afloat, but with more money going out than coming in, eventually the inevitable arrived and it was time to sell. Mind you, that nice Professor Bird was so kind and once he'd transformed the ground floor back into a home – kept the stable door too which was a nice touch – he'd promised not to change another thing about the thatched cottage. So based on that 'gentleman's agreement' and a further promise to take on Moira as a part time cleaner, her father agreed to sell.

Not that being divest of a focal point for gossip stopped it from happening. That Cheryl, from the pub for example, hadn't been seen for a while. Just upped and left apparently, she'd said to her friend Mable as they made their way down the narrow footpath towards the cottage. Always was a bit flighty so there were no surprises there that she'd gone. But as for the Professor. Well, what with being such an important man and oh so very handsome – she flushed at the thought – she was not unduly concerned that he hadn't been seen for a while. And besides, it gave her an excuse to spend a little more time in the cottage. There were those old cushions that needed the holes repaired and well, that kitchen sink needed a good bleaching so it did.

Saying 'goodbye' to her friend, she rummaged in her handbag for the key to the front door. Finding it eventually tucked under her purse, she tutted to herself and slid it into the lock.

My, that's strange, she thought as she turned the key and

realised it was already open. Not that it was really necessary to lock doors in the village and bless him, the poor love couldn't darn a sock so why would she be surprised that he'd left the door open. *Oh well, time for a cuppa before the day's work* was an adage she always adhered to as she hung her coat on a rack by the door.

'Oh my!' she exclaimed, grimacing at the awful smell as she made her way through to the kitchen. Her immediate thought was of a dead rat as she covered her mouth with a hanky *they don't 'arf pong, 'specially in the heat* but then, looking round she noticed a pile of broken crockery and glass had been swept into the corner alongside the dresser, *maybe a fox got in and the Professor had done his best to clear up.* 'Oh well, nevermind,' she muttered to herself as she took a step forward then pulled up short as her foot caught on something sticky. Using the worktop for support, she steadied herself and examined the underside of her shoe. Reaching for some kitchen roll to wipe off what looked like a blob of strawberry jam, she noticed a strange humming coming from the pantry. Had Ms Bingham been a Miss Marple fan rather than Percy Thrower, she might have stood back at that point and called the police, but instead curiosity got the better of her and having cleaned *whatever it was* off the bottom of her shoe, stepped forward and opened the pantry door.

CHAPTER 31

Unlike in the movies, negotiations take time and are never easy. Not everyone has a 'Dirty Harry' to call on and make their day and even if they did, they would never be used.

Trained in areas such as psychology, crisis intervention, active listening and incident management, the need for a police negotiator to strike up a rapport with hostage takers is of paramount importance. Likewise, to play for time, to offer one thing in exchange for another are also key elements to the management of a hostage scenario. Ultimately, the aim is to save lives and achieve a peaceful conclusion, but if that fails then to instil a false sense of confidence as the precursor to an assault can also be useful. But so far and with negotiations channeled only through Kamenev, it had been a long, uneventful night and we were running out of time. So, as midday approached and with only three hours to go till the deadline and no sign of Russia agreeing to the release of Aslan Barayev, Jim gave me the nod and I called Hammad on my mobile.

'How's it going?'

'All good,' he replied. It had been a rush job, but with the kind of pulling power behind this operation, not only had Sky come through with flying colours, but thanks to some inside knowledge, so had Pinewood Studios.

Seventeen miles west of central London and home to the 'Carry On' and 'James Bond' movie franchises, Pinewood was where I first met Bronagh. I'd been volunteered, as they did for these types of gigs at the time, to go along and help with some of the technical aspects of a movie based on the 1996 IRA bombing of Canary Wharf. As chief scriptwriter, and part of a familiarisation tour, Bronagh had introduced me to her best friend, Carol Ritchie, one of the SFX (Special Effects) team on the set. In all honesty, after the funeral I'd lost contact with Carol, but with the way things were panning out at the hotel, I'd hoped she wouldn't hold that against me as I'd dialled her number. She didn't. In fact she'd moved up a notch or two since then and now, as Head of SFX, she was working on the latest Bond movie.

'They're just sorting out the rushes,' Hammad continued,

'but I'm told they'll be ready before the deadline.'

'Keep on top of them, H, and remember, it's not meant to be a blockbuster!'

'Don't worry. Just remember in future, the name's Dosari, Hammad al-Dosari' he laughed and hung up, as I noticed a call waiting from Sir Henry.

'Yes, Sir?'

'Get back to the office now, Alex,' he said. 'Somethings come up.'

Despite the forecast looking grim for later in the day, Marty Farrow was looking forward to the next challenge. After a light workout and the summary demolition of a pile of bacon sarnies, an hour and a half after leaving the barracks, two land rovers pulled up in the car park of the Storey Arms. Once a pub, now a youth hostel, this was the official muster point at the foot of Pen y Fan where Farrow and his compadres debussed and gathered their kit together in readiness for the infamous fifteen mile 'Fan Dance' on the Brecon Beacons.

It had been several years since Farrow first underwent this challenge and although he believed himself to be fit as a butchers dog, once everyone was fully loaded with forty five pound

Bergens, rifles and water bottles and they'd trudged over to the iconic red phonebox that represented the start of the dance, he couldn't help but feel a little anxious as he looked towards the fifth member of the group.

DS (Directing Staff), Steve Hughes, another veteran of the Regiment was, for the purposes of this exercise, the de facto pacemaker. Not that raw recruits had this luxury. Their job was to keep up, finish in under four hours ten or return to their respective Regiments. Although this threat of expulsion was not there for Farrow and his group, that did nothing to diminish the inherent competitiveness and gentle rivalry evolving among them, as evidenced in the NCO mess the night before when Hughes was nominated by Mike Allen as 'chief babysitter for the SBS pussy.' Not that Farrow bit, but if there was ever an incentive for keeping all of them in sight, Hughes included, then that was it, he'd decided, as he'd set aside his half-finished pint of Guinness.

'Okay lads,' said Hughes with a sardonic grin. 'You know the score,' and with that, he was off like a long dog. Leaving the others to try and keep up on what was referred to, in military parlance, as a Tactical Advance to Battle or TAB, they set off in pursuit and fairly sprinted, at least that's what it felt like to Farrow, up the west slope of Pen y Fan.

Without waiting for a reply to his summons, the line had gone dead, a sure sign that whatever it was about was urgent. So having quickly updated Jim on Hammad's progress and passed on his mobile number, I left the hotel where, thanks to Di, I'd been able to grab a couple of hours shut eye during the night. Cutting through a succession of side streets, I emerged onto St Martins Lane and dropped down onto the northern perimeter of Trafalgar Square from where I could see the media circus had expanded exponentially since last evening. Avoiding the melee as local cops grappled with the traffic and the usual throng of onlookers, I passed the National Gallery, crossed the road in front of Admiralty Arch at the entrance to The Mall and was saying 'Hi!' to Di in less than five minutes from receiving the call.

'Grab a seat,' said Sir Henry without preamble as I walked in. 'Charlie's picked up something on *Atelier* I need you to look at.'

Joining Charlie at the conference table I reached for the coffee pot as he looked up from his laptop. 'Hi Alex,' he said, 'Thames Valley have logged a double murder on RMS.'

'The prison van drivers?'

'No. Two more and not so recent by the looks of it.'

Transferring a screengrab of the RMS page onto the big screen, I could see that one of the victims was Professor Alistair Bird.

Okay. That was a surprise. 'And the other victim?'

'Barmaid from the local pub, Cheryl something or other.'

'So let me get this straight,' I said as Sir Henry gazed at me over the top of his half-moon reading glasses. 'One…' I held up my right thumb. 'We've got the world's foremost authority on renewable energy, who happens to be a keynote speaker at the forthcoming World Energy Summit, murdered. Two…' index finger raised. 'Russia's former head of the SVR and confidant of President Ulyanov is taken hostage. Three…' middle finger. 'A Ukrainian scientist, formerly attached to Russia's Nuclear Weapons Programme is on the loose. Four…' Ring finger. 'Two unknowns who facilitated his escape, also unaccounted for, five…' Pinkie time. 'Khaled Hassan and Syed Wazir, also on the loose, both previously known to us as possible associates of the Leicester Square bomber and connected in some way or another to, six…' didn't bother with the other hand as still occupied with the coffee mug, 'Akram Murad, Minister of State for Immigration who happens to be the twin brother of another male who we know fuck all about!'

Sir Henry dipped his chin and raised his eyebrows like a pair of elevators above his specs.

I sighed. 'So what do we know about the murder, Charlie?'

'Found by the cleaner in the pantry. Barmaid shot,

298

execution style in the back of the head, but looks like Bird made a fight of it. Broken crockery, plenty of blood traces, but no sign of prints, other than those of Bird, the barmaid and the cleaner.'

'That'll be bar *person*,' admonished Di, as she came in with a fresh pot of coffee on a tray of delicious looking, doorstep, bacon and egg sarnies.

'Whatever you say, Di,' said Charlie with a grin as she placed the tray on the table.

'Motive?'

'Theft by the looks of it. Safe door's been left open and according to the cleaner the Professor was meticulous about keeping the safe locked at all times.'

'Do we know what's missing?'

'Nothing on the report so far, no.'

'Okay. What about the blood?'

'Looks like they made an effort to clear up after themselves, but as I said, the Prof obviously got stuck in so the lab should be able to get something back on DNA if they're in the system.' Pausing for a moment, he took a bite of sarnie, munched for a moment, then continued. 'The theory, according to the MO, is there had to be two involved. For no reason other than managing both Bird and the Cheryl woman, especially during what, according to the crime scene pics looks like a right royal dust up.'

Looking at the images on screen, I could see luminol spray had been used to pick up a series of blood splatters which appeared inconsistent with simply those of the victims. Used by crime scene investigators across the world, when sprayed evenly across a surface in the dark luminol activates trace elements of an oxidant which reacts with haemoglobin in the blood, causing it glow blue without the need for a UV lamp. Although this only lasts for about thirty seconds or so this is more than enough time for long exposures photographs to be taken and in so doing help Major Crime investigators to piece together exactly what took place during the intervening period prior to the Professor being killed.

'Anything else, Charlie?'

'No next of kin by the looks of it. Bird is, sorry was, holding down a position at Oxford's *Environmental Change Institute*.' He split the screen so he had the report from RMS on one side and the University website on the other. 'According to the website, he's the academic lead for an MSc/MPhil course in *Environmental Change and Management…* Hang on, there is something here… Oh yes, they've just posted a scan of an address book found in his study.' Again, he threw it up onto the screen. 'Looks like the Dean of his faculty is a guy by the name of George Thompson. Probably, as good a place to start as any if you want to follow it up.'

I did and looked towards Sir Henry for confirmation.

He nodded.

'Get hold of Thompson for me please, Charlie, and tell him I'm on my way.'

With that, I wolfed down the rest of my sarnie, took a glug of coffee and caught the car keys lobbed at me by Sir Henry. 'Jim's on rest day, so try not to prang it,' he said as I headed for the door.

Beads of sweat broke through Farrow's fatigues as he pushed hard to keep up with his compadres. Grateful for having Butser Hill on the outskirts of Portsmouth as part of his training, the chalk ridge hill and highest point on the South Downs offered terrain not dissimilar to the early stages of the run. That it was only just over two hundred and seventy metres above sea level, as opposed to the eight hundred plus of Pen y Fan, was not lost on him though as he concentrated hard on his breathing and blocking out the wind and first drops of rain predicted from earlier in the day.

Putting my foot down wherever possible, I weaved the Jag in and out of the beginnings of rush hour traffic. Why they call it rush *hour* when it's never just the one, beats me, but in fairness the covert blues and twos helped as I left Trafalgar Square behind and raced down the Mall towards Buckingham Palace. With a nod to Her Majesty as I passed Buckingham Palace, I went north on the Edgeware Road, west through White City, the home of London's first Summer Olympics back in 1908 – courtesy of another Mount Vesuvius eruption in 1906 apparently – and out of the city on the A40 before hitting the M40 where at last I was able to let the 3.0 L V6 engine fulfil its potential.

By the time they reached the top of Pen y Fan, the weather had closed in bringing with it a cold damp mist that enveloped the team as they traversed the peak. Ahead of Scanes and Barber, Farrow could just about make out Allen up ahead. Legs pumping like pistons, he was living up to his nickname of 'Duracell Bunny' as he disappeared down the far side of the hill onto Jacob's Ladder. The treacherous rocky descent was definitely not Jacob's dream 'staircase to heaven' from the Old Testament thought Farrow as he followed on. It was instead, a testament of men and now women's ability to overcome adversity. Not that anyone expected quarter from the DS, nor did they receive any as the mist cleared and they looped back around the upper then lower Neuadd reservoirs before continuing along an undulating stone vehicle track that had once been a Roman Road.

With the SAS and SBS needing to recruit no more than

thirty new members to their ranks each year, competition was fierce among the one hundred plus hopefuls that stepped forward to face this most grueling test of physical fitness and mental stamina. Widely regarded as the ultimate means to sort out the wheat from the chaff, on reaching the turnaround point where realisation kicked in that the whole thing had to be done again, this time in reverse, it was hardly surprising that on average only ten percent of the candidates were successful in achieving their personal dreams. With that thought in mind and Hughes now maintaining a steady pace, Farrow made the turn and with thighs burning bright like Blake's Tyger and sanity continually in question, he put his head down, picked up his pace and moved ahead of Allen.

An hour after leaving the office, I pulled up in front of the faculty building, took the Home Office crested log book out of the glovebox and left it on the dash. Fingers crossed, that would have to suffice for a parking permit as I walked through a pair of ancient portals that marked the entrance to Pembroke College. Looking round, at the combination of gothic, neoclassical architecture that surrounded the grassed quadrangle it felt like I'd just stepped into an episode of 'Morse' and could almost hear Wagner's 'The Flying Dutchman' echoing off the walls as I contemplated my next move. A signpost to the Dean's study would have been helpful. Thankfully my brief moment of frustration was addressed by a group of young gentlemen and ladies – kind of makes you think that way in this environment – who directed me towards an archway in the far corner of the quadrangle.

CHAPTER 32

With the FCP up and running, Major Keeble and trooper, Paul Campbell joined the CTSFO sniper on the flat roof of the Queen Elizabeth Concert Hall alongside Waterloo Bridge.

Son of Brigadier Gregor 'Gunner' Campbell, Paul was destined for Sandhurst from the moment he entered the gates of 'The Duke of York's, Royal Military School.' A born athlete and GB representative in the Biathlon at the London 2012 Olympics, Campbell's career was pretty much mapped out for him until his father was killed in a suicide bombing during a diplomatic mission to Bagdad. From that day onward, Campbell's life took a very different turn, choosing instead to utilise his skills for a different purpose which led him from the Paras to the Regiment where, as a sniper, he'd become responsible for numerous kills, many of which included would be suicide bombers.

'Any movement?' asked Keeble, as the Met sniper looked back from her perch behind the parapet.

'No, Sir,' she replied.

Constable Annie Davies had been a CTSFO since inception, her specialist skills honed from shooting tin cans on her parents farm in Shropshire. An animal lover, which, didn't extend to humans who deserved to meet their maker, meant Davies had refused the rabbit route suggested by her father in favour of attaching tin cans to fishing wire suspended from pulleys between trees, from which a homemade generator provided power to create moving targets. Hours and hours of practice spent in between shifts ultimately translated into the real world when, after seven years on patrol, she completed the selection board for attending the gruelling, eighteen week course at the Metpol Training Centre in Gravesend, Essex. Despite being part of a largely male dominated environment, she soon gained respect among her colleagues after coming top of her class, before swiftly going on to become the lead sniper within the Specialist Firearms Command.

Once the introductions were done, Keeble quickly addressed the *elephant on the roof* and the first thing on Davies mind when the two men had arrived. Her concerns were soon assuaged though as Keeble explained that the second sniper in his team had gone down with a virus and while all members of 'B' Squadron could be trusted to make the shot, having reviewed her profile he was happy for her to remain on point. That she was able to regularly embed ten consecutive rounds in a two inch circle over five hundred metres made this an easy decision for Keeble as Davies gratefully accepted her temporary role as Sniper Bravo-Two. It was also a decision which helped sooth any ego's within the Met High Command at having the job taken off them under such unusual circumstances.

Looking out across the river to the Savoy Hotel, Keeble noted Davies was using the Enfield Enforcer 7.62 sniper rifle. 'How do you fancy trying out a new toy?' he asked.

'Love to,' she said as Campbell, settling in alongside her, allowed her to shimmy back from the parapet and stand up to face Keeble.

Detaching the telescopic sight on her enforcer, she fitted the proffered Schmidt and Bender scope-sight to her rifle and returned to her perch alongside Campbell. Taking a moment to calibrated the new scope, she let out a low whistle and exclaimed quietly, 'Wow! That's one Gucci bit of kit. Where did you get it?'

'Pentagon's new technology,' he replied. 'Should help us work out who's who in the suite.' With that he thumbed his radio mike. 'Command to control, over?'

'Go ahead, over.'

'Make the call.'

'Roger.'

The Jetson laser did nothing to detract from the diagnostic capability of the scope as it cut through the curtains like a hot knife through butter. Monitoring the three infra-red thermal images from the suite, now accompanied by respective cardiac rhythms, Davies and Campbell watched carefully as one of the bodies moved to the telephone.

'That's interesting,' said Davies, looking back over her shoulder. 'Are we sure that's Kamenev on the phone?'

Keeble relayed the question to control and came back with an affirmative answer.

'For someone who's supposed to be a hostage, he's very calm,' she said, noting his heartbeat on the scope at just over 70 bpm. 'But what's really weird is the other two are hardly registering any different either.'

Keeble was aware of Kamenev's back story, which he suspected might, but only might account for his apparent lack of nerves, but he also knew from experience that terrorists, no matter how dedicated to their cause, always showed significant signs of stress when faced with the reality of such situations. Usually this would be picked up when speaking to them on the phone and although shielded to some extent from this by Kamenev being made to act as the go between, the levels identified by the Jetson laser simply didn't make sense. With a shake of the head, he dismissed that thought as one for the pencil pushers to work out in the post op investigation. For now though and while intriguing, he had a job to get on with as he indicated for Campbell to join him.

'Okay, Annie, stay sharp,' said Keeble as Campbell shimmied back from the parapet, and with a satisfied thumbs up from behind her back, Davies settled in for the wait.

Barely forty five minutes after entering the Dean's study, I was back on the A40 heading west, blues and twos again helping to carve my way through Oxford's city centre. Up to now, this whole shebang had felt like piecing together a jigsaw without any edges or corners. But at least now, with the information provided by George Thompson, things were beginning to make sense and while not completing the puzzle, it at last felt like we were moving in the right direction as I brought up the blue tooth display on the dash and speed dialled Sir Henry.

With Campbell left to take over from the other Met sniper on the roof of the Royal Festival Hall, Keeble returned to the FCP where

Mike Tizard was working a joystick in front of a bank of monitors. Known as *Ghost* among his contemporaries, Tizard was the Squadron's technical expert and Keeble's go to man when it came to the covert placement of audio and visual capabilities in preparation for an assault. A former member of the FBI's Hostage Rescue Team, Tizard had come over to the UK as part of an exchange scheme with the Regiment, but having met a girl, the rest as they say is history and so far as Keeble was concerned a good deal all round. In this instance, there was little Tizard could do in terms of getting close to the suite so instead he was remotely operating another new piece of kit recently acquired from the Pentagon. Hovering just above the cloud cover, the A-160T Hummingbird was a robot helicopter equipped with a 1.8 Gigapixel camera that cauterised the gloom to provide high quality live stream imagery of the hotel roof.

As with so many buildings in central London the hotel featured a central courtyard around which the various suites were located. At its centre, a glass domed atrium could be seen standing proud over 'The Thames Foyer' where the great and the good or in some instances not so good assemble daily for the Savoy's celebrated Afternoon Tea. The aerial view also made clear the two distinct roof levels, the entrance facing towards the Strand being one floor lower to that of the rear where the green tiled facade of the Penthouse Suites overlooked the river. Likewise, the shed like, single access point onto the roof was clearly visible to the far left hand side of the roof as viewed from the snipers vantage points on the other side of the Thames.

Alongside Tizard, Sergeant Major Mark Chapman looked on. Currently non-operational due to a ruptured achilles suffered during a training accident some six months ago, the former Colour Sergeant in the Royal Marines was, at forty three, Keeble's most experienced NCO and effectively his second in command. Normally at the forefront of any assault, Chapman's injury was largely healed and for the last week or so he'd been champing at the bit to get back in the saddle, a wish often expressed in colourful yet respectful language and one which was about to come to pass as Keeble placed a hand on his shoulder.

CHAPTER 33

Unlike the scrap of paper used by John Dellow to sign over control of the Iranian Embassy siege to Lieutenant-Colonel Rose in 1980, the revised protocol, laid out in the Metpol 'Gold' Commander's log book, effectively charted events from the moment Assistant Commissioner Pryde first received the call to action until now, when he officially relinquished police control of the operation to the Special Forces.

'Over to you, Ian,' said AC Dave Pryde as, with a flourish, he signed the last entry and proffered it for Maj. Gen. Walkerdine to countersign. Unlike in the old days when a tot of whisky would have sealed the deal, instead, both men shook hands and reached for their respective encrypted mobiles, Pryde's to update the PM and Walkerdine to set the wheels in motion.

Kamenev put the phone down, picked up the TV remote and indicated for his two captors to look at the television mounted on the wall. He selected Sky News just as the anchor, Stephen Dixon, appeared on the screen.

'Breaking news on the siege at the Savoy Hotel...

The image of the hotel appeared on the screen behind Dixon.

Following President Ulyanov's decision to release Aslan Barayev and in response to a special request from the Russian Ambassador, the UK Government have taken the unprecedented step of agreeing to step back from the siege at the Savoy Hotel in which Nikolay Kamenev, Russia's former head of their Foreign Intelligence Service, has been held captive.

The image behind Dixon changed to a mix of archive footage of the Dubrovka Theatre terrorist attack in 2020 with snow laden skies and iron gates to, as the strapline at the bottom of the screen showed, Camp No 17, Krasnoyarsk.

While not involved in the 2002 terrorist attack on Moscow's Dubrovka theatre during which over two hundred hostages died, Sky News sources can reveal that Aslan Barayev, the brother of Mosvar Barayev, the Chechen separatist leader responsible for the attack, was one of many followers swept up in the aftermath of the incident and who has since been held in a Siberian Prison Camp as a statement to others not to follow in his brother's footsteps.

As the iron gates to the prison opened, a figure, captioned as Aslan Barayev, appeared amidst a phalanx of prison guards.

When asked the reason for this move away from the UK's policy not to negotiate with terrorists, the Prime Minister's press secretary would not be drawn, simply stating it was for reasons of national security.'

Staggering slightly, Barayev was ushered towards a waiting, NATO liveried, helicopter. Shielding his eyes from the driving snow, he climbed unsteadily on board, turning briefly, as instructed by one of the guards, towards the cameras.

CGI is a wonderful thing thought Kamenev as he pressed the pause button on his remote control. Safe in the knowledge that not in a million years would Barayev be released he'd been intrigued to see how this little diversion would pan out. Not that it was over quite yet he knew as his two captors high fived each other. That the subterfuge was lost on them was of no significance to him. Nor did he have any feelings for their ultimate fate. How that would transpire remained to be seen, but more importantly, as the phone alongside him rang, he was satisfied that his immediate objective had been achieved.

A thumbs up from the negotiator and Keeble reached for the radio mike attached to his body armour. 'Command to Bravo-Three, over?'

Five miles south west of the FCR, Sergeant Major Chapman responded, 'Go ahead, over.' Having exchanged his nomex gear for a commercial pilot's uniform, Chapman was making his way across the tarmac of Battersea Heliport towards the waiting Dauphin 2 which had flown down from Albany Barracks.

'ETA, Chappers?' asked Keeble.

The rotors were already turning as Chapman stepped up into the co-pilot's seat. 'Four minutes and counting,' he replied as the pilot eased back on the collective and the D2 lifted smoothly off the tarmac.

'Roger that,' Keeble responded. 'Command to Snipers, radio check, over.'

'Sniper Bravo-One,' responded Paul Campbell from his perch on the roof of the Royal Festival Hall.

'Sniper Bravo-Two,' Annie Davies acknowledged a second later.

Two minutes later and with the rest of the team ready to go from the stairwell that led up to the top floor and from there the roof, Keeble gave his penultimate transmission as the D2 swept overhead and hovered above the hotel. 'Bravo Team, you are weapons free. Standard Operating Procedure, out.'

By the time I arrived, in record time, at the gates to Stirling Barracks, I'd updated Sir Henry and in turn been told of the events at the Savoy. Unlike so many other military establishments around the UK, I was directed to the main office building, not by a private security bod with nothing more than a clipboard in hand, but by one of two, those that I could see anyway, heavily armed sentries in combat fatigues.

Landing midway along the flat roof, some thirty metres from the access point in the far left corner, the positioning of the D2 ensured that both snipers had clear lines of sight for when the *Tangos* and *Hotel* emerged.

'Stand by, Stand by! Door opening,' reported Davies from the roof of Queen Elizabeth Hall.

'I have movement,' said Campbell, as three men appeared in the doorway.

Bunched together they turned left and shuffled along a clearly defined walkway towards the waiting chopper. '*Tango One* to the front, both hands on an AK47, *Hotel* centre, *Tango Two* to the rear, pistol in right hand, left on shoulder of *Hotel*.'

'I have *Tango One*,' relayed Campbell.

'*Tango Two*,' responded Davies, a millisecond later.

With all hands occupied and the threat of dead switches negated, Keeble breathed a sigh of relief as the Hummingbird confirmed the distinctive outline of the AK47 in *Tango One's* hands. Although weapons such as the Russian made AK47 were favoured by terrorists across the world, it never ceased to amaze Keeble why they would use them in close quarter situations. *Oh well, more fool them,* he thought as he watched Chapman step out from the co-pilot's seat and walk round to open the cabin door of the D2.

Using lasers to dial in both subjects, the snipers recalibrated respective ranges from their rooftop vantage points, but then, as Campbell's crosshairs centred on the base of *Tango One's* neck, Kamenev caught the back of his heel, sending both men tumbling to the floor.

'Sniper Bravo-One,' reported Campbell, '*Tango One* is blocked by the *Hotel*. I repeat *Tango One* is blocked by *Hotel*, over.'

Having returned to the cockpit, Chapman's earpiece chirped, 'Chappers, scratch your head if you have a clear shot on *Tango One*,' commanded Keeble.

A moment later, Keeble saw Chapman's left hand reach up to scratch the side of his head as his right hand disappeared down the side of the co-pilot's seat.

It was time... Keeble took a breath and pressed the transmit button, 'Command to Team, Strike, Strike, Strike.'

Breathing regularised, elbows moved slightly so that bone not muscle rested on the rubber mat beneath her, the mere passage of blood having the potential to skew her aim, Davies exhaled, pushed gently back on the double set trigger and the rifle roared sending a metre long muzzle flash out and towards the river.

Chapman's peripheral vision saw the flash a millisecond before the round entered *Tango Two's* skull just above the bridge of his nose. Barely pausing on its indefatigable course through the brain, the lethal projectile ripped out through the far side of the skull, sending out a cocktail of red spray and in the air before embedding itself into the bitumen.

While SOP was to neutralise the threat, part of Keeble's brief was, if possible, to find out more about the circumstances surrounding the hostage incident. In an ideal world that meant taking a terrorist alive, but as *Tango One* pulled himself up onto to his knees and brought the AK47 to bear on the prone figure of Kamenev, Keeble knew that wasn't going to happen as Chapman whipped his pistol out from behind the co-pilot's seat and sent two hollow point rounds into *Tango One's* left eye where, unlike the sniper round, they rattled round in his skull, turning his brain to blancmange.

With both terrorists no longer a threat, Chapman relayed, 'Clear,' over the radio as he stepped forward and kicked the weapons to one side. Expecting a reaction from Kamenev as he hauled him to his feet, he was surprised at the calm demeanour of the hostage.

'Are you okay?' Chapman asked, wondering if shock was kicking in.

'Yes, I am fine,' replied Kamenev, brushing off the front of his jacket as if he'd simply had a fall in the street.

Chapman shook his head as his earpiece chirped again.

'Good work, Chappers,' said Keeble, as the rest of the team appeared on the roof along with a group of CTSFOs. 'Hand over the hostage to the Met ASAP and get the boys back to Albany Barracks. Something else has come up!'

CHAPTER 34

Col. Truman arranged for everything to be ready on my arrival, so within twenty minutes of entering the gates, I was airborne, weaponised, suited and booted and on my way to the Brecon Beacons where, according to an update from DS Steve Hughes, the boys were on the final leg of the Fan Dance.

Another Dauphin 2 had been shipped in from RAF Credenhill specifically for this operation. Fitted with a revolutionary, near silent, rotor adapted from the Sikorsky RAH-66 Comanche helicopter, the need to remain undetected on our approach to the ultimate destination was going to be essential. For now though, as we descended onto a small crescent of land in front of the Storey Arms, it was clear to me that the overlap with events in London was no coincidence and with Sir Henry having briefed Major General Walkerdine on the events at Great Tew, I figured it wouldn't be long before Jim and his crew would be gearing up for a quick turnaround.

Under the watchful eyes of a group of hikers, Marty and the three members of 'E' Squadron quickly changed from civvies into black nomex fatigues, body armour, ballistic helmets and having checked their weapons, entered the cabin of the D2 as the heavens finally did what they'd been threatening to do all day and sent hikers skittling for cover.

With space for up to twelve passengers there was plenty of room to stretch out as the pilot warned us we were ready for take-off and with a chuckle, a rough ride.

'Might want to keep the barf bags handy, gentlemen.'

A moment later the twin turboshaft engines came to life and the four-bladed rotor began to turn. With the ceiling less than a thousand feet, the pilot pulled up on the collective and the D2 lifted off. A little uneven at first as the wind buffeted the chopper, the pilot made a tight turn, pushed the cyclic forward and nose down we were on our way.

On the outskirts of Southampton, Watch Manager, Tim Heptonstall, was coming to the end of his final ever shift at ATC Swanwick. Stood central to the open plan room of thirty plus, geographically aligned, 'Bananas,' the euphemism for the control desks on which radar tubes sat, he looked around with nostalgia at his team of men and women responsible for directing flights around the UK.

One of two air traffic control centres, the other at Prestwick in Ayrshire, Swanwick, in addition to catering for the complexity of air travel over London, also covers an additional two hundred thousand miles of airspace across England and Wales. Although used to the comings and goings of high profile visitors to the UK, the arrival of a succession of a US President always generated a combination of excitement and nerves for him.

Yesterday, the President's motorcade and Marine One arrived in the belly of the giant Boeing C-17 Globemaster at RAF Northolt and this afternoon, the man himself and his guest, the Canadian Prime Minister, in Air Force One at Stanstead. To the left of his own bank of tubes was a television, permanently tuned to Sky News, from which he'd watched the two leaders press the flesh with the waiting dignitaries then make their way across the tarmac to the Sikorsky VH-3C Sea King for the short hope south to Winfield House, the US Ambassador's residence on the fringe of Regents Park.

Nice way to travel thought Heptonstall as, having dropped off its passengers, he monitored Marine One's progress back to RAF Northolt, where it would remain until the conclusion of the Summit. Not that he'd be around for the return leg he thought, as he sat back to relax and enjoy the last few hours of his time in the hot seat. Taking a sip of tea from his 'Goofy' mug, a present from his daughter, Katie, and fellow survivor of his thirty years in the job, his moment of relaxation was about to be disrupted as one of the uniformed RAF controllers from the military desk approached.

Ever present to prevent potential conflict between civilian and military flights, the officer said, 'Got a call for you on line one, Tim.'

With a thumbs up, Heptonstall picked up and heard the familiar, yet unusually clipped, voice of Col. Phil Truman.

'We've got a Cat A flight heading south west from the Brecon Beacons towards the Scilly Isles, Tim, estimated altitude 18,000 feet.'

This wasn't the first time Heptonstall had dealt with Special Forces, but it was the first for this flight path and the first not to have received advanced warning as part of what he would normally have assumed was an exercise.

'Got it on the screen, Phil,' he replied, looking at the central tube in front of him.

'Needless to say, Tim, I need all civilian and military air traffic to be kept clear.

'Got it,' he replied.

Normally one for some light banter, this was the first time he'd received a call quite like this from the Colonel, so, as the line went dead, he looked up to the bomb proof ceiling from where an eight inch figurine of a golden Angel dangled from a length of fishing line. *If all else fails, at least we've got the Angel to watch over us* was the motto, something that Heptonstall hoped wouldn't be needed come the end of his final day.

Thirty five miles south west of Penzance in Cornwall, our destination was the Eastern Isles, a rocky outcrop of small islands two miles north of the Isles of Scilly. The distance from Hereford was 215 miles, so well within the parameters of the D2 which, at its current cruising speed of 150 knots, had a comfortable range of 514 miles or 447 nautical miles. With everyone listening in via headphones, I brought Marty and the team up to speed on the events in London, then moved on to my conversation with George Thompson.

It turns out that while Cornwall has been known for tin mining since the mid-1800s, lithium rich, geothermal fluids have led to significant areas of the County being underlain by large bodies of lithium rich granite, access to which can be gained via extraction boreholes supported by a relatively small number of processing plants on the surface. 'Very Eco-friendly,' as George put it yet. But with the vast majority of the world's lithium coming from the hard rock mines in Oz and beneath the Chilean salt flats, this still only represents about three percent of the earth's lithium resources.

That was until a subterranean aquifer was discovered which extends south west out into the Atlantic, to the Eastern Isles. Kept under wraps for fear of environmental activists learning of tests being undertaken to determine the viability of accessing and processing what was estimated as vast reserves of raw materials, the discovery was to have been announced by Professor Bird at the forthcoming World Energy Summit.

Apparently, the importance of this find couldn't be overestimated. For years now, scientists have been looking for ways to get round what George referred to as the fluctuating output of renewable energy sources produced by the wind, tides, solar and so on. 'After all,' he'd said, 'it's all well and good producing huge amounts of energy to feed the national grid, but without the ability to store that energy for when it's not windy or sunny, then we continue to be reliant on the likes of Russia for gas to heat our homes and the Middle East for oil to run our vehicles.'

As to why this this would lead to the professor's murder? George went on to explain that in addition to the discovery of the aquifer, a unique variant of the rare earth metal, Gallium, had been found at the same location. It turns out that when this particular REM is combined with lithium, it exponentially increases its storage capacity and longevity. In lay terms, the difference between an electric car travelling three thousand miles on one charge as opposed to three hundred and all wrapped up in a lithium battery no bigger than a Triple A.

No longer would the UK have to go cap in hand to China who currently hold the rights to eighty five percent of the World's REMs. Indeed, the quantities involved were such that it was impossible to estimate the number of years the supplies would last. Some experts believed it to be in the hundreds, others in the thousands, but what was certain was that every ounce of renewable energy produced by UK wind and solar farms, along with hydroelectric power stations could now be stored, transported efficiently and fully complement the LNG production of its soon to be partners in the US and Canada.

And he wasn't finished there. Not only would our road, rail and aviation industries benefit in terms of carbon zero emissions, this energy source could also feed a proposed super grid between the UK and Europe which would, by all estimates, eclipse Russia's Nord Stream pipeline into Germany and decimate Gazprom's oil and gas distribution across the continent, while at the same time having a similar impact on the need for oil from the Middle East.

George had also been careful to point out that this discovery also represents the key component of the UK's contribution towards the alliance with the US and Canada, without which, the Treaty, due to be signed by all three world leaders after the Summit tomorrow would undoubtedly be compromised.

So finally and having confirmed the six million dollar question that the location of the aquifer was among papers stored in Professor Bird's safe at home, I'd left Oxford with thoughts of cobalt radiation and contamination off the back of a dirty bomb rattling around my brain.

As the enormity of my conversation with George descended on the cabin, I retrieved a tablet from my rucksack and placed it on my lap so all could see and opened comms with Charlie in London. Despite the cloud cover, the satellite, zipping along at 17,000 mph and 435 miles above our heads, fast enough to get you from London to Paris in under a minute, provided live feed, crystal clear imagery of the rain sodden Scilly Isles.

Expanding the screen, I zoomed in on Great Auk, one of the islands to the north of St Martin's. At sea level and 3.5 square kilometres, the island's profile resembled more that of a sleeping Dromedary camel than the flightless bird which became extinct in the mid-19th century. Its single hump, some thirty four metres above sea level towered over the outstretched neck where several portacabins could be seen clustered together maybe forty or fifty metres to the north of a rectangular platform on which sat a deserted drilling rig. That some of the portacabins would be used as dormitories and others for recreation purposes, this explained the distance from what would be a lot of noise when the rig was in operation. At the camel's head, a narrow inlet opened out to a cove and small docking area from which supplies could be ferried to and from the island. In the mouth of the cove, a gin palace type motor boat was at anchor.

'Okay, Charlie,' I said, 'what have you got for us?'

Before he could respond, Sir Henry came on the line and confirmed 'B' Squadron were redeploying from London to the island.

'What's their ETA?'

'Approximately two hours behind you,' he replied, which for now at least, made it our show as the D2 continued on its parabolic arc, west south west, towards Great Auk.

Handing back to Charlie, he remotely took control of the imagery on the screen and moved the cursor to a small beach on the backside of the camel's hump.

'Distance from the LZ to the rig is two point four kilometres,' he said.

The cursor moved again, this time to the top of the hump and two rocky mounds.

'These large cairns should provide you with cover and

oversight of the facility.'

Tony Barber nodded at this observation.

'Have you been able to make contact with the facility, Charlie?' I asked.

'No, comms are down.'

That wasn't good, but half expected. 'We have we got on the boat?'

Panning right towards the cove, Charlie zoomed in on the bow of the cruiser and the name *Sunset Cruisers*. 'Chartered from Padstow Marina by two men and a woman. According to Marina security they'd asked for maps of the coast, the idea being to take a trip round the peninsular to its reciprocal Marina at St Mawes. Descriptions indicate that one of the two men could be the scientist.'

'Okay, Charlie, good job,' I responded. 'Can you dial back the footage to when the boat arrived at the island?'

The screen instantly split in two, the live feed remaining on the left of the screen while the image of now bustling activity around the rig appeared on the right.

Overcast, but with no sign of the rain to come, half a dozen rig workers were operating the giant drill on the platform monitored by, if white coats and clipboards are anything to go by, a couple of scientists. In contrast to this activity, there was very little going on round the portacabins. Presumably much of the technical work would be going on inside. Charlie again panned right towards the cover where two men in uniform appeared from a hut alongside the dock as the cruiser entered the cove.

'What sort of security do they have on the island, Charlie?'

I could hear keys being tapped as he did whatever he did to access the information.

'Private only, by the looks of it, Alex,' he responded a few moments later, as a woman edged her way along the gunwale to the front of the boat and dropped the anchor.

Given the importance of this discovery, it beggared belief didn't have a military presence on the island, but as always in such situations, hindsight really is a wonderful thing. Parking that thought for the time being, all eyes focused on the screen as a man, not the scientist and the woman, both in yellow smocks, pushed off from the back of the cruiser in a dingy. Tipping an outboard into the water, a puff of smoke indicated it had started first time.

'Any ID on these two, Charlie?' I asked, as the dingy puttered towards the dock.

'Nothing on facial recognition,' he replied, 'but I think it's fair to say they're not tourists.'

'The poor fuckers didn't stand a chance,' muttered Marty, as they tied up the dingy and stepped onto the dock. Approaching the security guards, Marty's prediction came true almost immediately as the smocks were swept to one side and the guards were mown down.

'Suppressed MP7s by the looks of it,' said Tony, his grip tightening on the handle of a toughened transit case used for transporting his snipers rifle.

Taking a moment to tip the guards over the side of the dock, they split up, the man turning left towards the rig platform, the woman straight ahead towards the portacabins.

Oblivious to what had just taken place only a few hundred metres away, the rig workers and scientists met the same fate after which they were dumped unceremoniously into the borehole.

Looking back to the real time footage on the left hand side of the screen, the couple could be seen returning to the dock from where they cast off and returned to the cruiser where a second male, evidently the scientist from the detention centre, appeared from the cabin holding a rucksack, about half the size of a Bergen. This gave me pause for thought as this was nothing like as large as the packing case taken from the container at the Strensham Service Station.

'Any thoughts on the size of the package, Charlie?'

'Probably travelled in a lead lined container,' he suggested.

That made sense... I guess.

'Okay, thanks, Charlie, keep us updated with anything new,' and with that, I signed off as the pilot's succinct warning came over the headphones, 'Five minutes, gentlemen.'

Having extended the arc to take us further west, a better angle from which to approach the island undetected, we dropped down from our cruising altitude and broke through the cloud cover into well... how can I put it. Shit weather. Driving rain again buffeted the chopper as we turned east and skimmed low over the Atlantic, the tops of white horses tickling the under belly of the D2 as through the gloom, the island came into view.

Approaching at about 30mph, dusk had come early due to the bleak weather conditions. Slowing rapidly as we reached the beach, the D2 went nose up, flared and dropped gently onto the rough sand. With waterproofs providing some protection from the weather, we decamped from the chopper and with a thumbs up to the pilot who would wait on our call for a pick up, we set off towards a goats path that wound its way to the top of the camel's hump and our rendezvous point between the two cairns.

CHAPTER 35

By the time we reached the summit, the rain had eased off to a heavy drizzle. Small mercies, I thought as I looked round. Swept clear of all but the hardiest vegetation, the sparse landscape of the island offered little protection from the elements and by little I really mean, none. That the cairns, some fifty feet apart, had withstood the attention of the Atlantic for however many centuries was testament to the makers of these ancient burial mounds. Not that they'd entirely escaped the ministrations of the elements. Scattered randomly across the hump, rocks from which the structures were originally built provided a haphazard array of cover from which Tony could set up unseen from below.

Discarding his waterproofs in favour of a ghillie suit, a

complex garment of rags designed to blend the wearer into the environment, Tony opened the transit case, assembled the snipers rifle then crawled forward to the ridge that overlooked the facility. Laying out a rubber mat on the rough ground, he set up the rifle on its bipod, flipped up the telescopic sight and adjusted the laser rangefinder.

'Two hundred and forty metres to the portacabins… three hundred to the rig,' he said, then panned left and right. 'All clear,' he announced a moment later.

On cue, I crawled forward to the ridge and looked down onto the rig's platform. Floodlights at each corner illuminated the giant drill and darkened borehole into which it descended. Stood proud and tall, yet abandoned and silent at the centre, it was the overspill from the beams of light that caught my attention. Extending to maybe fifteen or twenty metres beyond each of the four corners of the rig, the areas between the shafts of light created triangular pockets of darkness that would, I hoped, help us get close to the platform unseen. Looking across to the portacabins and despite the early onset of darkness, no lights shone from the windows.

Having seen enough, I edged back from the ridge and stood for a final weapons and radio check.

'Hold on,' whispered Tony. 'I have two male subjects approaching the rig from the nearest portacabin.'

'Any sign of the woman?' I asked.

'Negative,' he replied. 'The scientist has the rucksack.'

'Weapons?'

'MP7 still with the Russian. Can't see a sidearm, but like as not he'll have one. Nothing on the scientist.'

That figured. 'Any sign of movement on the boat?'

'Negative.'

After a final radio check, the digitally encrypted signal coming through loud and clear on the headsets attached to our ballistic helmets, I said, 'Okay, gents. Marty, you and Mark take the portacabins and Mike your with me. Eyes open for the female. Time to move.'

From behind the farthest of the two cairns, Svetlana Ivanov, crouched low as she watched the two groups of men move off in opposite directions. She'd chosen the spot for the same reason as the men in black. That she'd arrived too late to prevent them reaching the summit was unfortunate, but not insurmountable as she crept silently from her hiding place.

We arrived at the base of the hump on the far side of the rig platform from where I was able to confirm the overspill from the floodlights would give us the cover we needed to close in virtually unseen. With Marty and Mark on point at the portacabins, I tapped Mike on the shoulder and we slowly moved forward. The ground underfoot was like the rest of the island. A thin layer of grass covering a solid base meant the two men on the rig platform were none the wiser as we silently reached the edge of the overspill, each choosing a separate triangular pocket of darkness from which to make our approach.

Give or take the length of a cricket pitch, twenty odd yards in old money, the base of the rig was relatively low to the ground which meant I could see the scientist was kneeling down while the Russian stood over him, the MP7 hanging loosely from a sling on his shoulder.

Taking advantage of the wind whistling around the platform's stanchions, I checked in with Marty and Mark. 'Any sign of the woman?'

'Negative,' replied Marty. 'Bodies, but no sign of the woman.'

'Likewise,' responded Mark.

'Tony?'

'Negative,' came his immediate reply.

'Movement on the boat?'

Looking towards the summit, I pictured Tony switching his scope to night vision and traversing his rifle towards the cove. Not that I or anyone at ground level would be able to see this movement, but as one second bled inexorably into another, into another, into another, the silence was eventually broken as the sound of a text alert could be heard pinging out from the rig.

Not trusting the weather to entirely cover her approach, Svetlana Ivanov had tested each rocky footfall, one careful step at a time, as she'd worked her way slowly and carefully across the divide. Unaware of her approach, Barber was about to respond negatively to signs of movement on the boat when the suppressed MP7 spat out its lethal contents. Severing the spine at the base of his neck, the precision of the trajectory had two key purposes. The first to avoid any body armour and the second to prevent any accidental movement of the trigger finger.

Moving forward, Ivanov had dragged the body away from the ridge by its ankles, removed the ghillie suit and examined the rifle before slipping the suit over her head and assuming the sniper's position. Preferring the 7.62x52mmR Dragunov to the Accuracy International AX50 this was still an animal she could work with as she'd sighted on her first target then reached for her mobile.

*

Retrieving a mobile from his trouser pocket, the Russian looked down then instantly dropped out of sight as the ground to my left exploded. Only a few short metres away, Mike lay motionless, his helmet powerless against the overwhelming power and velocity of Tony's rifle. That I now knew the woman's location would mean nothing, unless I could make the most of the next four seconds, the time it would take for her to reload the bolt action rifle.

Hearing the alert, Farrow looked away from the portacabin window and across to the rig platform as the Russian hit the deck. With Scanes checking the portacabins nearest the dock, he intuitively looked towards the ridge as the muzzle flash illuminated the darkness, followed almost instantly by the crack of the rifle. His immediate thought was that Barber had been forced to take a shot before the strike command, but as he went to check in, his earpiece buzzed, 'Marty! The ridge!' as a shadowy figure leapt up from beyond the rig and charged forward, zig zagging in and out of the light towards the platform.

Although the lack of familiarity with the AX50 did nothing to affect the first round, the time it took to reload the bolt action rifle bought Ivanov's second target an extra few seconds.

'*Blyad*' (fuck), she growled as the figure disappeared under the lee of the platform.

Panning left away from the rig, Ivanov sought alternative targets, adjusting the night vision on the scope to pick out a luminous green figure alongside one of the portacabins. Down on one knee and as the weapon in the figure's hands moved up towards the ridge, Ivanov's finger tightened on the trigger and Newton's theory of relativity kicked in.

With every action having an equal and opposite reaction, the burst of adrenalin caused by her anger at missing the second target, travelled down from the pectoralis muscle in Ivanov's armpit, through the subclavian, axillary and brachial arteries before diverting at the elbow and pulsing through the radial and ulnar arteries. The deviation caused by the hormone rush was only slight, but sufficient to divert the flight of the .300 round by a fraction of a degree and save Scanes life as it ripped through his shoulder instead of his head.

Watching the figure fly backwards into the wall of the portacabin was the last thing Ivanov saw as thirty rounds from Farrow's c8 carbine traced its way up through the darkness, tore into the ridge, disintegrated the AX50 and sent multiple shards of metal and rock through Ivanov's unprotected skull.

*

Trusting the carbine to have done it's work, I skidded to a halt at the base of the platform and reached for the metal rungs of a ladder that would take me up top.

Zhukov looked up as a figure in black, holding an assault rifle, appeared on the platform. With the scientist's work, Zhukov knew he had time for just one of two choices. To go for a weapon or fling the rucksack towards the borehole. Knowing failure to complete the mission would ultimately lead to his death, he chose the latter as three rounds drilled into his chest.

Hitting the Russian centre mass, I watched as he was thrown backwards, the trajectory of the rucksack altered as it released from his hand and looped in the air. Spinning right as it dropped short and bounced off the deck, I threw myself forward and reached for the trailing straps as the rucksack slid beneath the guardrail protecting the borehole. And I would have made it were it not for my body armour catching on the grilled platform and pulling me up short as bloody thing tipped over the edge and disappeared from view.

CHAPTER 36

While 'B' squadron's fast turn-around from Albany Barracks to Farnborough International Airport was not unusual, the threat of a possible nuclear device on UK soil certainly was. It also accounted for the sombre mood in the cabin of the Lockheed Martin C130 Hercules as each man in their own way prepared silently for the mission ahead. They were after all professionals who knew there was no point in wasting energy worrying about something for which they had no control. Not yet at least. So as Major Keeble unbuckled his safety harness in the knowledge this would probably be his last operation, he looked round into the eyes of each and every member of his team, a deep sense of pride coursing through his body as the tailgate lowered slowly in readiness for the jump.

*

Getting to my knees, I thumped my fist on the platform and looked up to see the scientist staring at me. Expecting the worst, I got to my feet and walked over to the borehole. Disconsolate would be a good word, pissed was better, as I looked down into what I expected to be a gaping hole. But it wasn't. Maybe ten or fifteen feet down, an inspection platform ran round the inner circumference of the borehole and there, alongside the bodies of the rig workers and scientists was the rucksack.

Turning back to the cowering figure of the scientist, I pointed a finger at him, *'zalyshaysya tam, de ty ye'* (stay right where you are) and with that, looked round for a ladder that would get me down to the platform without breaking a leg. There it was on the far side, hidden from view by the drill. So with another backward glance at the scientist who in fairness was rooted to the spot, I trotted round the perimeter and slid down the ladder onto the platform.

Without knowing the evolving situation below, the HALO (High Altitude Low Opening) drop was considered the best option for a silent approach to the island. So, at thirty thousand feet, each man equipped with oxygen, shuffled forward towards the tailgate of the Hercules and without hesitation dove out and into the abyss. Leading from the front Keeble quickly reached terminal velocity, the point at which air resistance force and weight are equal and speed becomes constant. Two minutes later, they broke through the cloud cover at six thousand feet where improving weather conditions allowed them to continue in freefall for a further three thousand feet before deploying their chutes and forming up on a glide ratio of 2.5:1 on their approach to the island.

Making my way round the inner circumference of the borehole, I stepped between the bodies of the rig workers and scientists, a deep sense of sadness and regret overwhelming me that we'd been unable to get to them in time and prevent this tragedy. Shaking my head, I knew there was nothing I could do for them now and moved on towards the object that would ultimately determine all our fates.

Lights from the rig platform were clearly visible in the otherwise pitch black surroundings and with the rest of his team stacked in formation above, Keeble adjusted the toggles on his chute and steered a path towards the drop zone.

With the rucksack on one shoulder and carbine slung on the other, I climbed up the inspection ladder and made my way back around the borehole...

What the fuck!

Unaware of my presence, the hunched figure of the Russian was on his feet, just, and staring intently at the back of the still cowering scientist. That the answer to my silent expletive was my stupidity at not having checked for body armour was plain to see as he limped forward, a bloodied left arm clutched tightly to his chest as his right brought the MP7 to bear on Kyryukhin's exposed back.

At two hundred feet, Keeble watched the scene below unfold. Unable to reach for a weapon while in descent, he again adjusted the toggles, this time directing the ram-air canopy away from the drop zone and towards the platform.

Slowly, carefully, silently I placed the rucksack on the platform and reached for the Glock on my utility belt. Why was the Russian so focussed on Kyryukhin? Surely his job was done? Perhaps he might be able to diffuse the device? I certainly hoped so, but so far as the Russian was concerned it now lay at the bottom of the borehole, so why was he still so interested in him? Like so many things about this wretched business, it didn't make sense – or did it!

*

Optimal weather conditions would have made landing on the platform relatively straightforward, but as Keeble flared his chute, a gust of wind blew him sideways, threatening to wrap him around one of the floodlight gantries.

It must have been the Russian's peripheral vision that picked up my movement. Turning his head towards me for a moment he grimaced then smiled as I flipped the retaining clip that held the Glock in place. He must have realised I had no time to release my weapon as he shook his head. A movement that caused him to shudder then turn his attention back to Kyryukhin. Using the sling on his shoulder to steady the MP7, he slipped his finger from the trigger guard onto the trigger.

Missing the gantry by a fraction, at least that's what it felt like to Keeble, he regained control of the chute, tugged once more on the toggles and despite knowing it was going to hurt, let go of the toggles, pulled down on the quick release shoulder buckles on his harness and freed the canopy.

Like an avenging Angel, a shadow flashed across the floodlight beam and slammed the Russian. Sending both men flying, the MP7 spilled from his already tenuous grasp and skidded out of reach across the platform. Lying motionless for an instant, he stirred then rolled to one side and reached for a pistol strapped to his belt.

'*Ne delay etogo!* (Don't do it!),' I shouted, hoping the decision he was about to make was one that would provide the answers to my questions.

CHAPTER 37

It didn't and as further shadows came to earth around the rig, I turned away from the body of the Russian, two hollow point rounds leaving just the scientist to unravel the mystery. Laying down my weapons on the platform, now wasn't the time for any confusion over who was friend or foe, I looked across to Jim who was gingerly, getting to his feet.

'That was close,' he said as he limped over and looked down at the Russian.

'Thanks to you,' I said gratefully.

'Is that what I think it is?' he asked, looking at the rucksack.

'Where about to find out,' I replied.

'Perimeter secure, Sir,' said one of the troopers as he climbed up onto the platform.

'Casualties?' asked Jim.

'Mike Allen,' I replied quietly.

'And Scanes,' said the trooper. 'Shoulder's fucked. Won't be doing press ups anytime soon, but the SBS guy is looking after him.'

At least that was some good news, I thought, as I turned to the trooper, 'You'll need to check the ridge,' the tone of my voice reflecting the likelihood of what would be found.

'Get some people up there,' said Jim.

'Roger that,' replied the trooper as I retrieved my weapons, picked up the rucksack by its straps and indicated for Jim to follow me over to the scientist who was sitting back on his haunches, staring at the dead Russian.

'Yak vas zvaty?' (What is your name?)

'Oleksandr Kyryukhin,' he replied, quietly.

That was a start. I was half expecting him to say Mikola Virastyuk as I looked across at the Russian and said, *'Zaraz vin ne mozhe nashkodyty tobi.'* (He can't hurt you now).

'*On ne mozhet, no drugiye mogut*' (He can't, but others can), he replied.

'*Tvoya rodyna?*' (Your family?).

He nodded.

'*Vasha rodyna v bezpetsi, Oleksandr*' (Your family is safe, Oleksandr).

He raised his head, a momentary flicker of hope in his eyes, replaced instead, a second later, by a shake of the head, '*Ni, tse nemozhlyvo,*' (No, that is not possible).

'*Vashu druzhynu svaty Yuliya, a dvoye ditey – Yaroslava ta Bohdan,*' (Your wife's name is Yuliya and your two children are Yaroslava and Bohdan), I responded, eager to put his fears to rest and get on with the job to hand.

'How… how do you know that?' he blurted.

Previous background checks on Kyryukhin showed he spoke English. Hardly surprising really given his line of work, but it was important for him to offer this information freely, trust being vital considering what I hoped was about to take place.

'So you speak English?' I smiled.

'Yes, yes, but you say my wife is safe?'

'Yes and your children.'

'But how?'

I quickly explained how we'd been able to establish his identity and our suspicion that his family may have been used as a means to make him cooperate with the Russians.

'But how can I trust you?' he responded sceptically.

I reached for my satellite phone and made the call.

Answered instantly, I listened for a moment then said, *'Dobra, dyakuyu. Bud laska, khvylynochku,'* (Okay, thank you. One moment please) and passed the phone to Kyryukhin.

The exchange was quick and as Kyryukhin handed back the mobile tears flowed freely down his cheeks. 'Please,' he said and reached out for me to hand him the rucksack.

Placing it on the platform, Kyryukhin loosened the ties around the top and slid the sides down to reveal an aluminium case about the size of a standard airline carry on. Not that I had any idea what a nuclear device looked like, I did know a timer when I saw one as he opened the lid to reveal a digital display registering 43:59... 43:58... 43:57... as it counted down relentlessly towards zero.

Alongside the timer and above what looked like the casing for a small artillery shell embedded in foam, plus what you might expect in terms of wires and other items no doubt linked to a triggering device, was a keypad, not dissimilar to those you'd expect to find on a tablet. Wasting no more time, Kyryukhin leant forward and tapped out a sequence of letters and numbers on the pad, pressed enter and again sat back on his haunches. The digital timer continued for a few more seconds then stopped at 43:26.

'It's done,' he said, his initial joy at knowing his family were safe, replaced by a vision of sadness.

'What's wrong?' I demanded.

'There is another,' he replied.

'Where?'

'I don't know.'

I took a deep breath… 'Okay, what *do* you know?'

He looked at the dead Russian then up towards the ridge. 'They took me to a house where a man, an Arab, came with two devices. This one,' he pointed to the suitcase, 'and another I had to prime ready for the timer to be activated.'

'Where was the house?' I asked as Jim was already turning away to radio in the D2 on the far side of the island.

'I don't know,' he replied. 'In the countryside, near to where we got the boat.'

'Is it still there?'

'No, the Arab took it with him?'

'Oleksandr. I need you to think. Is there anything you saw or overheard which might help us find out where he was going or where the second device was to be detonated.'

He paused for a moment, his eyes tight shut, lids flickering as if trawling back through the archives of his mind. 'He talked of today being the day of reckoning and by the grace of Allah the infidels would pay – or something like that. I'm sorry.'

'Today or the day he left the house?'

'No, today,' he insisted.

Again, this wasn't making sense for a whole host of reasons. 'Why were you needed here and not wherever the other device is to be activated?'

'This one is more complex. It has a cobalt casing which requires greater finesse during the activation phase.'

'So this is a dirty bomb designed to contaminate the reservoir?'

'And the aquifer which leads to the mainland, yes.'

'Are both devices the same?'

'No. The other is only thermo nuclear,' he said, as if 'only' made it any the less lethal.

'And the yields?'

'They are the same. One kiloton?'

Remembering Charlie's briefing, I said, 'Which makes the blast radius half a kilometre.'

'Approximately, yes.'

CHAPTER 38

In the time it took for the satellite phone to connect, less than a minute, thoughts continued to race through my mind.

Rarely is a crime committed where motive is not involved and this situation was no exception.

If the device in front of us had detonated, the alliance which threatened the economy of Russia and the Middle East would be over. Simply put, we'd have no chips to play in the game, leaving the US and Canada to ply their trade across the World without the support of the UK. That China were also in the mix due to the discovery of the REM 'Gallium' was also a factor for consideration. But, if this device was discovered or failed to detonate for whatever reason, how else could the alliance be prevented?

There had to be a contingency plan, hence the need for a second device. But where could it be planted to have the desired effect of not only achieving this aim, but also to deflect blame away from those responsible?

The World Energy Summit, when all three leaders would be present was the obvious choice, but we'd already discounted that due to so many other key players being present. At the end of the day, the destabilising effects of taking so many leaders out of the game out in one hit would be devastating and could easily backfire. So, no that couldn't be the strategy. On top of that, if this device had detonated as planned then the US President and Canadian Prime Minister could have been whisked away on Marine One to Stanstead and from there, back across the pond on Air Force One.

So that left just the one conclusion.

The second device had to detonate at the exactly the same time as the first which, according to my watch, was in thirty two minutes.

And two questions.

Where was it?

How could we find it in time?

Frankie picked up immediately, 'How's it going?'

'Where is he?'

No doubt sensing the urgency in my voice she dispensed with any pleasantries, 'Hang on a sec…'

I could hear radio chatter in the background as she spoke to the lead surveillance officer. A moment later she came back on the line.

'According to his schedule he's due to be in meetings all afternoon.'

'Please check with his PA, Frankie.'

Another few precious minutes ticked by until, 'He's gone.'

'What do you mean he's gone.'

'He was down to attend a Home Affairs Select Committee meeting this afternoon, but failed to show.'

'GPS on his phone?'

Although we'd been able to get clearance from the Surveillance Commissioner to bug Murad's office and cover the GPS on his phone, elsewhere in the House was off limits.

'Showing that it's still in his office.'

'Get onto ANPR, Frankie, and see if we can pick up his car.'

'No point,' she replied. 'It's still in the car park.'

'And nothing from the watchers outside?'

'No nothing. What's going on, Alex?'

'Sorry, Frankie, no time,' I said, looking back at Oleksandr who was on his knees, hands clasped in prayer.

CHAPTER 39

Named after the eponymous W.G. Grace, 'The Grace Gates,' had been welcoming fans to Lords since 1923 and today had been no exception as thirty thousand noisy fans in a vast array of colours, fancy dress and other paraphernalia packed the ground for England's second day/night match of the ODI series against Pakistan.

With the visitors having chosen to bat first and setting a respectable total of 325 for 7, England were making steady progress at 195 for 3 after thirty eight overs. At the end of the next, they'd progressed to 201 off the back of a four and a couple of quick singles when the dulcet tones of David 'Bumble' Lloyd could be heard over a thousand and one earpieces, prompting the crowd to roar in approval as the image of Kumar Sangakkara, Sri Lankan cricketing legend and newly elected President of the MCC appeared on big screen. Sipping from a glass of champagne, he looked out from the members pavilion and with a huge smile, waved in response then turned to the gentleman sat next to him.

'It's a shame the Minister was unable to stay for the second innings,' said Sangakkara. 'This is looking like it could go down to the wire.'

'Yes indeed,' replied the Chairman. 'Called away on Government business, I understand.'

The penny had dropped almost as soon as I hung up on Frankie and saw Oleksandr praying.

"By the grace of Allah..."

Freudian slip or simply a coincidence, it was enough to trigger memories of Murad's attendance at the Rosebowl, chief of which being the list of up and coming ODIs on the TV screen in the suite.

To the west of Regents Park and according to map tools, the home of English cricket lay within a half kilometre of Winfield House, the US Ambassador's residence and current location of the US President and Canadian Prime Minister. A further call, this time to Sir Henry, took a few more precious minutes off the clock, but confirmed, not only was Murad on the VIP guest list for the second ODI, according the Chairman, a personal friend of Sir Henry's, he'd left the ground after the first innings on some form of Government business.

As to where he might have planted the device, I was sure it wouldn't be at the ground. After all, why would a Minister of State turn up at social event carrying a piece of luggage? There was always the chance he'd simply rented a property or left the device in a car, but his was still at Westminster. Besides, this seemed unlikely given the plethora of CCTV in the area that would be examined in any post incident investigation. So if he wanted to retain anonymity and continue in his role and who knows go even further up the food chain to create more havoc, then these two options were unlikely. Not impossible, but unlikely and with time disappearing fast, unlikely was all I had left as I again reached for the Satellite phone.

With Sir Henry cracking on with the evacuation of the US President and Canadian PM from Winfield House, the first call confirmed my suspicion as to the probable location of the device and the second left me sick to my stomach.

CHAPTER 40

TWENTY MINUTES AND COUNTING

A mottled green Land Rover raced out of the gates to Albany Barracks and skidded onto Prince Albert Road as the 'Beast' pulled up in front of Winfield House. At the same instant and twelve miles north west of the US Ambassador's Residence, 'Marine One' was scrambled from RAF Northolt.

Weighing in at over twenty thousand pounds, not even the hermetically sealed, armoured 'Beast' with run flat tyres and five inch thick bullet-proof windows could withstand the force of a one kiloton blast. So with the Security Service literally dragging both world leaders out of the Residence and dumping them in the back of the limousine, nothing was going to get in their way as the convoy of black Cadillac SUVs burst through the gates to Winfield House. Covering the limousine's top speed of 60 mph and with sirens blaring, the cavalcade raced north through St John's Wood and beyond Swiss Cottage by which time, much to the amazement of late evening shoppers, Marine One was landing in the unfamiliar surroundings of the Brent Cross shopping centre car park.

Tongue lolling out the side of his mouth like a slice of ham and tail beating a steady rhythm on the back seat of the Land Rover, Scrumpy was oblivious to the urgency of the situation as he took in the wonderful smells of London Zoo floating across from Regents Park. Not that the same could be said for Jill Dennison who, riding shotgun, had feet jammed in the footwell of the Land Rover and fingernails dug deep into the sides of her seat.

'Yes, alright! There's no need to make a fuss!' shouted Capt. Vingoe above the noise of the six cylinder engine as she cut in front of a classic Ford Capri and bounced off the kerb.

Slowing slightly for a set of traffic lights at the Avenue Road crossroads, she shot across the junction, raced ahead for a quarter mile, took the final roundabout on two wheels before finally screeching to a halt in front of the hotel entrance.

'Had a boyfriend once who had one of those,' said Vingoe as she stepped down onto the pavement.

'One of what?' asked Dennison as she let Scrumpy out of

the back.

'A Capri. Drove it into a ditch – not sure he ever forgave me!'

TEN MINUTES AND COUNTING

Whether it was the dramatic arrival, the uniform or more likely the Sig Sauer strapped to Capt. Vingoe's hip, there was no objection from the doorman as two women and a dog ran passed him through a pair of ornate doors and into the hotel's gleaming lobby of the hotel. Resplendent in white marble, the art deco surroundings reminded Dennison of a bygone era where the likes of Agatha Christie's fictional hero, Hercule Poirot, might otherwise have taken afternoon tea.

'Can I help you?' asked a startled receptionist as she looked up from her computer. 'Oh, I'm sorry, but no dogs are…'

'It's okay, Lesley, they're with me,' said a voice from the far side of the lobby as a smartly dressed man in a navy blue suit strode across the marble floor. The name on his lapel badge read, Dave Hulbert, Head of Security. Mid to late fifties, receding hairline, goatie with flecks of grey and hazel eyes, he had the bearing so common to those of a services background.

'This way please, ladies,' he said calmly as he gestured for the women to follow him across to a bank of three elevators.

'Come on Scrump's, it's okay,' said Dennison stopping short as he pulled back on his lead and firmly planted his backside on the marble floor. 'Scrumpy! We haven't got time for this, now come on.'

Sliding him reluctantly along the polished floor, Scrumpy eventually got the message, stood up and reluctantly followed Dennison across the lobby as Hulbert waved a card in front of a panel to the side of the central elevator.

'Must have been my driving,' said Vingoe looking down at Scrumpy as the doors opened and they stepped inside. Pressing the button for the eighth floor Hulbert said, 'Sir Henry, called,' then by way of explanation, 'he was my Detective Chief Super back in the day.'

'Did he tell you what this was about?' asked Dennison as the doors opened and Hulbert led them down the corridor towards a suite at the end of the corridor.

'He did,' he replied, as Vingoe unclipped the Sig and Dennison drew another from inside her jacket, courtesy of the Barrack's armoury.

'Thank you for not doing a runner,' said Dennison.

'Not in my DNA,' he replied, nodding at the firearms, 'but you won't be needing those. The Minister was seen leaving by the late shift doorman. Told him he was off to the cricket and wouldn't be back till late.'

'Better safe than sorry,' replied Dennison as she exchanged Scrumpy's lead for the electronic master key card and then, painfully aware of the potential for a booby trap, took a deep breath before waving the card in front of the sensor on the door and stepping into the suite.

FIVE MINUTES AND COUNTING

The suite was empty and having let Scrumpy off his lead, it quickly became clear there was nothing for him to get excited about.

He checked everything in no time. Not that there was much to check. Just the usual items you'd expect of a guest on a one night stay. Toiletries in the bathroom, change of underwear and a small black canvas holdall, but no sign of an aluminium suitcase or what might have been inside. So now, having done his job, Scrumpy was sitting down looking up at Dennison, panting expectantly.

'What's up matey?' she said looking down, her anxiety levels peaking as she checked her watch. The delay between whatever time was left from the counter on the island and now meant that although the timing wasn't precise, it was too close for comfort.

Forcing herself to focus, she sat on the edge of the bed and took a few more precious moments to try and clear her head then... 'Oh Shit!'

Calling for Scrumpy, Dennison jumped up and raced out of the suite leaving Vingoe and Hulbert in her wake. Ignoring the elevator, she took the stairs three at a time, cursing herself on each landing until they burst back out into the lobby and ran back over to the reception desk.

TWO MINUTES AND COUNTING

As the once head of Hampshire's dog section, part of Dennison's role had been to sign off on the unit's extended bomb training programme. For Scrumpy and the other Springers in the section, this saw them become Vapor Wake K9s. With up to three hundred million olfactory receptors in their noses compared to humans with only six million, their brains are devoted to analysing smells and proportionately speaking are forty times larger than that of their handlers. So when VW K9s sample the air, they pick up even the most minute heat plumes given off by explosive particles, including those found in detonators needed to trigger a bomb.

Under normal circumstances, Dennison knew she should have recognised the signs and again silently cursed herself for not having done so when they first entered the lobby. But she also knew that now wasn't the time for recriminations. Instead, she just hoped it wasn't too late as she knelt down in front of Scrumpy, ruffled his ears, unclipped his lead and said, 'Go on Boy, seek.'

Tail wagging furiously, Scrumpy spun round and flew behind the reception desk. Sweeping aside objections from the startled receptionist, Dennison followed him into a back office where, in full on search mode, he homed in on a pair of desks set back to back at the far end of the room. Skidding to a halt, Scrumpy sat down and stared at the side of a black, carry on style suitcase case protruding from between the desks.

Not aluminium was Dennison's first thought as she said, 'Good boy,' and rushed forward. *But then why would it be*, was her second as she knelt down beside Scrumpy. Her third was *let's hope it's the same inside or we're...* as the receptionist appeared followed by Hulbert and Vingoe. 'Where did this come from?' she demanded.

The receptionist hesitated until Hulbert snapped, 'Tell her what she needs to know!'

'The, the, the Minister...'

'The Minister, what!' snapped Dennison.

He, he said he was going to the cricket and left it for his Secretary to collect. I'm sorry,' she said, her cheeks flushing as she began to cry. 'I just thought, being an MP, it wouldn't be a problem.'

Why didn't he just leave it in his room, was the first thing that sprung to mind as Dennison pulled the case out from the recess between the desks and carefully lay it on the floor. Perhaps a final piece of subterfuge or was it better, no not better, more effective for the device to detonate at ground level rather than on the eight floor? She had no idea. What she did know and with a final check of her watch as she flipped open the catches on the lid, there was no chance of 11 EOD, the Explosive Ordnance Disposal, getting here on time, so whatever happened in the next few moments was down to her – good or bad.

THIRTY SECONDS AND COUNTING

Relief swept through Dennison as she lifted the lid. The inside was identical to the picture sent to her mobile from the island. It was hard to believe the innocuous looking object was capable of such devastation. But capable it was as the devil in the detail of her visit to MI6 with Charlie came to mind.

On a flipchart stand in the corner of Julie Cloke's office was the vertical outline of an object much the same as the one in front of Dennison.

'Okay, Darlings,' she said, grabbing a black marker pen to draw a circle in the neck of what looked like a small artillery shell. 'This little ball here is what they call the fission primary stage, fuelled, probably by Uranium-235, while here,' she drew a beaker

*like shape beneath the ball, 'is the fusion secondary stage that
contains the thermo nuclear element of the device, probably
deuterium and tritium given its likely origin.'*

*Changing the black marker pen for red, she continued.
'Now here's the good bit... when the fission primary stage
detonates, its temperature soars,' she coloured in the ball using the
red marker pen. 'This causes it to glow intensely with thermal x-
rays that flood the void around both stages. The radiation case that
lines the inside of the shell casing keeps the x-rays in check until
the plutonium spark plug in the base of the beaker implodes. This
causes the secondary stage,' she pointed at the beaker just to be
sure they were paying attention, 'to compress like a squashed coke
can and begin a fission chain reaction, after which... well, BOOM
really. Not that you need to worry about that darlings, as you'll be
vaporised instantly and won't feel a thing.'*

So with that thought in mind, Dennison flexed the fingers of her
right hand and with the mobile in her other hand carefully tapped
in the seven digit combination of letters and numbers that
accompanied the image from the island.

CHAPTER 41

TWO WEEKS LATER

Nobody likes loose ends, least of all when doing business with terrorists.

Praises to Allah, assurances of fidelity and commitments to a cause mean very little when fingernails are extracted, airways drowned or testicles are connected to fifty thousand volts. Indeed, the Sheik knew only too well that the architects and purveyors of such atrocities would be shown no mercy should the subsequent investigation point in their direction. That this was unlikely to happen mattered not to Prince Ali bin-Sayed as the Sheik knelt before him, his head bowed in supplication and readiness for the *Sulthan's* overtures.

As the ceremonial scimitar hovered above his neck, the

Sheik was minded of a phrase used by Dr Joseph-Ignace Guillotine to describe the parting of one's head from its shoulders. Nothing more than the feeling of *'a refreshing coolness,'* he'd said when proposing his invention to the French government as a gentler means of execution. Well that was something to look forward to, he thought, as bin-Sayed interrupted his rumination.

'I am of course grateful for your efforts,' said bin-Sayed, his tone failing to convey any degree of sincerity as he took a sip of tea from a small decorative glass. 'But,' he looked to the figure in black, poised to send the Sheik on his journey to Allah, 'those efforts were unsuccessful and for that my friend, one of us must pay.' So with a flick of his hand and a nod to the executioner, bin-Sayed turned away.

Two thousand miles north, Nikolay Kamenev sat in an armchair opposite President Vasily Ulyanov. Diplomatic immunity had assured him of an uneventful return to Russia as was the trip to the President's dacha on the outskirts of Moscow.

'We came close,' said Ulyanov, dressed in readiness for his attendance at the Bolshoi later that evening.

'We did,' Kamenev replied, wiping the palm of his hand on his trouser leg. 'But not close enough.'

That he'd been searched on arrival was not unexpected,

even for a person of Kamenev's stature. What was unusual was the continued presence of Pavel Gusev. Personal Assistant to Ulyanov on paper, Gusev was in reality a former Spetsnaz Colonel and bodyguard to the President.

'No indeed,' replied Ulyanov.

For the second time in as many weeks Kamenev knew what was coming as the GSh-18, 9mm semi-automatic pistol appeared in Gusev's hand. There was no suppressor fitted, a testament to the sound proofing of the President's study, something which Kamenev knew only too well Ulyanov had taken full advantage of since his succession to the seat of power.

'I am genuinely sorry,' said Ulyanov to his former trusted confidant as he rose from his chair and adjusted his bow tie. Smoothing the front of his white dress shirt down over his belly, he tucked it into the top of a cummerbund then, turning away from Kamenev, walked over to a bank of French windows from where an expansive view of the forest could be seen beyond.

Fifteen hundred miles west, Frankie Cervera and Alpha Team were again mobile. Akram Murad had dismissed his driver and pool car in favour of his Lexus. Leaving Parliament Square behind, he turned left into Whitehall and drove north towards Trafalgar Square.

Looking down from the window of Sir Henry's office, it wasn't lost on any of us that the request from the Russian Ambassador to involve the SAS was designed to draw the Regiment away from Hereford and delay any potential deployment to the Eastern Isles. To all intents and purposes, a hoax scenario right out of Sun Tzu's playbook. Proving it however, was entirely another matter.

There was also the issue of the second device and its proximity to a mass gathering. This was all about obfuscation and as sure as eggs are eggs, every Tom, Dick and Harry would have come out of the woodwork claiming responsibility for such an attack and in so doing cloud the real motives and perpetrators behind such an atrocity. But again, knowing it was one thing, proving it was another.

Even the proximity of Albany Barracks to the epicentre of the detonation could have been a factor in the planning process. It's no secret that over the years the Regiment's activities across the world have led to them attracting numerous enemies for whom revenge or at least the pretense of revenge would have seemed attractive. But again, the same problem.

Bottom line, that the evidence trail would undoubtedly point to Russia, the Middle East and perhaps even China as key beneficiaries from such a disaster, none of that would matter to the likes of Ulyanov any more so than to his predecessor in the aftermath of the Skripal affair. So while the world would condemn the attacks, without direct proof, the likelihood of repercussions would be slim.

It's said that one's life flashes before you when death is on your doorstep, but as the Sheik listened to the *faisal*, the sound of the Sulthar scything through the air, no such thoughts were on his mind. Nor, a millisecond later, were they on the mind of Prince Ali bin-Sayed as his head, relieved of its body, bounced just the once before rolling to a stop at the feet of his now risen guest. Followed a moment later by a thud as the unencumbered corpse collapsed to the floor, the double doors on the far side of the room opened.

The Sheik had always admired the English euphemism known as 'hedging one's bets,' something which he'd adroitly achieved by informing the Crown Prince of bin-Sayed's plans. That the plot had been allowed to go ahead was something that would never come to light of course nor would his own life be threatened, at least not for as long as the recording of his discussions with the Crown Prince, in front of whom he now bowed, remained secure in a Swiss vault.

That the poison took a few minutes to penetrate the waterproof layer of the epidermis was all Kamenev needed to wipe it from his hand. The same however, could not be said for Pavel Gusev. His mistake had been shaking the outstretched hand on Kamenev's arrival at the Dacha and now, as he collapsed to the floor, the GSh-18 fell from his grip and dropped with a gentle thud onto a rug that separated the two armchairs.

Hearing the unexpected noise, Ulyanov turned from the French windows and looked first in surprise at Gusev's body then in shock as Kamenev rose from his armchair, slipped on a glove and picked up the pistol.

Kamenev could see the questions racing through Ulyanov's mind as the President looked towards his desk.

Could he reach it in time?

Could he open the top left hand drawer in time?

Could he chamber a round and fire in time?

The answer to all three questions was of course 'No.' So with a resigned shrug Ulyanov said, 'You won't get away, you know that, Nikolay.'

'Perhaps, perhaps not, but better than the alternative,' replied Kamenev as he raised the weapon and fired.

The first round hit Ulyanov in the chest sending him staggering back into the French windows. Made of armour plate glass, again nothing could be heard from outside as Ulyanov slumped to the floor, a crimson rosette blooming on his otherwise pristine white dress shirt.

'You really didn't have to do it, Vasily,' said Kamenev, a modicum of regret in his voice as he walked forward and delivered the second and third round into the top of his former President's head. 'But those who live by the sword...'

Although not a religious man, Kamenev couldn't help but feel Matthew 26:52 was a fitting epitaph for Ulyanov as he opened the French Windows and stepped out into a gathering mist, so common in this part of the world.

The lights turned from amber to green as Murad, murmuring quietly to himself, eased down on the accelerator and crossed the traffic lights from Charing Cross Road into Tottenham Court Road. Frustrated by yet another failure, he calmed himself by reciting verses from the Quran. That his interpretation of the holy book was diametrically opposite to the vast majority of Muslims across the world was a common misnomer among Jihadists, as was his belief that the infidels failure to recognise his role in the failed mission was Allah's will. But for now, as he circumvented Hampstead Heath and drove through Wood Green, he began to relax as he turned into Tottenham High Street and pulled up outside his destination.

*

As to what we *could* prove, well that was entirely another matter. Despite the whole thing having at times made my head spin and although his brother was in the wind, for the time being at least, so far as Murad's culpability was concerned, the ducks had eventually lined up in a row. So with the paper trail complete and the need to avoid a public scandal, the decision was made for Murad's fate to rest in the hands of Jim Kirby, the Attorney General and three Supreme Court judges.

Stepping out of the Jaguar, Murad stretched, crossed the pavement and opened the door from where, as always, he was greeted by the humble owner of the premises.

'I am sorry, Minister,' said the owner, immediately bowing to his most esteemed guest.

'What is it my friend?' asked Murad.

'I am afraid Omer has been taken ill...'

EPILOGUE

THREE MONTHS LATER

The G700 Gulfstream landed smoothly on a private airstrip 200km south of Beijing. The lone passenger paused momentarily in the doorway before descending the short flight of stairs onto the runway. The rear passenger side door of a black Hongqi saloon was held open for him by a stone faced individual in a jet black button down suit, white shirt and black tie. Accepting the unspoken invitation, he stepped inside and made himself comfortable as he was whisked away to a secluded villa on the outskirts of Cangzhou, part of China's Hebei province.

Despite its pretext at the collective good of communism and not dissimilar to its counterpart in Moscow, Chinese Politburo members see no reason why they should follow the doctrine of the masses, a philosophy which explained the luxuriant surroundings in which the guest now found himself.

Left to wait for several hours, he occupied himself by exploring a vast library of communist literature that looked out onto grounds which he suspected, but could not see, were heavily guarded. At the centre of the room a single copy of Mao's 'Little Red Book,' took pride of place in a large display cabinet. That so many millions could have been charmed by this egotistical monster and sexual pervert, did not surprise him, for history is awash with such tyrannical leaders, many of whom from his own part of the world. But what did surprise him was that even now, in this modern era, there remained countries such as this and its neighbour to the south where the populace continued to follow this path of blind faith in their leaders.

Still, to debate the whys and wherefores of such brainwashed societies was not the reason he was here. For as darkness fell, signs of activity around the villa heralded the arrival of the person from whom the invitation, accompanied by a deposit of one million dollars into his Cayman Islands account, had been delivered.

As a line of headlamps wound their way up the drive, he

was summoned to the far side of the villa where double doors opened into a huge gallery of Chinese artifacts dominated, again at its centre, by the statue of a Chinese warrior, the body of which was a writhing serpent engulfed in a sea of bodies.

'Gonggong, the Water God,' said the voice of a cultured man who had silently entered the room. 'My apologies for having kept you waiting.' The man bowed his head.

Interesting, thought the guest as he returned the gesture, keen to ensure he bowed just a little lower than his host. In preparation for this trip he had taken time to study and memorise all members of the Politburo, of which this man was not one.

'My name,' said the man, 'is Zhao He.'

At a guess, the guest estimated him to be in his mid-fifties, well groomed, as is so typical of the hierarchy in this country and with the smooth skin of one used to, how should he put it he thought, being pampered.

'I represent certain interested parties,' he continued, 'who are keen, shall we say, to continue the work undertaken by you and your brother.'

The guest's eyes narrowed.

'Forgive me,' the host said quickly. 'I am sorry for your loss.' Again, he bowed his head. 'We would like to offer you the opportunity to avenge his death and rid the world of its capitalist ideals.'

Though his face remained placid, the guest cringed inwardly at this idealistic rhetoric, but if his host were to be true to his word, then he was interested and for the first time since his arrival on Chinese soil, the Sheik spoke, 'How can I be of service?'

Zhao He studied his guest for a moment longer then asked, 'What do you know of viruses?'

ACKNOWLEDGEMENTS

As always, there are a great many people to thank for their help in pulling together an otherwise disparate storyline into something resembling a novel.

Lorna Dennison-Wilkins and Tim Heptonstall for the finer points of scuba diving and air traffic control. Dr Alistair Bird for his insights into the world of renewable energy. Sophia 'Ronnie' Luce, Nick May, Nikki Berry and Joyce Turness for subjecting themselves to the arduous task of proof reading, each of whom offered insightful comments which made me realise I needed to change a few, actually a lot of things, and Dr Steve Watts whose encyclopedic knowledge of 'lots of stuff' helped put some much needed meat on the bones as the story progressed.

Likewise those who kindly lent me their names for a whole host of characters, even if most of them sadly met their demise. Gary Bushell, Alan Hillary, Olivia Hardwick, Isabel Erlebach, Jill Kingston nee Dennison, Nici Matthews, Jim and Mary-Jane Kirby, Marty Farrow, Steve Hughes, Phil Truman, Paul 'Murtan' Truman, Frankie Cervera, Pam Dibben, Doug Palmer, Tony Ellis, Nyree Mills, Paul Bright, Bill Mason, Charlie Sinclair, Roy Folland, Julie Cloke, Dr Alistair Bird, Dr Cheryl Rodgers, Carol Ritchie, Tony, Ally and Jordi Barber, Mike Allen, Annie 'Get Your Gun' Davies, Mark Scanes, Paul Campbell, Ian and Kate Walkerdine, Stephen Radley, Jim Keeble, Mike 'Leebek' Keeble, Mark Chapman, David Pryde and Dave Hulbert.

And finally, I'd also like to tip my hat to the late, great Tom Clancy without whom I would not have found the inspiration for this novel.

Printed in Great Britain
by Amazon